SILICON SHACKLES

SILICON SHACKLES

A Novel

Saheed Adepoju

This is a work of fiction. Names, characters, places, and incidents are products of the author's imagination or are used fictitiously. Any resemblance to actual events, locales, or persons, living or dead, is entirely coincidental.

Inspired by true events.

Copyright © 2026 by Saheed Adepoju
All rights reserved.

No part of this publication may be reproduced, distributed, or transmitted in any form or by any means, including photocopying, recording, or other electronic or mechanical methods, without the prior written permission of the author, except in the case of brief quotations embodied in critical reviews.

ISBN 979-8-9041-7453-8 (ebook)

First edition, 2026

Printed in the United States of America
www.prossess.com

For Dayo. Keep being Freeman.

Prologue

The stand-up is at 9:15, and I am late because the 880 had opinions this morning.

This is not unusual. The 880 always has opinions — about merging, about the distance between vehicles, about the particular audacity of the Honda Civic in the far left lane doing sixty-two in a seventy zone with the calm conviction of a driver who has decided that their schedule is everyone's schedule. I have driven this freeway five days a week for six years, and in that time I have developed a relationship with it that resembles a long marriage: predictable resentments, occasional beauty, the knowledge that neither of us is going anywhere.

I park at 9:11. Badge swipe. The lobby smells like it always smells — coffee and the synthetic optimism of a building that believes natural light and exposed concrete are a substitute for happiness. I take the stairs because the elevator is slow and because Remi told me last month that I should move my body more, and the stairs are the only exercise I can fit between the parking garage and the sprint to my desk, where my laptop is already open and Slack is already blinking and Marcus has already posted in the team channel: *stand-up in 4 min, who's got updates?*

I have updates. I always have updates. I am a senior software engineer, and the nature of the job is that there is always something to update — a ticket closed, a review submitted, a deployment scheduled, a dependency upgraded, a meeting about the meeting about the thing that will eventually become a feature if the roadmap doesn't change, which it will, because roadmaps in this industry are less maps than suggestions, drawn in pencil, on napkins, by people who will not be in the room when the napkin is read.

I settle into my chair. Fourth row from the window, left side. The chair is ergonomic in the way that everything in this building is ergonomic — designed to support you in a posture the designers have determined is optimal for productivity, which is a different thing from comfort but which the company treats as the same thing, because productivity is what they are paying for and comfort is what they tell you they are providing.

"Kolade, you're up."

"Finished the caching layer refactor yesterday. PR is up. Need eyes on the migration script — Priya, if you have time this afternoon. No blockers."

"Nice. Dapo?"

*

Twenty-three miles east, on a screen in a home office in Dublin, California — because Dapo works hybrid, Tuesdays and Thursdays in the office, the rest from the desk Chinwe helped him set up in the spare bedroom with the window that faces the backyard and the fence he promised to stain in April — Dapo unmutes.

"Morning. I've got the pipeline monitoring dashboard at ninety percent. The latency metrics are pulling correctly now. I need to validate against production data before I push to staging. Should have it ready for review by Thursday."

His voice is steady, measured, the voice of a man who has learned that stand-ups reward brevity and punish improvisation. He has been in this industry for fourteen years — long enough to understand that the daily stand-up is not, despite its name, a meeting where people stand. It is a ritual. A proof of life. A fifteen-minute ceremony in which engineers demonstrate that they are present, productive, and moving forward, and the demonstration is more important than the movement, because the movement is invisible — it happens in the code, in the commits, in the quiet hours between meetings when the real work gets done — and the stand-up is the place where the invisible is made briefly, performatively, visible.

He mutes. He takes a sip from the thermos — stainless steel, his initials etched on the bottom, DKO, a Christmas gift from Chinwe, who had it engraved at a shop in Pleasanton because Chinwe does not give gifts that are generic. The coffee inside is the way he makes it every morning: strong, no sugar, a habit inherited from his father, Emmanuel, who drank his coffee the same way in the flat on Bode Thomas Street in Lagos while reviewing the day's inventory in a notebook with a blue cover.

Through the window, the Dublin hills are golden-brown in the June light. The backyard needs attention — the fence, the overgrown jasmine, the patch of lawn where Sade set up the sprinkler last weekend and left it running long enough that the ground is still soft. These are the things he sees but does not process, the background texture of a life that is functioning so well it does not require his active attention. The mortgage is paid. The children are at school. Chinwe left for the dental office at 6:50 with the punctuality of a woman who regards lateness as a character flaw. The coffee is hot. The stand-up is done. The day is a system, and the system is running.

*

I eat lunch at my desk. This is not a confession — this is a description of the industry. In the cafeteria, the food is free, which is the company's way of saying *please do not leave the building*. The salad bar has eighteen toppings. The espresso machine speaks Italian. There is a kombucha tap that I have never used and do not intend to use, because I am a man from Surulere and the fermented beverages of my childhood were not served on tap and did not come with a flavour called *ginger-turmeric bliss*.

I eat the salad. I review Priya's comments on the PR. I respond to a Slack message from my manager about the Q3 planning offsite, which will be held at a hotel in Napa because the company believes that strategic thinking requires a change of scenery and a wine list. I decline a meeting about a meeting. I accept a meeting about a deployment. I move a ticket from *In Progress* to *In Review*. I move another ticket from *Backlog* to *In Progress*. The board updates. The pipeline runs. The system holds.

At 2:30, my phone buzzes. WhatsApp. The *Naija Tech Bros* group.

Emeka Obi [2:31 PM]

Bros who is going to Wale's barbecue Saturday?

Wale Bakare [2:32 PM]

If you're asking if there will be suya the answer is yes

Dapo Olusanya [2:33 PM]

I'll be there. Chinwe is bringing jollof. Nobody touch the jollof until I arrive.

Kolade Adeyemi [2:34 PM]

Remi says she's making puff puff. Yemi says he's bringing his appetite. These are the only two facts I have been authorised to share.

Emeka Obi [2:35 PM]

The Adeyemis are a household of discipline and I respect it ■

I lock the phone. I smile. The smile is real — not the stand-up smile, not the meeting smile, but the one that comes from the specific pleasure of a WhatsApp thread where the men you came up with in this country are talking about barbecue as though barbecue is the most important thing happening this week. And maybe it is. Maybe the most important things are always the ones that happen between the meetings and the stand-ups and the deployments — the suya and the jollof and the laughter of men who have known each other long enough that the laughter does not need to prove anything.

*

Dapo picks up the children at 3:45. This is the hybrid-day privilege — leaving early enough to be the parent at the school gate, the one the children see first, the one who asks *how was your day?* and receives, from Femi, a thirteen-year-old's monosyllable (*fine*) and from Sade, a ten-year-old's unabridged monograph on everything that happened between 8 a.m. and 3:30 p.m., narrated with the enthusiasm of a child who believes every detail is essential and who is, in Dapo's private assessment, absolutely correct.

"Amara's dog had puppies," Sade says from the back seat. "Six puppies. They're so small, Baba. They fit in your hand."

"All of them?"

"No. One at a time. Don't be silly."

He drives. The 580 carries them east, toward Dublin, toward the house on Amaryllis Court with the broken ceiling fan he has been meaning to fix since February and the wooden cross above the kitchen doorframe that Chinwe's mother sent from Ibadan when they bought the house. The hills are gold. The traffic is light. Sade is describing the puppies' colours with the specificity of a field researcher cataloguing a new species, and Femi has his earbuds in and is looking at his phone, and Dapo is driving with one hand on the wheel and the window cracked because the June air in the East Bay has a quality he has never been able to name — warm but not heavy, dry but not harsh, carrying something that might be jasmine or might be the eucalyptus from the hills or might just be the particular scent of a geography that has decided to be kind today.

He pulls into the driveway. The Accord is not in the garage — Chinwe is still at work. He unlocks the door. The house receives them the way it always does — the cool of the tile in the entryway, the hum of the refrigerator, the specific silence of a home that has been empty for seven hours and is now, with the arrival of its people, beginning again.

Sade goes upstairs. He hears her door, then the creak of her bed, then the sound that means she has opened the book she is reading — a ritual, an after-school decompression that mirrors his own need, at the end of a day, to sit quietly in a space that does not require anything of him. Femi opens the fridge, assesses the contents with the critical eye of a thirteen-year-old who believes the household should stock more of everything, and retreats to the living room with a yoghurt and the expression of a boy who has negotiated a compromise with himself.

Dapo stands in the kitchen. The cross is above the doorframe. The ceiling fan is broken. The light through the window is gold. He is alone for a moment — the specific, brief aloneness of a parent between the arrival of the children and the arrival of the spouse, the ten-minute window where the house is his and the quiet is a gift.

He opens his laptop. He checks Slack. He checks his email. He checks the monitoring dashboard for the pipeline he built — green across the board, the metrics holding, the system doing what he designed it to do. He closes the laptop.

He makes coffee. He stands at the counter and drinks it — strong, no sugar, from the thermos with his initials — and he looks at the backyard through the window. The fence. The jasmine. The soft patch of lawn from the sprinkler Sade left running. The small, imperfect evidence of a life that is working.

This is a Monday in June. A week from now, none of this will be true.

But today the coffee is hot, and the pipeline is green, and the children are home, and the cross above the doorframe catches the afternoon light in a way that makes it glow, and Dapo Olusanya stands in his kitchen in Dublin, California, in the life he built, and does not know that it is borrowed.

I leave the office at 5:47. The 880 carries me south, toward Fremont, toward the house with the cracked driveway and the red door and the air freshener shaped like a small tree that Remi hung from my mirror three years ago and that I said was foolish and that she kept anyway. The drive takes twenty-six minutes. I do not call anyone. I do not listen to anything. The freeway is my decompression chamber — the twenty-six minutes between the man who sits in the fourth row from the window and the man who walks through the red door and becomes a husband, a father, a person whose name is spoken by people who love him rather than people who need his updates.

I pull into the driveway. The porch light is on. Through the kitchen window, I can see Remi moving — the silhouette of a woman who is always in motion, always building, always making the house into the thing it is supposed to be for the people who live inside it.

I get out of the car. I walk to the door. Yemi's music is coming through his window — bass, something I do not recognise, something that belongs to him and not to me, and the fact of it, the privacy of a fifteen-year-old's chosen sound, is a kind of growing up that I witness daily and cannot slow.

I open the door. The house smells like stew — Remi's tomato stew, the one with the scotch bonnets she handles with the bare-fingered confidence of a woman who was raised in a kitchen where the peppers were respected but not feared. Dara is at the table with a book. Remi is at the stove. The light is the warm overhead I have been meaning to replace — the fluorescent, the one she has asked about three times, the one that makes everything look like evidence.

"How was your day?" she asks.

"Fine," I say. "The stand-up was fine. The code review was fine. Marcus wants to do Q3 planning in Napa."

"Napa."

"Napa."

She gives me the look. The look that says: *your company is spending money on a hotel in wine country for people to discuss a spreadsheet, and my company is spending money on hand sanitiser that smells like artificial lavender, and this is the economy we live in.*

"Wash your hands," she says. "Food is ready."

I wash my hands. I sit down. Dara does not look up from the book. Yemi comes down when called — the earbuds removed, the appetite present, the contribution to dinner conversation limited to responses of three words or fewer, delivered with the economy of a boy who is saving his language for people who are not his parents.

We eat. The stew is good. The rice is the way Remi makes it — each grain separate, because Remi believes that sticky rice is a moral failing and I have learned, over nineteen years, not to disagree. We eat and we do not talk about the Q3 offsite or the pharmacy schedule or the mortgage or the school fees or the transfers to Lagos. We talk about Dara's book (the dragon is good; the people are boring), about Yemi's football practice (coach is making them run hills; Yemi has opinions about hills), about the barbecue on Saturday (Remi is making puff puff; I am making myself available).

The ordinary. The unremarkable Tuesday evening of a family that is, by every measure available to us, fine. The house is paid for — this month. The children are fed. The stew is good. The man at the head of the table has a job and a salary and a title and a badge that lets him into a building where people need his updates, and the woman at the other end has a schedule and a paycheck and a legal pad in the drawer where she tracks the numbers, and the numbers work. The numbers have always worked. The numbers are the reason we are here, in this house, in this neighbourhood, in this country, eating this stew — and the numbers, next week, will be the thing that falls.

But not tonight. Tonight the stew is good, and Dara's dragon is flying, and Yemi has opinions about hills, and Remi is watching me across the table with the expression that means she is content, or close enough, and the closeness is enough.

This is the life. This is the golden cage. And we do not know, sitting inside it, that the door has already been unlocked from the outside.

PART ONE

The Golden Cage

Chapter One

The Morning

The Tuesday starts with eggs. I want to say it starts with something more significant—a premonition, a catch in the air, the way the light falls wrong through the kitchen window—but the truth is less cinematic than that. It starts with eggs, and Remi standing at the stove in her scrubs, and the particular sound of oil popping in a cast-iron pan that has been in her mother's family longer than our marriage has existed.

I am at the kitchen table with my laptop open, pretending to read Slack, but I am watching her. I do this sometimes—watch my wife move through the ordinary machinery of our morning—and I don't think she knows, or if she knows, she has decided not to ruin it by saying so. She cracks the second egg one-handed, the way her mother taught her, and the yolk slides into the oil without breaking. A small perfection. The kind of thing nobody applauds but everybody misses when it stops.

The house smells like plantain. She is frying dodo alongside the eggs because Yemi has a maths exam today and Remi believes—with the unshakeable conviction of a Yoruba woman who has opinions about breakfast—that a child cannot think clearly on cereal alone. I tried once to suggest that Cheerios and milk constituted an adequate Tuesday morning. Once. The look she gave me is still paying rent in my memory.

"Kolade. Your coffee is getting cold."

"I know."

"Then drink it."

I drink it. It is, in fact, cold.

Yemi comes down the stairs in his school uniform, backpack already on, earbuds in, existing in the selective deafness of a fifteen-year-old boy who has perfected the art of being present without being available. His sister, Dara, follows three minutes later, which is her way of establishing that she operates on her own schedule. She is twelve and has recently developed the habit of reading at the table, which Remi tolerates on school mornings because the alternative—arguing with a child who has inherited her mother's stubbornness and her father's talent for justifying it—is not worth the energy before 7 a.m.

"Good morning, Daddy."

"Morning, sweetheart. You have everything?"

"Mm-hmm." She doesn't look up from the book. It is something with a dragon on the cover. I decide this counts as communication.

I close the laptop. I eat the eggs, the plantain, a piece of toast that I don't need but take because leaving food on a plate in this house is an act of mild treason. Remi sits across from me with her own plate and her phone propped against the salt shaker, scrolling through something—the pharmacy schedule, a WhatsApp thread, the weather. We don't talk much during breakfast on weekdays. We have been married long enough that silence is not absence; it is just the sound of two people who have said enough to each other that they don't need to fill every minute with proof.

I rinse my plate. I kiss her on the side of the head, near the temple, where her hair is pulled back tight. She smells like shea butter and the faintly clinical undertone of whatever hand sanitiser they use at the pharmacy. She pats my arm without looking up.

"Drive safe."

"Always."

This is the script. We say it every morning. It means more than it sounds like, but neither of us has ever tried to explain that, and I think we are right not to.

*

The commute from Fremont to Santa Clara takes forty minutes if the 880 is merciful, which it rarely is at 7:45 on a Tuesday in June. Today I am in the right lane behind a Tesla whose driver is either texting or having a spiritual experience, because the car drifts at the precise speed designed to make every other vehicle on the freeway reconsider its life choices.

I do not mind the traffic. I know this makes me unusual. Most people in this office treat the commute like a wound they have to redress every morning, but for me the car is the one place where I am not a husband, not a father, not a senior software engineer on a team that builds infrastructure nobody outside the company will ever see or thank us for. In the car, I am just a man with a steering wheel and forty minutes of NPR and the particular quality of Bay Area morning light that turns the hills east of the freeway the colour of bread crust. Golden, almost. If you don't look too closely at the dead grass.

I think about the sprint review at ten. I think about the Jira ticket I left open yesterday—a caching issue in the notification pipeline that is not urgent but has been sitting in my peripheral vision for three days like a bill on the counter. I think about whether Yemi studied for the maths exam or just told us he did, which is a distinction I have learned to interrogate with the careful diplomacy of a man who remembers being fifteen and lying about exactly the same thing.

I do not think about anything that will happen after 9 a.m. I want to be clear about this. There is no foreshadowing in my body, no tremor of intuition. The morning is ordinary and I am inside it the way a fish is inside water—completely, without thinking about the medium.

The office is a three-storey glass building in a business park that could be anywhere in Northern California. Beige exterior, manicured succulents, a lobby with the kind of abstract art that exists to prove someone considered aesthetics without actually committing to taste. I badge in. The light on the reader turns green. I walk past reception, past the micro-kitchen with its shrine to oat milk and sparkling water, past the empty standing desks of people who are either remote today or have quietly stopped showing up since the last round of performance reviews.

My desk is on the second floor, near the window. I chose it three years ago when the team moved from the SoMa office, and I chose it because the window faces east, which means morning light, which means I can sit down with my coffee and my stand-up notes and feel, for the first twenty minutes of the day, like a man who is exactly where he is supposed to be.

I open Slack. I open my email. I open the terminal and pull the latest from main, because this is what I do, every morning, in the same order, with the same muscle memory that Remi uses to crack eggs one-handed. Routine is not glamorous, but it is the architecture of competence, and I have spent fifteen years building mine—brick by brick, commit by commit, meeting by meeting—until the structure is so familiar I could navigate it blindfolded.

At 8:47, I send Dapo a message: *Omo, you see this caching ticket? I go close am today or e go follow me home.*

He doesn't reply immediately. I don't think anything of it.

At 8:52, I refill my coffee from the machine near the stairs. I exchange a nod with Priya from the data team, who is carrying a bowl of overnight oats and looking at her phone with the expression of someone who has just received either very good or very bad news and hasn't decided which.

At 8:58, I sit back down.

At 9:01, the notification comes.

*

Dapo Olusanya woke at 5:40 a.m. the way he always did—not to an alarm, but to the internal clock of a man whose body had learned that the day would not wait for him to be ready. He lay still for a moment, eyes open, staring at the ceiling fan that had not worked since February. He had told Chinwe he would fix it. He had not fixed it. The fan hung above them like a small, domestic accusation, its blades furred with dust, and every morning he looked at it and every morning he added it to the list of things he would get to, the list that grew the way lists do when a man is employed and busy and tells himself that time is the one resource he will eventually have more of.

Chinwe was asleep beside him, turned away, the comforter pulled up to her chin despite the June warmth. She slept like that—sealed, contained, as though even in unconsciousness she was protecting something. He watched the slow rise of her shoulder and felt the specific tenderness of a man observing his wife in the last moments before the day claims her. She would wake at six-fifteen. She would shower, dress, make breakfast for the children with the quiet efficiency of someone who has turned motherhood into a logistics operation. She would ask him if he wanted the car today or if he was driving himself, and he would say he was driving himself, because he always drove himself, because the car was the one space that was his.

He rose without making the bed. He brushed his teeth with the door closed, watching his face in the mirror with the detached appraisal of a man checking equipment before a shift. Forty-two years old. The grey at his temples had arrived the previous winter, not gradually but all at once, as though his hair had received a memo he had not been copied on. He wore it without complaint. Chinwe said it made him look distinguished, and he had chosen to believe her, which is a form of trust that married people extend to each other like small, daily loans.

Downstairs, he made coffee—French press, two scoops, water just off the boil—and stood at the kitchen counter while it steeped. The house was quiet. Femi and Sade would not surface for another thirty minutes. Through the kitchen window, the Dublin hills were still dark against a sky that was just beginning to suggest light at the eastern edge, the way a page begins to suggest the sentence before the words appear. He liked this hour. It was the only hour that belonged entirely to him, before the children needed things, before Chinwe's day began its machinery, before the freeway demanded his attention and the office demanded the rest.

He ate two slices of toast with peanut butter. He checked his phone—three WhatsApp notifications from the family group in Ibadan, a reminder about Femi's orthodontist appointment, an email from the school about a fundraising gala he would attend because Chinwe had already RSVP'd. He opened LinkedIn, scrolled for thirty seconds, closed it. He opened the weather app. Seventy-four degrees, clear. A Bay Area June morning doing what it does best: being so beautiful it feels like a dare.

He left the house at 6:50.

The drive from Dublin to Santa Clara was the 580 to the 680 to the 237, forty-five minutes if the merge at Sunol went smoothly, an hour if it did not. Dapo drove a grey Camry, 2019, paid off—one of the few financial facts in his life that did not keep him awake. The car was clean in the way that a man's car is clean when he uses the drive as a decompression chamber: no crumbs, no water bottles, no evidence of children. The only personal item was a small wooden cross hanging from the rearview mirror, a gift from his mother on the day he left Lagos, which he kept not because he was especially devout but because removing it would require an explanation he did not want to give.

He listened to nothing on the drive. Not music, not podcasts, not the news. The silence was a choice, though he would not have described it that way. He would have said he preferred to think in the morning, to organise the day in his head before it began, and this was true, but it was also true that the silence served a second purpose: it was the space where he practiced. Practiced being fine. Practiced the answers he would give if someone at the office asked how things were going—*Good, busy, you know how it is*—and the smile that accompanied them, the one that was close enough to real that nobody had ever questioned it.

The merge at Sunol was clear. He arrived at the office at 7:38.

He badged in. The light turned green. He walked through the lobby, past the same abstract art, past the same micro-kitchen, up the same stairs to the second floor where his desk sat four rows from the window, further from the glass than Kolade's, a fact that had once bothered him and now did not, because a man can only carry so many small grievances before the weight of them becomes the thing that tires him more than the work.

He set his bag on the desk. He opened his laptop. He connected to the VPN, opened Slack, opened Jira, opened the data pipeline dashboard that showed him, in real time, the health of systems he had built or maintained or inherited from engineers who had left before him. Green across the board. Everything running. He took a sip of the coffee he had brought from home in a thermos Chinwe had given him two Christmases ago—stainless steel, insulated, with his initials engraved on the bottom in a font so small you had to turn it over to read it. A private thing. A tenderness hidden where only he would see it.

He checked his email. He read through the morning's pull requests. He reviewed a junior engineer's migration script with the careful, generous attention of a man who remembered what it was to be new, to submit work and wait for someone senior to tell you whether you were good enough. He left three comments, all constructive, all kind. This was the version of Dapo that the office knew—measured, competent, quietly excellent—and it was not a performance, exactly. It was him. But it was also a selected frequency, the way a radio plays one station while the full spectrum hums beneath.

At 8:47, Kolade's message appeared in Slack: *Omo, you see this caching ticket? I go close am today or e go follow me home.*

Dapo read it. He almost smiled. He began to type a reply—something about how the ticket had been sitting there long enough to qualify for tenure—and then stopped. Deleted the draft. He would reply after stand-up. There was time.

There was, he believed, always time.

At 8:55, he stood to refill his thermos. The floor was filling now—engineers arriving in ones and twos, the low murmur of a workday assembling itself. He nodded at Marcus from platform, at Suki from the ML team, at the new hire whose name he had learned and then immediately filed in the part of his brain where names went to be retrieved later, always later.

At 8:59, he sat back down.

He opened Slack.

*

The message is in #general. It is from someone whose name I recognise but have never spoken to—a VP of something, people operations, human capital, one of those titles that sounds like it was designed by a committee that couldn't agree on what the job actually was. The message is pinned. There is a thread beneath it already—fourteen replies in the first minute, which I know because I watch the number climb the way you watch a car accident assemble itself in the mirror.

The message does not say the word *layoff*. It says *restructuring*. It says *difficult decisions*. It says *impacted employees will receive a calendar invite with further details shortly*. It uses the phrase *moving forward* twice in three sentences, as though forward were the only direction available, as though anyone in this building had been consulted about the route.

My hands are on the keyboard. They have not moved. I am reading the message for the second time, and what I notice on the second read is what I missed on the first: the Slack channels are disappearing. Not all of them. But the ones I can see—the team channels, the project channels, the ones with inside jokes in the names that nobody outside the team would understand—are going grey, one by one, like lights shutting off in a building being closed for the night.

I look at my phone. There is no calendar invite. Not yet.

I open a DM to Dapo. The cursor blinks. I type: *You seeing this?*

I watch the screen. Three dots appear. Then nothing. Then three dots again.

Then his reply, six words that I will carry for the rest of my life the way a man carries a photograph of a house he used to live in:

Koly. I just got the invite.

I look at my own inbox. I refresh. I refresh again.

There it is.

*

Dapo stared at the calendar invite. It had arrived at 9:03 a.m., two minutes after the Slack message, with the punctuality of something that had been scheduled long before this morning, long before this week, queued in some system by someone who would never sit across from him and say the words to his face. The subject line read: *Your Meeting with People Operations — 10:00 AM*. No agenda. No context. Just a time, a virtual room link, and his name.

He read it twice. He closed the laptop. He opened it again.

Around him, the floor had gone quiet in a way that was louder than noise—the particular silence of forty people reading the same message at the same time and understanding, each in their own body, what it meant. Someone near the window said *what the fuck* in a voice so calm it sounded rehearsed. Someone else laughed, the short, airless laugh of a person whose nervous system has chosen the wrong response and cannot correct it in time.

Dapo looked at his thermos. At the initials on the bottom he could not see from this angle but knew were there. He thought about Chinwe, who was probably driving the children to school right now, the Accord moving through Dublin Boulevard traffic, Femi in the passenger seat looking at his phone, Sade in the back with her headphones on, and none of them knowing. None of them knowing that the architecture of their life had just received a memo, and that the memo was already two minutes old, and that he was sitting in a chair four rows from the window reading it for the third time because reading it again might change what it said.

It did not change what it said.

He picked up his phone. He opened the message from Kolade—*You seeing this?*—and typed his reply. He pressed send. He put the phone face down on the desk.

Then Dapo Olusanya, senior data engineer, husband, father of two, son of a man in Ibadan who had sold fabric at Dugbe Market for thirty years so that his boy could sit in a glass building in California and build things with his mind instead of his hands—Dapo Olusanya placed both palms flat on the desk, the way a man places his hands on a surface when the room has begun to move and he needs to confirm that something, at least, is still solid.

The desk held.

Everything else had already started to fall.

Chapter Two

The meeting lasts eleven minutes. I know this because I watch the clock on my laptop the way a man watches a meter running in a taxi he cannot afford — not because the number will change the destination, but because counting is the last thing left that feels like control.

The woman from People Operations has a name I will not remember by the time I reach the parking lot. She has a face built for delivering news that isn't hers — sympathetic without being soft, professional without being cold, the precise calibration of someone who has done this forty times today and will do it forty more before lunch. She speaks from a script. I can hear the edges of it, the places where the sentences have been sanded smooth by Legal, where the word *terminated* has been replaced by *separated* and *fired* has been buried under *impacted* and the whole thing sounds like a weather report for a disaster someone else is having.

I nod in the right places. I ask one question — about the severance timeline — because asking a question means I am processing this like a professional, like a man who understands that even the end of something has logistics. She answers. Twelve weeks, prorated. COBRA details to follow. A box will be sent for personal items, or I can arrange a time to come in. She says this the way a landlord tells you the lease is up: factually, without cruelty, but with no interest in where you go next.

When she says *We wish you the best, Kolade*, I close the laptop.

I do not slam it. I want you to understand that. I close it the way I close it every evening — gently, with both hands, the screen meeting the keyboard with the soft click I have heard ten thousand times. And then I sit at my desk, in the chair by the east-facing window, in the morning light I chose three years ago because it made me feel like a man who was exactly where he was supposed to be, and I sit there for four minutes and twenty seconds doing nothing at all.

Four minutes and twenty seconds. I counted.

This is what they do not tell you about the moment it happens. They do not tell you that the building continues. That the air conditioning hums at the same frequency. That the micro-kitchen still smells like oat milk and someone's reheated dal, and the abstract art in the lobby is still proving nothing to no one, and the badge on your lanyard still has your photo on it — the one from orientation, three years younger, a version of you that signed the offer letter with a pen he brought from home because he wanted the moment to feel significant. They do not tell you that the world does not rearrange itself around your loss. It just keeps going, indifferent, the way a freeway keeps carrying cars long after the accident has been cleared.

I pick up my bag. I leave the laptop on the desk because it is not mine anymore — it was never mine, I understand now, in the way that the desk was never mine and the badge was never mine and the morning light was just light, indifferent to who sat in it. I take my phone, my car keys, the mug Dara made me in ceramics class last spring — slightly lopsided, with *DAD* painted in letters that lean to the left, as though even the word is bracing for something.

The elevator is empty. The lobby is not. There are people standing near reception in the particular cluster of those who have just received the same news and are deciding, collectively, whether to be angry or stunned or practical. I recognise faces. Priya from the data team, holding her phone in both hands like a prayer book. Marcus from platform, jacket already on, moving toward the door with the purpose of a man who has decided that leaving quickly is a form of dignity. A woman from design whose name I know but cannot reach right now — it is somewhere in the part of my brain that has gone quiet, the part that files names and meeting times and sprint priorities, the part that was working an hour ago and is not working now.

I do not stop. I nod at Marcus. He nods back. We do not speak because there is nothing to say that the nod does not already contain.

The parking lot is bright. June in the South Bay has a quality of light that is almost aggressive — clear, warm, the kind of sunshine that makes shadows sharp and leaves nowhere to hide. My car is in the same spot I parked it this morning, four hours and eleven minutes ago, when I was a senior software engineer with a caching ticket to close and a wife who said *drive safe* and a life that worked. The car is a Honda Accord, dark blue, 2021, still three years from being paid off. It is the most expensive thing I have ever owned that is not the house, and right now it is the only space in the world that is mine.

I get in. I close the door. The silence is immediate and total, the way silence is in a car when you have not turned anything on and the world outside is muffled by glass and steel and the particular insulation of a vehicle designed to make you feel that you are moving through the world without being touched by it.

I do not start the engine. Not yet.

My phone buzzes. Then again. Then three times in quick succession, the staccato of a WhatsApp group waking up.

I look at the screen. The Naija Tech Bros group — the one Dapo started two years ago, thirty-seven members, mostly Nigerian engineers at companies across the Bay — is already on fire. Messages scroll faster than I can read them. *Who got hit?*

and *Bro I just got the email* and *Is this legal?* and *Anyone know a good immigration lawyer?* and then, from someone I don't know well, the message that sits in my chest like a stone: *Guys, what happens to H-1B if you lose the job?*

I am not on H-1B. I am naturalised. I have the blue passport, the one my father held in his hands at my swearing-in ceremony and turned over twice, as though he needed to verify that a thing this small could carry this much weight. But I read that message and I feel it in my body anyway, the old fear, the one that predates citizenship, the one that lives in the part of you that remembers what it is to be conditional. To exist in a country that can revoke you.

I put the phone face down on the passenger seat.

I start the car.

*

The 880 northbound is the only freeway in the Bay Area that I have ever loved, and I use that word carefully. It is not beautiful. It runs through Milpitas and the salt flats and past the kind of industrial parks that exist to remind you that someone, somewhere, is manufacturing something you will never think about. But at 1:47 on a Tuesday afternoon, when the commute traffic has not yet begun and the lanes are open and the hills to the east are the colour of dried grass, the 880 is the closest thing I know to mercy. It asks nothing of you. It does not require a decision. You enter, you stay in your lane, you follow the road until it becomes the place you live, and for those twenty-six minutes you are suspended — not home, not work, not anything. Just a man in a car, moving.

I drive the way I always drive: right lane, three miles above the speed limit, hands at ten and two because my father taught me to drive in a borrowed Peugeot 504 on Ikorodu Road and some lessons live in the body longer than the man who gave them. The radio is off. I cannot listen to anything right now. Not NPR, not music, not the sound of another human voice telling me about a world that is still functioning. The silence is not comfortable. But it is honest, and honest is what I can manage.

I pass the 237 interchange. I pass the salt flats where the water is the colour of rust and the air smells like something old and mineral. I pass the Fremont exit sign and I do not take it. I stay on the 880 for three more exits — Stevenson, Auto Mall, Mowry — because taking the exit means arriving and arriving means deciding what to say and I am not ready. I am not ready for any of the sentences that are forming in the back of my throat like weather I cannot stop.

Remi, I lost my job.

No. Too blunt. Too much like a confession. She will hear the word *lost* and her face will do the thing it does when she is calculating — not money, not logistics, but the distance between what I have told her and what is actually true. She has been married to me long enough to know the difference.

Remi, the company did layoffs. I was included.

Better. More clinical. The passive voice doing its work, distributing the blame across a system instead of a person. *Included* — as though it were an invitation. As though someone chose me for something.

Remi, we need to talk.

Worst of all. Four words that have never in the history of any marriage preceded anything good. She will set down whatever she is holding and look at me and the looking will be worse than the telling.

I take the Mowry exit. I loop back south. I take the 880 again, retracing the same stretch I just drove, past the same salt flats and the same dead grass and the same exits, and this time I take Stevenson because I cannot drive forever, even though part of me — the part that is not a husband or a father or a man with a mortgage and two school fees and a car payment — wants to.

The surface streets of Fremont are quiet the way they always are in the early afternoon. The light is different here than it is in Santa Clara — softer, filtered through the eucalyptus trees that line the residential blocks, the kind of light that makes a neighbourhood look like a photograph of itself. I turn onto our street. I pull into the driveway.

I do not go inside.

*

I sit in the car for forty minutes. Remi texts twice. I watch the dots appear and disappear on my phone like they have somewhere better to be.

The first text arrives at 2:23: *Yemi needs new school trousers. The grey ones. I'll stop at Target after work unless you want to go.*

The second, four minutes later: *Also we're low on groundnut oil. And Dara wants that cereal with the bear on the box. I forget the name.*

I read both messages. I do not reply. I watch the screen go dark, then light up again as another WhatsApp notification scrolls across the top — someone in the group posting a link to an article about severance negotiation — and then dark again. The phone lies on my thigh like a small, warm animal that does not know it is carrying the worst news of my life.

The driveway is twelve feet wide and twenty-two feet long. I measured it the week we moved in, not because the measurement mattered but because I was a man who had just bought a house in America and measuring things was the only way I knew to make it real. The concrete has a crack running from the left edge to a point roughly two-thirds across, a fracture I have been meaning to fill since last spring. The air freshener hanging from the rearview mirror — a cardboard pine tree, the green one, bought at the Shell station on Paseo Padre three months ago — has lost its scent. It turns slowly in the still air of the car, moved by nothing I can see.

The October light — no. The June light. I have to be careful here, because I am telling you this from a place where the months have blurred, where this Tuesday has been replayed so many times that it has started to borrow details from other days. But it was June. I know it was June because the jasmine along the fence was in full bloom and the smell came through the cracked window like a small, unearned kindness. June, and warm, and the kind of late afternoon where the sky is still high and blue and completely indifferent to whatever is happening beneath it.

I think about my father.

Not the version of him that I tell stories about — the Lagos civil servant with the pressed trousers and the proverbs for every occasion, the man who could make a room of arguing uncles go quiet with a single raised hand. I think about the version I saw once, through the crack of a bedroom door in our flat in Surulere, the night he came home after the ministry let him go. I was nine. I did not understand the economics of what had happened, but I understood the geometry of it — my mother at the stove, stirring something with too much focus, and my father at the table with his hands flat on the surface, the way you put your hands down when you need to feel something solid.

He sat like that for a long time. And then he stood, and he walked to where my mother was, and he said — in a voice so steady I can still hear the effort it took to make it so — *We will manage.*

That was it. Three words. No drama, no collapse, no negotiation with the facts. Just a statement of intent from a man who believed, with the particular faith of his generation, that endurance was the highest form of love. That you walked through the door and you said the thing and the saying of it was enough to make it true.

I am not my father.

I know this the way you know the shape of your own hands — completely, without looking. I am not the man who walks through the door and names the problem and trusts the naming to hold. I am the man who sits in the driveway for forty minutes with the engine off, watching texts appear and disappear, rehearsing sentences he cannot say, counting the cracks in the concrete because counting is the only language he has for fear.

My father would have been inside by now. He would have kissed my mother's forehead. He would have eaten whatever she made and complimented it and waited until the children were asleep to sit with her at the table and say the hard thing in a low voice. And maybe that is what love looked like in Surulere in 1993 — immediate, declarative, built on the understanding that a family is a boat and the man's job is to say *we are taking on water* before the water reaches the children.

But this is Fremont in June, and the water is not visible yet, and the boat looks fine from the outside, and I am sitting in a Honda Accord that I will not be able to make payments on in four months if nothing changes, and the jasmine smells like grace I have not asked for, and my wife is at work texting me about school trousers and groundnut oil because she does not know that the architecture of our life received a memo this morning and the memo is already five hours old.

I pick up the phone. I type: *I'll get the trousers. And the oil. Don't worry about it.*

I press send. I watch the blue checkmarks appear. I put the phone down.

It is the first lie. Not the last. But the first one has a weight the others do not, because the first one is the one you choose with your whole body. The others follow like current — once the water finds the crack, it does not ask permission to keep moving.

*

At 3:04, I open the car door. The air outside is warmer than the air inside, and the difference registers on my skin like a change in pressure, like stepping from one room into another. I stand in the driveway with my keys in my hand and I look at the front door — the red one, the one Remi chose because she said a red door meant welcome, and I teased her about it, called it superstition, and she said *Kolade, not everything has to be rational*, and she was right, and I told her she was right, and we painted it together on a Saturday in April, three years ago, while Yemi and Dara sat on the lawn eating popsicles and offering critiques of our brushwork.

The door is six steps away.

I have built databases that serve fourteen million users. I have debugged systems at 2 a.m. while the on-call Slack channel pulsed with the panic of engineers half my age. I have sat in rooms with directors and VPs and explained, calmly, why the architecture I designed would hold, and I was right, and it held, and nobody thanked me because infrastructure is invisible until it breaks.

Six steps. The red door. Remi on the other side, probably home by now, putting groceries away, or starting dinner, or sitting on the couch with her feet up and her phone in her hand, scrolling through something, waiting for me the way she waits for me every evening — not anxiously, just knowingly, the way a person waits for a thing that has always come.

I take the first step.

I am not going to tell her tonight. I know this already. I know it the way I knew, sitting in the parking lot in Santa Clara, that the nod I exchanged with Marcus would be the last honest thing I did today. I am going to walk through the red door and I am going to kiss my wife on the side of the head and I am going to eat whatever she has made and I am going to ask Dara about her book and Yemi about the maths exam and I am going to be the man they expect me to be for one more evening, because one more evening is what I can carry.

Tomorrow I will tell her. Or the day after. Or when I have a plan — yes, that is it, I will make a plan first, a spreadsheet, a list, an architecture for what comes next, and then I will sit her down and say *Remi, here is what happened, and here is what I've already figured out*, and she will see that I have it under control, that the boat is taking on water but I have already found the bucket.

This is what I tell myself as I walk the six steps.

I reach the door. I put my hand on the handle. The metal is warm from the sun.

Inside, I can hear the television. Dara's laughter — high and sudden, the kind of sound that has no history, that belongs entirely to the present tense. The clatter of something in the kitchen. The ordinary machinery of a house that does not know what I am carrying, that will not know tonight, that I will protect from knowing for as long as I can, because this is what I was taught, because this is what men like me do, because the silence feels like shelter even when it is the thing that will, eventually, bring the roof down.

I open the door.

Chapter Three

The boy who would become Dapo Olusanya — senior data engineer, husband, father, man who placed his palms flat on a desk in Santa Clara when the world shifted — that boy was born in a two-bedroom flat in Yaba, Lagos, on a Thursday in March, during a rainstorm that knocked out the power for six hours. His mother, Folake, told this story at every birthday, every graduation, every gathering where the arc of her son's life needed a beginning. *The light went out the moment you came*, she would say, pressing his face between her hands the way she held fruit at the market — testing for ripeness, for readiness. *And when NEPA brought it back, you were already here. Already in a hurry.*

He grew up in the flat above his father's shop on Bode Thomas Street, where Emmanuel Olusanya sold fabric — ankara, aso-oke, guinea brocade — to women who came from as far as Abeokuta and Ijebu-Ode because Emmanuel's eye for pattern was, in the language of his customers, *correct.* The shop was narrow, barely wider than a man's outstretched arms, but Emmanuel had organised it with the precision of a man who understood that the difference between a successful business and a failed one was not the size of the space but the intelligence of its arrangement. Bolts of fabric stood upright in wooden racks he had built himself, sorted by colour, by weight, by the occasion they were meant to serve. He could pull any bolt in under ten seconds. He timed himself. He taught Dapo to time himself too.

This was the first lesson: order is not luxury. Order is survival.

The flat had a parlour, a kitchen with a two-burner stove, and two bedrooms — one for his parents, one for Dapo and his younger brother, Kunle. The bathroom was shared with the family downstairs, the Adenirans, whose patriarch kept a transistor radio tuned permanently to highlife and news, so that the sound of King Sunny Ade drifted up through the floor tiles like weather. The electricity came and went on its own schedule. The rent Emmanuel paid on the first of every month with the ceremonial gravity of a man settling a debt of honour.

Dapo's childhood was not poor. He would resist that word later, when Americans asked about Lagos with the particular curiosity that meant they were imagining something from a documentary. His childhood was *managed*. Resources were finite and known, and the intelligence of the arrangement was what made the difference. There was always food — his mother's cooking was an event, each meal assembled with the focus of a woman who believed that feeding her family well was a theological act. There were always clean uniforms. There was always enough. But enough meant that the margins were thin, and thin margins meant that any disruption — an illness, a month when the customers did not come — could turn enough into something else entirely.

He learned to read the household the way his father read the shop: by what was present and what was absent. He learned that his father's laughter at dinner — generous, full, the laugh of a man who wanted his sons to believe the world was stable — sometimes had a different texture on nights when the closed-door conversations had been longer than usual. He learned that worry, in his family, did not announce itself. It dressed in pressed trousers and sat at the head of the table and said *eat, eat* and did not explain why the portions on its own plate were smaller than everyone else's.

This was the second lesson: the man provides. The man does not discuss the cost of providing. The cost is his to carry, privately, the way the beams of a house carry the roof — structurally, invisibly, and with no expectation of thanks.

*

The scholarship arrived the way most transformations do — not as thunder but as paper. A letter on cream-coloured stationery, delivered to the flat on Bode Thomas Street in his final year at King's College. His mother opened it because Dapo was at school, and when he came home she was sitting in the parlour with the letter on her lap and her face arranged in an expression he had never seen — not joy, not shock, but something closer to the look a person has when they are holding something so fragile that even celebrating could break it.

Full scholarship. Four years. Electrical engineering. A university in Ohio whose name his father pronounced three different ways before settling on a version delivered with absolute confidence. Emmanuel stood in the shop that evening and told every customer who came in. He told the Adenirans. He told the suya man at the junction. His voice cracked at the edges with a pride so large it could not fit inside the steadiness he usually maintained.

My son. America. Full scholarship. The boy did it.

Dapo stood in the corner of the shop and felt something he would spend twenty years trying to name. It was the sensation of a door opening — not just for him, but for everyone who had ever folded fabric in this shop or eaten his mother's rice or sat in the parlour watching NTA on the television with the cracked screen. The scholarship was not his alone. It belonged to the flat, the shop, the street. He was not going to Ohio. He was being *sent* to Ohio. And being sent meant that the sending had a return address.

The night before he left, his mother cooked the way she cooked for Christmas — egusi with stockfish and ponmo, jollof rice with enough pepper to make your eyes water, fried plantain cut in the diagonal slices she insisted tasted better than the round ones. *E get things wey your book no fit teach you*, she had said, and she was right, and twenty years later, eating plantain in his house in Dublin, sliced round by his own hand because Chinwe did not share his mother's geometry, he could still taste the difference.

After dinner, his father took him to the balcony. Lagos at night — generators humming at different pitches, music from three directions, the particular percussion of a city that never fully slept. Emmanuel stood with his hands on the railing and said nothing for a long time. Then he placed both hands on Dapo's shoulders and said, in Yoruba, the thing that would sit in Dapo's chest like a second heartbeat for the rest of his life:

Do not come back the same.

Not: do not come back. That was the difference. Emmanuel was not sending his son away. He was sending him forward, into a version of himself that the flat on Bode Thomas Street could imagine but could not build. And the instruction was clear: the investment was large, the margins were thin, and the return was not optional.

Dapo nodded. He did not cry. His father did not cry. They stood on the balcony and looked at the street and the understanding between them was as solid and as silent as the railing under their hands.

*

Ohio was cold. Not cold the way Lagos was occasionally cool during harmattan, when the dust from the north settled on windshields like a fine, red commentary on the weather. Cold the way a country is cold when it has decided, structurally, that winter is a season people should simply endure — minus twelve in January, wind that cut through the secondhand coat he had bought at a Salvation Army three blocks from campus, ice on the pavements that turned every walk to class into a negotiation with gravity.

He survived Ohio the way he survived everything that came after: by studying. Not studying as a preference but studying as the operating system of his existence, the foundational layer upon which every other function ran. He was in the library by 6 a.m. most mornings, in a carrel near the heating vent, with his textbooks and a thermos of coffee he made in the dormitory kitchen because the campus coffee cost $1.75 and $1.75 was not nothing when your stipend had to cover books and food and the calling card he used every Sunday to phone his mother.

He graduated summa cum laude. His mother wept on the phone. His father said *well done* in a voice so even it sounded like a man trying not to break a window with the force of his own pride.

Then began the years that no one at the graduation ceremony had explained.

The H-1B years. The years of paper and waiting and the particular anxiety of a man whose right to exist in a country depends on a document that expires, that can be denied, that sits in a filing cabinet in some government office being processed by a person who does not know his name and will never know the weight it carries. He worked first at a small firm in Columbus, then at a consulting company that moved him to San Jose, then at a startup that promised equity and delivered eighteen-hour days and a CEO who called the team *family* in the same speech where he announced that the Series B had fallen through.

Each job was a rung. Each rung was a document. Offer letter, employment verification, I-797 approval notice, visa stamp — a bureaucracy of belonging that reduced a man's life to a stack of papers, each one asserting, in the language of federal regulation, that he was allowed to be here. He kept every document in a fireproof safe he bought at Home Depot the month he arrived in California. The safe sat in the closet of his apartment in Sunnyvale, then in Milpitas, then in the house in Dublin — travelling with him like a portable country, the one stable territory in a landscape of contingency.

The green card took seven years. Seven years of premium processing and RFE responses and a lawyer in San Jose whose hourly rate was more than Dapo's father earned in a week at the shop on Bode Thomas Street. When the approval came — a letter, again, cream-coloured, the bureaucracy apparently faithful to its stationery — he sat in his car in a parking lot in Milpitas and held it in both hands and felt something release in his chest that he had not known was clenched. Not joy. Relief. The specific relief of a man who has been holding his breath for seven years and is finally permitted to exhale.

He called his mother. She prayed over the phone for four minutes straight, a prayer so detailed in its gratitude that Dapo wondered if God kept notes. He called his father. Emmanuel said: *Now build.*

*

He built.

The house in Dublin was a four-bedroom on a cul-de-sac with neighbours from Gujarat, from Guangzhou, and a white man named Craig who grew tomatoes in his front yard. The mortgage was $7,200 a month, a number that would have been unimaginable to the boy on Bode Thomas Street but that the man in Dublin carried with the same invisible discipline his father had carried the rent — paid first, paid on time, paid before anything else, because the house was not a house. The house was proof. Proof that the scholarship had worked, that Ohio had worked, that the H-1B years and the green card years and the eighteen-hour days had accumulated into something you could stand inside and say: *I built this. From there to here. I built this.*

The mortgage was the largest number in his life, but it was not the only one. School fees for Femi and Sade — private, because adequate was not a word their children's future could afford. Chinwe's Accord, two years into a five-year loan. The credit cards, managed but present, carrying the accumulated weight of dental work and the trip to Disneyland that Sade had wanted for her birthday, the trip he had said yes to because saying no to his daughter's face required a kind of strength he did not possess.

And there was Nigeria. Nigeria was not a line item on any spreadsheet, but it was the most consistent expense in his life, as regular as the mortgage and more emotionally expensive. His mother's medical bills — the blood pressure medication, the knee that needed surgery, the hospital in Ibadan where you paid before they treated you. Kunle's children's school fees, because a good job at a bank in Lagos was not a good job at a tech company in California, and the exchange rate was a canyon that swallowed the comparison. The cousin who needed capital for a business. The uncle whose roof leaked. The neighbour's son who needed *just a small help, Dapo, you know how it is.*

He knew how it was. The requests came through WhatsApp with a regularity that was almost tidal — each one prefaced with a greeting, an inquiry about his health, a compliment about his success, and then the pivot, the careful turn toward the ask, delivered with the delicacy of people who understood that asking a man for money was an act that required choreography. He never said no. He adjusted the amounts, sometimes. He delayed, occasionally, citing *cash flow* in a way that sounded technical enough to forestall follow-up questions. But he never said no, because saying no would mean admitting that the life they imagined for him — the American life, the tech salary life — had margins thinner than they knew.

The phone was the instrument of this double life. The same device that connected him to Chinwe and the children and his Jira tickets also connected him to the other life, the one that lived in the 234 country code, the one that expected him to be what they had sent him to become. His success was not individual. It was communal property. And communal property cannot declare bankruptcy.

*

He met Chinwe at a friend's wedding in Houston, seven years before the morning in Santa Clara. She was a bridesmaid. He was a groomsman. The pairing was logistical, not romantic — they stood next to each other in photographs that would end up in an album neither of them owned. But during the reception, at a table near the back where the aunties' supervision was thinnest, she turned to him and said, with no preamble: *You look like a man who would rather be reading.*

He laughed — not the professional laugh, not the measured one, but the real one, the one that came from the part of him that his colleagues had never heard. She was right. The fact that she could see this in the way he held his glass of Chapman like a prop in a scene he had not auditioned for told him something about her attention that he found, immediately and without reservation, extraordinary.

She was an accountant from Enugu who had come to America on her own terms — no scholarship, no sponsorship, just a plan and a stubbornness she described, without irony, as *Igbo common sense*. She understood money not as abstraction or anxiety but as a material that could be measured, allocated, and controlled. Here was a woman who could see the spreadsheet of a life and understand its architecture — the load-bearing walls, the decorative ones, the places where the structure needed reinforcement.

They married fourteen months later. His father wore an agbada so white it seemed to generate its own light, and at the Lagos reception he gave a toast that lasted eleven minutes and covered the entire history of the Olusanya family, from the grandfather who had farmed in Oyo to the grandson who had gone to America and built a life that brought honour to them all. Dapo listened with his hand on Chinwe's knee under the table, and what he felt was not embarrassment but vertigo — the sense of being lifted by a narrative larger than himself, carried by it, unable to set it down.

Chinwe was the person who came closest to seeing him. She knew about the remittances, though not always the amounts. She knew he lay awake some nights staring at the ceiling fan that did not work, and she knew not to ask what he was thinking, because the asking would require an admission that the man she had married — the man with the plan, the man who built systems —

was not as solid as he appeared.

She did not ask. This was not neglect. It was the contract they had built together, unconsciously, over seven years — a contract that said: I will trust the version of you that you present to me, and you will trust that my trust is not ignorance but choice. It was a generous contract. It was also, in the way of all contracts built on incomplete information, fragile.

*

The morning the Slack message appeared, the morning Dapo placed his palms flat on the desk and felt the surface hold while everything else began to fall — the first thing he thought was not about the mortgage or the school fees or the cars.

The first thing he thought was his father's hands on his shoulders on the balcony in Lagos, and the instruction that had never been rescinded, that lived in his chest the way the wooden cross hung from his rearview mirror — not because he was devout but because removing it would require an explanation he did not want to give.

Do not come back the same.

He had not gone back the same. He had gone forward, and forward, and forward, building and providing, converting every hour of his life into evidence that the investment had paid off, that the boy from Bode Thomas Street had become the man his father's toast described. And now the structure was shaking, and the only language he had for this moment — the only language his childhood had given him, the only language the balcony and the shop and the church and the culture had ever taught him — was silence.

He could not say *I am struggling*. The sentence existed in English. He knew the words individually. But assembled, in that order, spoken aloud in his own voice, they described a man he did not have permission to be. Not from his father. Not from his mother. Not from the cousins whose WhatsApp messages assumed his permanence. Not from the community at church, where the men's fellowship asked *How are you, brother?* and the only acceptable answer was *We thank God.* Not even from himself — because the self he had built was an architecture of competence, and competence does not crack. Competence does not sit in a parking lot at Ohlone College applying for jobs on campus Wi-Fi. Competence does not stare at letters from the bank's legal department and file them in the glove compartment as though neatness could hold back what they contained.

Competence provides. It provides until it cannot, and then it is silent, because silence is the last thing a provider controls when everything else has been taken.

Dapo removed his palms from the desk. He picked up his thermos — Chinwe's gift, his initials on the bottom — and took a sip of coffee that had gone cold. He stood and walked to the bathroom and locked the door and placed both hands on the edges of the sink and looked at his face in the mirror the way he had looked at it that morning in Dublin — the detached appraisal, the checking of equipment.

The grey at the temples. The jaw his mother said came from his father. The eyes that Chinwe had once told him were the eyes of a man who was always building something, even when he was sitting still.

He straightened his collar. He adjusted the face. He unlocked the door.

The floor was emptying — people leaving with boxes and laptop bags and the particular posture of those who have been told their presence is no longer required. Dapo walked back to his desk. He opened Slack and typed a reply to Kolade's message about the caching ticket, casual, professional, revealing nothing, because revealing nothing was the one system he had built that had never, in forty-two years, failed him.

It would not fail him now. He was certain of this the way his father was certain the rent would be paid, the way his mother was certain the shape of the plantain mattered, the way the boy on the balcony was certain he understood the instruction, that the weight was manageable, that the margins would hold.

He picked up his phone. Three WhatsApp notifications from the family group in Ibadan. He opened the chat. His mother had sent a photograph of the new tiles in the kitchen — the kitchen he had paid to renovate last March — and beneath it, the message: *My son, see how fine. God bless your hands.*

He typed back: *It looks good, Mama. Very fine.*

He did not mention the calendar invite. He did not mention the Slack message. He did not mention that the hands she was blessing were the same hands that had pressed flat against a desk thirty minutes ago, searching for something solid.

He closed the chat. He put the phone face down. He looked at the pipeline dashboard — green, green, green, all systems running — and he waited for ten o'clock.

Chapter Four

I last three days.

I want to tell you it was longer — that the weight of it built slowly, that the lie had time to settle into the architecture of the house the way moisture settles into a foundation before the damage shows. But the truth is less patient than that. Three days. Tuesday to Friday. Seventy-two hours of performing the man I was before the calendar invite, and by Friday evening my body has decided, on my behalf, that it is finished.

It is 8:47 p.m. The children are upstairs. Yemi is in his room with his headphones on, doing whatever fifteen-year-old boys do when they have negotiated an extra hour before lights-out. Dara is in bed already, or pretending to be — she has entered the phase where she reads under the covers with a book light she thinks we don't know about, and Remi and I have silently agreed to let her, because a child who hides reading is a problem we are happy to have.

Remi is in the kitchen.

She is not cooking. This is important, because Remi in the kitchen is usually Remi cooking, and Remi cooking is a specific state of being — purposeful, rhythmic, the kind of movement that makes a room feel governed. But tonight she is standing at the counter with her back to me, sorting the week's mail into two piles. Bills to the left. Everything else to the right. I have watched her do this every Friday for nineteen years, and tonight the ordinary machinery of it — the sound of envelopes being opened, the small decisive tear she makes across the top, never the side — tonight it sounds like someone keeping time.

The kitchen light is the overhead one, the fluorescent that Remi has asked me to replace with something warmer three times. I have not replaced it. Under its flat white gaze, everything looks clinical — the granite counter, the stainless steel sink, the wooden knife block Remi's mother sent from Lagos that holds five knives we use and two we don't. The room does not flatter. It reports.

I am standing in the doorway. I have been standing here for almost a minute, which is long enough that she knows I am here and has chosen not to turn around. This is how Remi signals that she is aware of your presence but has not yet decided to make room for it. It is not coldness. It is triage. She is finishing one thing before she begins another, and I have always admired this about her — the way she moves through tasks sequentially, completely, while I am the man who opens seven browser tabs and completes none of them.

"Remi."

She does not turn. "Mm."

"I need to talk to you."

Now she turns. Not quickly — there is no alarm in it — but with the deliberate rotation of a woman who has heard that sentence before and knows it never precedes anything she wants to hear. She sets the envelope down. She looks at me. Her eyes do the thing they do, the quick scan from my face to my hands to my posture, reading the whole paragraph of me in a single glance.

"Okay," she says. And then, because she is Remi: "Sit down."

I sit. The kitchen chair scrapes against the tile and the sound is too loud for the room. She pulls out the chair across from me, but she does not sit in it immediately. She folds the dish towel that was on the counter. She places it on the rack by the sink. She adjusts the towel so it hangs evenly. Then she sits, and her hands come together on the table in front of her, fingers laced, the way a person sits when they are bracing for something and want their body to be still while they receive it.

I look at her hands. I think about how to begin. I have rehearsed this — in the car, in the shower, in the four-minute walk from the driveway to the front door that I have stretched to eight minutes every evening this week. I have scripted sentences, revised them, discarded them, built new ones. None of them are right. The right words for this do not exist in any language I speak, because what I need to say is not just *I lost my job* but *I have been lying to you for three days* and *I am afraid* and *I do not know what comes next*, and those sentences are different sizes and they don't fit in the same mouth at the same time.

"Tuesday," I say. "When I came home on Tuesday."

"Yes."

"I didn't come from work. I mean — I came from the office. But I wasn't working."

Her fingers tighten. Slightly. Barely. But I see it.

"The company did layoffs. Six hundred people. Across all departments." I pause. "I was one of them."

The kitchen is so quiet I can hear the refrigerator cycling, that low electrical hum that lives beneath every other sound in the house but that you only notice when every other sound has stopped.

Remi does not speak. Her face does not collapse or harden or do any of the things I had prepared for. Instead, it goes still — profoundly, deliberately still — the way a body goes still when it is processing something that requires every available resource. Her eyes stay on mine. She does not blink. I watch her receive the information the way a wall receives a nail: with resistance, and then with accommodation, the material rearranging itself around the new fact.

"Tuesday," she says. Not a question. A coordinate.

"Tuesday morning. Nine o'clock."

"And today is Friday."

"Yes."

"So for three days you have been —" She stops. She unlaces her fingers and places her palms flat on the table and I feel something lurch in my chest because the gesture is so close to what I imagine Dapo's palms on the desk looked like that I have to close my eyes for a second. When I open them, she is still looking at me.

"What have you been doing?" she asks. "During the day. While I'm at work."

"I've been home. Mostly. I've been — looking at job boards. Updating my résumé." This is partially true. I have done these things. I have also spent an hour and forty minutes sitting in the car in the Costco parking lot on Tuesday afternoon, watching a man load bulk toilet paper into a minivan, because the parking lot was the only place where I didn't have to perform anything for anyone.

"Your laptop," she says. "You've been on it every evening. I assumed you were working."

"I know."

"You let me assume that."

"Yes."

She stands. Not dramatically — she doesn't push the chair back or let the legs scrape. She stands with the controlled precision of a woman whose body needs to move but whose mind has not yet decided where. She goes to the sink. She turns the tap on. She fills a glass of water, drinks half of it, sets it on the counter. The tap is still running. She turns it off. These small actions take maybe fifteen seconds, and inside those fifteen seconds I can see her rearranging something — not the facts, which are already landing where they need to land, but her response to them. She is choosing what to say. She is editing in real time.

When she comes back to the table, she does not sit. She stands behind her chair with both hands on the backrest.

"The severance," she says. "How much."

"Twelve weeks. Plus whatever PTO I had accrued."

"That takes us to —" She is calculating. I can see her doing it, her eyes moving slightly to the left the way they do when she is working numbers, and I remember that this is the woman who balances the household budget on the first of every month with a yellow legal pad and a mechanical pencil, who can tell you the exact amount of every recurring bill we have and when it debits. "September," she says. "Maybe early October, if we're careful."

"Remi —"

"The mortgage is sixty-eight hundred. Yemi's school is forty-two hundred a month. Dara's is thirty-eight. The cars, insurance, the—" She stops. She takes a breath. It is not a dramatic breath. It is the breath of a person who has started a list and realised, mid-list, that the list is a cliff and she is already halfway over the edge. "My salary alone won't cover it. You know that."

"I know."

"So what's the plan?"

And there it is. The question I have been dreading — not because I don't have an answer but because the answer I have is the wrong shape. The plan I have built in my head over the past three days is a plan designed for one person. It involves a spreadsheet, a job search timeline, three recruiting contacts from LinkedIn, a revised budget that I have not yet committed to paper but that exists in the mathematical part of my brain like a blueprint waiting for a foundation. It is a reasonable plan. It is a competent plan. And it is a plan that has no room in it for Remi, because admitting that I need her help with this is a sentence I have not yet learned to say out loud.

"I'm going to start applying next week. Aggressively. I've already reached out to a few people."

"Who?"

"A recruiter at Google. Marcus — you remember Marcus, from the platform team — he's connected me with someone at his new company. And I'm going to work the Nigerian network."

"Okay." She nods. Then: "And in the meantime?"

"We tighten up. Reduce discretionary spending. I'll look at the budget this weekend."

"You'll look at the budget."

"Yes."

"The budget I've been managing for nineteen years."

I hear it. The edge. Not anger — Remi does not do anger in the way I was raised to understand it, the loud, percussive, Lagos version where everyone knows where they stand because the volume has made the territory clear. Remi's anger is architectural. It is load-bearing. It shows up as precision, as the sharpening of every word until each one carries exactly the weight she intends and not a gram more.

"That's not what I meant," I say.

"What did you mean?"

"I meant I'll put a plan together. For what we cut, what we adjust. A timeline."

"And I'll — what? Wait for the plan? Receive it? Like a memo?"

"Remi."

"No, I'm asking. Because from where I'm standing, you had three days to tell me, and you used those three days to build a plan *by yourself*, in your head, in this house where I also live and pay bills and raise children, and now you're presenting it to me like —" She stops again. Her hands tighten on the chair back. I watch her knuckles.

"Like what?" I say, even though I know. I know because I can feel it, the thing she is circling, the shape of the accusation that she is too strategic to deliver bluntly because bluntness would let me deflect it.

"Like you don't need me," she says. Her voice is even. Quiet. The quietness is what gets me. "Like this is something that happened to *you*, and I'm just — nearby. Observing."

The refrigerator hums. Somewhere above us, a door closes — Yemi, probably, going to the bathroom. The house continues its nighttime sounds, the settling, the small creaks that I used to find comforting and now hear as the building's own private accounting, every joint and beam carrying its specific weight.

"That's not fair," I say, and even as I say it I know it is the wrong sentence — not wrong because it is untrue, but wrong because fairness is not the unit of measurement this conversation needs. Remi is not talking about fairness. She is talking about partnership, about the distance between a man who carries things alone and a wife who is asking to help carry them, and the thing pressing against every sentence I speak — the thing I can feel in my jaw, in my shoulders, in the way I am gripping my own knee under the table — is the knowledge that she is right and that being right does not make it easier to let go.

"I know it's not fair," she says. "I didn't say it was fair. I said it's how it feels." She pulls the chair out and sits. Something in her posture has shifted — not softer, but more settled, the way a person settles when they have decided to stay in a hard conversation instead of leaving it. "Kolade, do you remember when Dara had the ear infections? Back-to-back, three months, she was two, and you were at that startup with the lunatic CEO and you were working fourteen-hour days?"

"I remember."

"Do you remember what you said when I told you I needed you to take her to the ENT? You said, *I'll handle it.* And then you went to work and I took her to the ENT and I sat in the waiting room filling out the insurance forms and I handled it, because *I'll handle it* meant *I'll think about it and then not do it and you'll do it anyway.*"

"That was twelve years ago."

"It was a pattern twelve years ago. It is still a pattern." She says this without bitterness. She says it the way you'd read out a measurement. "You carry things alone and you call it strength and the rest of us work around you."

I want to argue. The reflex is immediate, muscular — a response so deeply wired that it precedes thought. I want to say: *I carry things alone because that is what I was taught. Because my father carried things alone and his father before him and the whole architecture of manhood I was handed is a structure built for one, a house with no windows, and I have been living inside it so long that I do not know how to open a door without feeling like the walls will come down.* I want to say this, and I don't, because saying it would require an honesty I am not yet capable of, not fully, not at 9 p.m. on a Friday in a kitchen lit by a fluorescent bulb I keep promising to change.

What I say instead is: "I'm telling you now."

She holds my gaze. Three seconds. Five. "Yes," she says. "You are."

It is not forgiveness. It is not resolution. It is acknowledgment — the simplest, most difficult thing two people in a marriage can offer each other. She is saying: *I hear you. I am angry. I am here.*

The silence that follows is the loudest sound in the room.

*

What happens next is not a plan but the beginning of one, and the difference matters. Remi pulls the yellow legal pad from the drawer beneath the phone dock — the same pad she uses for the monthly budget, the same mechanical pencil, the eraser cap already worn to a nub — and she begins writing numbers. Not asking me for them. Writing the ones she already knows, because she has always known them, because the architecture of this household has never been a secret she needed me to reveal. She writes the mortgage. The school fees. The car payments, both of them. Insurance. Utilities. The credit card minimums. The number she sends to her mother in Abeokuta every month, which I have never asked about and which she has never hidden.

I watch her write. Each number lands on the paper like a small, precise weight being placed on a scale.

"Your unemployment," she says, without looking up. "Have you filed?"

"Not yet."

"File tomorrow." This is not a suggestion. It is the voice of a pharmacy technician who counts pills for a living — exact, intolerant of delay, aware that dosage and timing are not separate concerns. "California EDD. You'll need your last pay stub and the separation notice."

"I know how to file for unemployment, Remi."

She looks up. The pencil stops. "Do you?"

I don't answer, because the question is not really about unemployment. The question is: *Do you know how to accept help? Do you know how to be in the room with someone who is trying to solve the same problem you are, without needing to solve it first, without needing to arrive at the answer alone so you can deliver it like a gift instead of sharing it like a burden?*

I don't know. I am learning.

"I'll file tomorrow," I say.

She nods. She writes something on the legal pad — a note to herself, not to me — and then she puts the pencil down and looks at the numbers and I watch her face do the mathematics of our life, the addition and subtraction that will determine what shape the next three months take, and I see the moment when the total registers. She does not say the number. She does not need to. The distance between what comes in and what goes out is a geography we both understand now, a landscape with no landmarks, and we are standing at the edge of it together.

"We'll need to talk about the school," she says.

"I know."

"Not tonight."

"No."

"But soon."

"Yes."

She looks at me across the table. The fluorescent light does nothing kind to either of us, but I am not looking for kindness right now. I am looking at my wife, who has just received the worst news of our marriage and has responded not by falling apart — Remi does not fall apart, she has never fallen apart, she is built from a material I do not have a name for — but by pulling out a legal pad and a pencil and beginning the work of figuring out what comes next.

And I love her for this. And I resent her for this. And the two feelings exist in the same breath, in the same room, under the same inadequate light, and I do not know how to hold them both except to sit here and let them press against each other like tectonic plates beneath a surface that looks, from the outside, like solid ground.

✳

It is almost eleven when we turn the kitchen light off. The legal pad stays on the table, the numbers face-up, because Remi has decided — without saying so — that the numbers will be there in the morning, that they are not the kind of problem you put away in a drawer. We have not resolved anything. We have named the wound and measured its edges and decided, together, that it will not kill us tonight.

Remi goes upstairs first. I stay in the kitchen for another few minutes, standing at the counter where she stood earlier, sorting the remaining mail she didn't finish. Bills to the left. Everything else to the right. My hands do the work automatically, and I am grateful for the automation, for the way the body continues its small tasks even when the mind is somewhere else entirely.

My phone buzzes on the counter. I glance at it. A WhatsApp notification from the Naija Tech Bros group — someone posting about a job opening at Salesforce, a link followed by three prayer-hands emojis. Below it, a message from Dapo, sent twenty minutes ago: *Koly, you dey? Call me when you get chance. No rush.*

No rush. The words sit on the screen with the casual weight of a man who has not yet told his own wife, who is still carrying the news alone, who believes — the way I believed until an hour ago — that silence is a room you can live in indefinitely.

I put the phone face down. I turn off the kitchen light. In the darkness, the room holds its shape — the counter, the chairs, the yellow legal pad with its column of numbers glowing faintly in the light from the hallway. The house is quiet the way houses are quiet when the children are asleep and the adults have said the hard thing and the air between them is not clean but is at least breathable.

I go upstairs. Remi is in bed, on her side, facing the window. She is not asleep. I know this the way I know most things about her — not from evidence but from nineteen years of sleeping beside a body whose rhythms I can read in the dark.

I get into bed. I do not touch her. She does not turn. But she reaches one hand behind her, across the mattress, and leaves it there — palm up, fingers open, in the space between us. Not reaching for me. Just making the space available. Saying, without saying: *I am here. I am still here.*

I take her hand. Her fingers close around mine. The grip is firm and warm and says nothing and everything.

We lie like that — two people in a house they may not be able to keep, holding hands in the dark, with a legal pad full of numbers on the kitchen table below them and two children dreaming above and a friend's message glowing on a phone neither of them will answer tonight.

We are not okay.

We are still in the same room.

Chapter Five

The drive home from Santa Clara took longer than it should have. Not because of traffic — the 680 was open past Sunol, the merge clean, the hills moving past the Camry's windows with the unhurried patience of a landscape that did not know what he was carrying. It took longer because Dapo missed the Dublin Boulevard exit. He watched the sign appear and recede in the mirror and did not correct the mistake immediately. He stayed in the right lane for another two miles, past Stoneridge, past the signs for Pleasanton and Livermore, before pulling off and looping back the way a man loops back from a sentence he has started and cannot finish.

He had been rehearsing on the 580. The words had come in drafts, each one discarded before it reached his mouth. *Chinwe, I need to tell you something.* Too dramatic. *Chinwe, the company restructured today and my role was affected.* Better. Corporate. The passive voice doing its work, distributing the agency across a system instead of a man. But *affected* could mean anything — a delay, a title change, a transfer — and he did not want to introduce ambiguity into a sentence that was already doing more work than it could bear.

By the time he pulled into the driveway — 6:14 p.m., later than usual — he had settled on a version. He had held it in his mouth for the last seven minutes, testing its edges, its weight, the way it sat against his teeth. It was not the truth. But it was adjacent to the truth, close enough that a reasonable man could stand on it without falling, and Dapo was, above all other things, a reasonable man.

He turned off the engine. Through the windshield, the house looked the way it always looked at this hour — the porch light on, the living room window lit with the warm yellow that meant the lamps were on and the overheads were off, which meant Chinwe had finished cooking and had moved to the part of the evening where the house was allowed to be soft. Her Accord was in the garage, pulled forward to the precise mark on the concrete she had measured with painter's tape their first week in the house, because Chinwe did not estimate distances. She confirmed them.

He picked up his phone. No new emails from recruiters. Three notifications from the family WhatsApp. He did not open them.

He got out of the car.

*

The smell met him at the door. Egusi. He knew it before he crossed the threshold — the earthy, dense sweetness of melon seeds simmering with palm oil and stockfish, the smell that was not just food but biography, the entire history of his mother's kitchen in Yaba folded into a pot on a stove in Dublin, California. Chinwe's egusi was not his mother's. She used spinach where Folake used bitter leaf, and she did not pound the melon seeds by hand but blended them, a concession to efficiency that his mother would have considered a moral failing. But the smell was close enough. It always was.

Chinwe was at the stove, weight on her left foot, right hip slightly cocked, wooden spoon moving in the slow circles that meant the egusi was at the stage where it could not be left alone. She wore the grey cotton dress she changed into on days when the office had been long, and her hair was pulled up in a wrap tied without a mirror — the knot slightly off-centre, a small imperfection she would have corrected if she had been looking.

She did not turn when he came in. This was not indifference. It was the particular focus of a woman who understood that egusi at this stage was a negotiation between heat and patience, and that looking away was a concession the pot would punish.

"You're late," she said. Not an accusation. A coordinate.

"Traffic on the 680."

"Mm. Wash your hands. Food is almost ready."

He set his bag on the chair by the door. He washed his hands at the kitchen sink, standing beside her, close enough that his arm brushed hers. She shifted slightly to make room, the way two people shift in a space they have shared long enough that accommodation is automatic.

The sentence was sitting in his chest like a stone he had swallowed on the freeway. It was there, solid and specific, pressing against the base of his throat, and the longer he stood in the warm kitchen with the egusi steaming and Chinwe's elbow moving in its slow rhythm and the house doing what houses do at this hour, the harder it became to say. Not because the words were difficult. Because of what the words would do to this room — this specific room, at this specific hour, with the food at this specific stage and his wife's face in this specific state of unsuspecting calm. The words would change the air. And once the air was changed, it could not be put back.

He would tell her. He would. But not standing at the counter while she cooked. He would tell her properly. After the children were in bed. After the house had gone quiet. He would tell her the way a man tells his wife something that matters: deliberately, with the next steps already mapped, so that the news arrived not as a wound but as a problem with a solution attached.

This was not a lie. This was timing.

He opened the cabinet and took down two plates.

*

Femi came downstairs at the sound of plates being set. He appeared in the doorway the way thirteen-year-old boys appear — suddenly, entirely, as though assembled from available materials and delivered to the threshold fully formed. He was wearing a T-shirt from a coding camp Dapo had sent him to last summer in San Jose, the one that cost two thousand dollars for the privilege of imagining your offspring's future. The shirt was too small now. Femi was growing at a rate that made Dapo feel as though he were watching a time-lapse of his own body — the same shoulders, the same long arms, the same way of standing with his weight slightly forward.

Chinwe served. The egusi went into a deep bowl, the pounded yam into another. She brought out a small dish of fried plantain — sliced diagonally, the way Dapo's mother cut it, the way he had mentioned once, years ago, and that Chinwe had absorbed into her repertoire without comment, without fanfare.

They sat. Chinwe said grace — short, Catholic, efficient. *Bless this food. Bless this family. Amen.* Femi's amen came a beat late, his eyes already on the bowl. Dapo's came on time, the word forming automatically in his mouth while the rest of him was somewhere else entirely — on the 680, in the ten o'clock meeting where the woman from People Operations had used his name twice and both times it had sounded like a word being erased.

He ate. The egusi was good — it was always good — and the act of eating was a relief, a physical task that required his hands and his mouth and enough attention to create the appearance of presence. He tore the pounded yam the way his father had taught him — right hand, a small piece rolled between the fingers, pressed into the soup, lifted — and the ritual was steadying.

"How was work?" Chinwe asked.

The question arrived the way it arrived every evening — casually, between bites. He had the answer ready. He had been carrying it since the 580.

"Actually," he said. He set the pounded yam down. "I've been meaning to talk to you about something."

Chinwe looked up. Her face was open, attentive — the face of a woman who had not yet been given a reason to rearrange it.

"The company is going through some restructuring. My team was affected. They're eliminating a number of senior positions."

"Your position?" Her spoon was suspended between the bowl and her mouth.

"My role, yes. It's — they're calling it a restructuring, but essentially, I'm between opportunities right now."

Between opportunities. The phrase tasted like plastic. It was a phrase from LinkedIn, from networking events, from the curated vocabulary of men trained to describe unemployment the way estate agents describe small rooms — not as what they are but as what they could become. It did not describe a man who had sat in a bathroom at his former office with his hands on the edges of a sink, checking his own face for damage.

Chinwe set her spoon down slowly, with the controlled precision of a woman who needed her hands free. "When did this happen?"

"Today."

This was true. It had happened today. The fact that it had happened at nine o'clock and it was now six-thirty, and that he had spent the intervening hours driving in circles on the 880 and sitting in a Walgreens parking lot staring at a job board — these were details. They were the kind of details that would shift the conversation from *news* to *confession*, and he did not want a confession. He wanted an exchange of information between two adults, calm and structured, with the emotional register of a meeting that ends on time.

"Dapo." Something in her frequency had shifted. "Are you okay?"

"I'm fine. It's not ideal, obviously. But these things happen. The whole industry is going through it — Google, Meta, everybody. It's cyclical."

He was speaking the language of the market now. *Cyclical.* As though the cycle would complete itself while he waited, the way seasons complete themselves, and at the end of the rotation he would be standing in the same place, employed, providing, the structure intact.

Chinwe watched him eat. She was measuring the distance between what he had said and what he had not said. Chinwe was an accountant. She worked with numbers that either balanced or did not, and she had the accountant's instinct for gaps — the sense that a ledger was showing her one column when there should be two.

"What's the severance?"

"Twelve weeks. Plus accrued PTO."

She nodded. The nod was not acceptance. It was acknowledgment — receiving the data, filing it, reserving judgment. Except she did not have the full picture. She had the picture he had given her, which was accurate in its components and misleading in its frame, the way a cropped photograph can show you a room without showing you the fire.

"I've already started looking," he said. "A few people in my network are at companies that are hiring. Data engineering is still in demand."

"Good." She picked up her spoon. She ate. The conversation, in its surface mechanics, was functioning — two adults discussing a setback. The orthodontist who had overcharged them. The car accident. The month when the dishwasher and the water heater failed in the same week. They had managed. They always managed.

"I'll probably have something within a few weeks," he said. "A month at most."

Femi looked up from his plate. "Did you get fired?"

The word landed like a glass dropped on tile. *Fired.* A thirteen-year-old's word — blunt, unsheathed, carrying none of the corporate padding adults wrapped around it.

"No," Dapo said. "The company eliminated the position. It's different."

"How is it different?"

"Femi." Chinwe's voice was soft but final. The boundary was drawn. Femi looked at his mother, then his father, and whatever he saw in the geometry between them was enough. He returned to his plate.

*

He picked up Sade from Mrs Obi's at seven twenty-eight. She climbed into the back seat with her backpack and a bag of chin chin, because Mrs Obi expressed affection through fried dough the way other women expressed it through words. Sade was ten, small for her age, with Chinwe's cheekbones and Dapo's quiet way of entering a room as though she had already studied it from a distance.

"How was Amara's?"

"Good. We watched a movie."

"Which one?"

"The one with the dog that talks."

"Was it good?"

"The dog was funny. The people were boring."

He smiled. It was a real smile — the first since nine o'clock that morning — and it came from the part of him that was not performing. He glanced at her in the rearview. She was looking out the window, chin propped on her hand, watching the streetlights pass with the thoughtful attention of a child who was always, quietly, cataloguing the world.

She did not ask about his day. She was ten. His day was a room in the house of adulthood whose door she had not yet learned to open. He was grateful for this. Grateful that the contract between a father and a ten-year-old required less disclosure, less of the careful architecture of partial truth.

Two blocks from home, she fell asleep. Her head tilted slowly to the left, her hand dropped from her chin, her body surrendering to the specific gravity of a child who has been safe enough, for long enough, that sleep is not a decision but a reflex.

He carried her inside. She was heavier than he expected — heavier than the last time, which he could not remember, and this troubled him, the idea that there had been a last time and he had not known it, that the ordinary acts of fatherhood were passing through his hands like water.

Chinwe met him in the hallway. She looked at Sade's sleeping face and her expression softened in the way it only softened for the children — the full, unguarded tenderness she held in reserve, that she rationed with the discipline of a woman who understood that love, like any resource, was more powerful when it was concentrated.

He laid Sade on her bed, removed her shoes, pulled the comforter up. She murmured something he couldn't make out and settled. He stood in the doorway and looked at the glow-in-the-dark stars she had stuck to the ceiling last summer — a constellation of her own invention, a private sky. The stars glowed faintly green in the dark, a weak, persistent light.

He closed the door.

*

The house went quiet the way their house always went quiet — in stages. Femi's door at nine-fifteen. The dishwasher starting its cycle. The bathroom light switching off.

Dapo lay in bed and stared at the ceiling fan that did not work.

Chinwe was beside him, reading on her tablet — articles from financial sites, *The Balance*, *NerdWallet*, the kind of reading other people found tedious and that Chinwe found calming. Numbers soothed her.

"Dapo."

"Mm."

"We should look at the budget this weekend. If we're going to be on one income for a few weeks, I want to see the numbers."

"Okay."

"I'll pull the statements tomorrow. I need your last three pay stubs and the severance letter when it comes."

"I'll get them."

She turned off the tablet. The room went dark except for the hallway nightlight — the one they had installed when Sade was four and afraid of the dark, the one nobody had removed because removing it would mean admitting that the daughter who needed it was becoming the daughter who did not.

"It's going to be fine," she said, facing the ceiling. "You're good at what you do. Someone will snap you up."

Snap you up. The phrase had a brightness to it that belonged to the woman who had married a senior data engineer whose salary she could build a life around. She was not wrong to be confident. His résumé was strong. His skills were current. Men with his experience did not stay unemployed for long. This was the rational case. And Dapo believed the rational case the way a man on a bridge believes the engineering — not because he has inspected the cables but because the alternative is unthinkable.

"A few weeks," he said. "Maybe a month."

"Call Emeka. At Databricks. Didn't he say they were hiring?"

"I'll reach out tomorrow."

"Good." She turned on her side, facing away. "Goodnight."

"Goodnight."

He listened to her breathing change. Four minutes. He counted, the way he counted everything now, as though assigning numbers to the dark could make it measurable. Her breathing deepened. Her shoulder rose and fell in the slow cadence of sleep. She was gone, trusting the day to hold, trusting the man beside her to be what he had always been.

He lay awake.

The ceiling fan hung above him, motionless, its blades furred with dust he could not see but knew was there. He had told Chinwe he would fix it. February. It was June. Four months of looking at it every morning, adding it to the list that was no longer a list of household tasks but something heavier — a catalogue of things deferred, each item pressing against the next like books on a shelf loaded past its capacity.

He reached for his phone. The screen lit the room briefly, held close to his chest. He opened LinkedIn. His feed was a wall of announcements — people starting new roles, celebrating promotions, the curated joy of a platform that monetised optimism. Each post was a small, bright window into a life that was working, and each one made the dark around him darker.

He closed LinkedIn. He opened the job board. Senior data engineer, Redwood City. Staff data engineer, Sunnyvale. He read the descriptions systematically, matching requirements against his own inventory. Two of the three were reasonable. He bookmarked them. He would apply tomorrow.

Tomorrow. The word was doing a lot of work tonight. Tomorrow he would update the résumé. Tomorrow he would call Emeka. Tomorrow he would file for unemployment — though he had not told Chinwe this, because *unemployment* was a word that carried weight she did not need to feel, not yet, not while the severance was still a buffer between them and the edge.

He put the phone face down on his chest. He stared at the fan.

His heart was beating faster than it should have been. He noticed this the way he might notice an anomaly in a dashboard — a metric slightly outside its expected range, not alarming, not yet, but present. He took a breath. Another. The beating did not slow. It sat in his chest like a second clock, the two rhythms slightly out of sync in a way only he could perceive, only in the dark, in the specific silence of a house where everyone was asleep and the man who was supposed to be asleep was lying on his back with a phone on his chest and a heartbeat he could not quiet and a ceiling fan that did not work and a wife who believed him and children who did not know and a sentence — *I am struggling* — that sat in his throat like a bone he could neither swallow nor cough up.

He closed his eyes.

Sleep did not come. Not for a long time. And when it finally did — in that borderland between consciousness and surrender where the body overrules the mind — it came not as rest but as retreat, the temporary withdrawal of a man who would wake in five hours and stand at the counter in the dark and make his coffee and rehearse the day's performance before the audience arrived.

The ceiling fan hung above him. The dust settled. The crack held his weight, for now.

For now.

Chapter Six

The group already has a name by Wednesday morning. Someone — I think it was Emeka, though Emeka will deny this later with the theatrical innocence of a man who knows exactly what he did — has changed the WhatsApp group name from *Naija Tech Bros* to *Severance Package FC*. Below it, the group description reads: *We move. (Where exactly, nobody knows.)*

I see the name change on my phone at 6:47 a.m., sitting in the kitchen before Remi comes down, in that brief window where the house belongs to me and the coffee is still hot and I can look at my phone without performing anything for anyone. The name makes me laugh. Not the big laugh — not the one that comes from the belly and surprises the room — but the quiet one, the one that escapes through the nose, the laugh of a man who has been holding his breath and has been given, by a joke he did not ask for, temporary permission to exhale.

I scroll up. The group has been active since midnight. Thirty-seven members, and at least a dozen of them have been talking through the small hours — the insomniac shift, the men who lie awake in houses across the East Bay and the Peninsula while their families sleep, turning their phones into the only room where what happened can be discussed without the weight of being watched.

The messages are layered the way WhatsApp messages always are in Nigerian groups — overlapping, interrupting, three conversations happening simultaneously like traffic at a Lagos roundabout where nobody yields but everybody, somehow, gets through.

Chidi Nwosu [12:14 AM]

Bros who has the recruiter contact at Stripe? The one that was posting on LinkedIn last week. Tall guy. Igbo name.

Wale Bakare [12:15 AM]

Every Igbo guy on LinkedIn is posting about Stripe

Chidi Nwosu [12:15 AM]

■ I said tall

Emeka Obi [12:17 AM]

Stripe is on freeze bro. My guy there said they're not backfilling senior roles till Q4

Tola Balogun [12:21 AM]

Not true. I have a phone screen with them Thursday

Chidi Nwosu [12:22 AM]

TOLA. Thursday? You just got laid off Tuesday.

Tola Balogun [12:23 AM]

Applied three hours after the email. What am I waiting for? Mourning period? ■

Wale Bakare [12:24 AM]

This one is not serious ■

Emeka Obi [12:25 AM]

Tola please share your LeetCode routine because some of us are still on the denial stage

Tola Balogun [12:26 AM]

I don't do LeetCode. LeetCode is for people who don't know how to talk. Interview is conversation. You tell them what you built and why it mattered. That's it.

Chidi Nwosu [12:27 AM]

Spoken like someone with no mortgage

Tola Balogun [12:27 AM]

Spoken like someone who sleeps at night ■■■■■

I read this exchange the way you read a weather report when the storm has already passed your house but is heading toward someone else's. Tola's ease does not sting the way I expected it to. Not now. Not after Friday night with Remi, after the legal pad and the numbers and the hand she left palm-up on the mattress. I have told the truth — not all of it, not the deepest parts, not the places where the fear sits like sediment at the bottom of a glass I keep trying to drink from — but enough that the act of reading Tola's confidence does not feel like an accusation. It feels like watching someone who is travelling light pass someone who is travelling heavy, and understanding, without resentment, that the difference is not talent. It is luggage.

Tola is twenty-nine. Single. Rents a one-bedroom in Mountain View with a roommate who works at Apple. No children. No mortgage. No mother in Abeokuta waiting for the monthly transfer. No father's instruction sitting in her chest like a second heartbeat. Tola has herself, her MacBook, her gym membership, and the frictionless mobility of a person whose life can be packed into two suitcases and relocated in a weekend. She will be fine. She will be fine because her version of fine requires only herself.

I do not envy this. I want to be clear. I have Remi. I have the children. I have a house with a red door and a driveway I measured the week we moved in. These are not burdens. They are the architecture of a life I chose, and I would choose it again, every morning, without hesitation. But the architecture has weight. And the weight is what makes the fall different.

I keep scrolling.

Jide Adeyinka [1:03 AM]

Guys honest question. Anyone know what happens if you can't make mortgage while on severance? Is there a grace period or does the bank just come for your neck

Emeka Obi [1:05 AM]

Talk to your lender before you miss a payment. They have forbearance options. Google "loss mitigation" + your bank name.

Jide Adeyinka [1:06 AM]
I'm asking for a friend
Wale Bakare [1:06 AM]
We're all asking for a friend ■

Nobody replies for four minutes after that. The silence on a WhatsApp group at 1 a.m. is not the same as silence in a room. In a room, silence has texture — you can feel the other person breathing, shifting, deciding whether to speak. On a screen, silence is absence. The chat holds its last message the way a page holds its last sentence, and you cannot tell if the people on the other side are thinking or sleeping or staring at their ceiling fans in houses across the Bay Area, counting the minutes the way I count cracks in the driveway.

Then someone posts a meme. A stock photo of a man in a suit sitting at a desk with his head in his hands, and the caption reads: *When you update your LinkedIn to "Open to Work" and your auntie in Lagos calls to ask why you're advertising your shame.* Three laughing emojis follow. Then four more. Then Wale sends the one with the coffin dancers — the Ghanaian pallbearers, the meme that has outlived its era and become a permanent fixture in the visual vocabulary of men who need to laugh at things that are not funny.

I screenshot the meme. I don't send it to anyone. I just hold it, the way you hold a receipt from a restaurant you went to on a good night — not because the paper matters but because it is proof that the night happened, that laughter was possible, that a room full of men who had lost the same thing could still make each other laugh at 1 a.m. on a Wednesday.

I put the phone face down. Remi's footsteps on the stairs. The day begins.

*

Dapo read the same messages at 5:52 a.m., standing at the kitchen counter in Dublin with the French press steeping and the house still dark around him. He had been awake since four. The ceiling fan — the broken one, the one he had not fixed — had become a kind of clock in the dark, a fixed point his eyes returned to while his mind moved through rooms he could not enter during the day: the mortgage statement, the orthodontist bill, the email from the school about next year's tuition deposit, due July 15th.

He opened WhatsApp with his thumb and the group's new name — *Severance Package FC* — appeared at the top of his chat list like a headline he had not subscribed to. He scrolled from the beginning, reading each message with the systematic attention he gave to pull requests, missing nothing, noting everything, cataloguing the information the way his father had catalogued fabric — by type, by weight, by the occasion it was meant to serve.

Chidi needed a recruiter contact. Emeka said Stripe was frozen. Then Tola.

Tola had a phone screen on Thursday.

Dapo read the message twice. He read Tola's follow-up — *What am I waiting for? Mourning period?* — and the laughing emoji that followed it, and something moved in his chest that was not quite envy and not quite admiration but the specific discomfort of a man watching someone navigate the same terrain at a different speed. Tola moved through the world the way data moved through a well-designed pipeline — efficiently, without bottlenecks, each stage completing before the next one required input. Dapo had built systems like that. He knew the architecture. He also knew that the architecture worked because the inputs were clean, and Tola's inputs were clean in a way that his own had not been since the day he signed the mortgage, since the day

Femi was born, since the day his father placed both hands on his shoulders and said the thing that had never been rescinded.

He did not resent Tola. The feeling was subtler than that, harder to name — the feeling of a man who understands the engineering of someone else's lightness and knows it cannot be replicated because the specifications are different. Tola had designed her life for speed. Dapo had designed his for load-bearing. Both designs were valid. But only one of them survived a disruption without structural damage.

Chidi Nwosu [12:27 AM]

Spoken like someone with no mortgage

Dapo stared at the message. The truth of it sat in the air above his phone like steam from the French press — visible, temporary, already dissolving. He wanted to type something. He opened the keyboard and his thumbs hovered over the glass and for a moment he could feel the shape of the words he wanted to say: *Bros, the mortgage is $7,200 a month and the severance runs out in September and I have not told Chinwe how bad it is and I don't know how to start.* The words were there, fully formed, pressing against the screen like passengers against a closed door. He could feel their weight in his thumbs.

He typed: ■■

Two laughing emojis. The minimum viable response. Enough to register presence without revealing position. He pressed send and watched the message appear beneath the others and felt the specific relief of a man who has participated without being seen — the relief that would, in the months to come, become his primary mode of engagement with the group, with the church, with Chinwe, with every room and screen and conversation that asked him how he was doing. Fine. We thank God. ■■.

He kept scrolling.

Jide Adeyinka [1:03 AM]

Guys honest question. Anyone know what happens if you can't make mortgage while on severance?

Dapo read the message and his hand tightened around the phone. Not dramatically — the French press did not rattle, the counter did not shift — but with the quiet intensity of a man who has just heard his own question asked by someone else's voice. Jide was in Milpitas. Three children. Wife taught at a community college. Dapo did not know the details of Jide's mortgage, but he knew the neighbourhood, and he knew what houses in Milpitas cost, and the mathematics were close enough that Jide's question could have been extracted from the part of Dapo's brain that he had walled off since Tuesday morning.

Anyone know what happens if you can't make mortgage while on severance?

He read Emeka's reply about forbearance and loss mitigation. He read Wale's response: *We're all asking for a friend.* He did not laugh. The joke was accurate in the way that only jokes between men in crisis are accurate — not because it was funny but because it named the thing everyone was pretending not to feel, the way a doctor names the disease so the patient can stop calling it *that pain in my chest*.

He closed the app. He poured the coffee. He drank it standing at the counter in the dark, and in the silence of the house — the refrigerator cycling, Chinwe's breathing through the ceiling, the nightlight in the hallway casting its faint yellow glow — he made a decision. Not the decision he should have made. Not the one that Kolade would make, imperfectly but actually, on a Friday night in a kitchen with a fluorescent light and a wife who refused to be excluded. Dapo's decision was quieter, and more dangerous, and it sat in his body the way the mortgage sat in the filing cabinet: neatly, invisibly, accruing.

He would not tell the group. He would not tell Chinwe the full truth. He would manage this the way he managed everything — systematically, privately, with the discipline of a man who had been taught that competence does not crack. He would apply to jobs. He would optimise his résumé. He would prepare for interviews with the methodical intensity he had given to every challenge since Ohio — the scholarship, the H-1B, the green card, the mortgage. He had solved every one of them. He would solve this.

The coffee was hot and bitter. He drank it. The house held its silence around him like a room with walls he could not see.

*

By the weekend, the group has developed its own rhythms. I watch them the way I once watched the patterns in a codebase I was learning — the recurring functions, the hidden dependencies, the parts that look decorative but turn out to be load-bearing.

Mornings belong to the job hunters. Between 6 and 9 a.m., the group is a feed of links — LinkedIn postings, Lever applications, the occasional direct referral from someone whose cousin's friend's former colleague is a hiring manager at Databricks or Confluent or one of the companies that are still growing while the rest of the industry contracts. The links arrive with commentary, brief and practical: *This one is legit, I know the hiring manager* or *Don't bother, they ghosted me after the third round* or, most often, *Forwarding in case*, which is the WhatsApp equivalent of leaving a door open without promising what is behind it.

Afternoons are quieter. The job hunters have retreated into their applications and their LeetCode sessions and the particular exhaustion of performing competence on a screen for eight hours when the audience is a hiring manager who does not know your name. The messages that come in the afternoon are logistical — questions about COBRA, about California EDD, about whether severance payments affect unemployment eligibility. Emeka, who worked in fintech before the layoff and has the particular fluency of a man who has read the fine print on everything, answers most of these with the patience of a community college professor, the kind of patience that costs nothing and saves everything.

Evenings are different. The evenings belong to the men who cannot sleep.

> **Segun Ajayi** [11:47 PM]
>
> Anyone else just sitting in their car in the garage? No? Just me? Cool cool cool
>
> **Wale Bakare** [11:48 PM]
>
> Bro WHY are you in the garage
>
> **Segun Ajayi** [11:49 PM]
>
> Because the WiFi reaches and my wife thinks I'm checking the tire pressure
>
> **Emeka Obi** [11:50 PM]
>
> ■■■ tire pressure at midnight
>
> **Segun Ajayi** [11:51 PM]
>
> The tires are very important Emeka

I read these messages in bed, beside Remi, who is asleep or near-asleep, her hand no longer reaching across the mattress — not because the gesture has been withdrawn but because it has been replaced by something else, something sturdier, the quiet proximity of a woman who has decided to stay in the room even when the room is uncomfortable. She knows I am on my phone. She does not ask. This is the new contract between us — not the old silence, which was a wall, but a newer silence, which is a window left open. She can see me, and I can be seen, and neither of us needs to narrate what is visible.

Segun's joke about the tire pressure makes me smile. It also makes me want to call him, to say something that the group cannot hold — something about the particular loneliness of a married man sitting in a car he is still paying off, pretending to be somewhere he is not, performing even his solitude. But I do not call. That is not what the group is for. The group is the in-between — more honest than the dinner table, less honest than the 2 a.m. conversation a man has with himself. It is the room where you can say *I am sitting in my car at midnight* and have twelve men respond with laughing emojis and everyone understands that the laughter is not about the joke. The laughter is the sound of men recognising each other in the dark.

Tola Balogun [Saturday, 2:14 PM]

Update: Stripe phone screen went well. Moving to onsite next week.

Chidi Nwosu [2:15 PM]

Already?? Tola what are you eating

Tola Balogun [2:16 PM]

Confidence and protein shakes

Emeka Obi [2:17 PM]

■

Wale Bakare [2:18 PM]

Make sure you negotiate the RSUs o. Don't let them lowball you because you're eager

Tola Balogun [2:19 PM]

I know my worth. They will pay me or I will walk.

Jide Adeyinka [2:22 PM]

■■

There is a pause after Jide's message. Seven minutes. An eternity in a group that usually responds in seconds. I notice it because I am counting — because counting is the thing I do when I am trying to understand the shape of a silence. Seven minutes in which thirty-seven men read Tola's update and weighed it against their own. Seven minutes in which every man in this group did the private mathematics of comparison — where he was versus where Tola was, how many applications he had sent versus how many had replied, the specific distance between his own progress and the young woman in Mountain View who had applied three hours after the layoff and was already moving to the onsite round.

Then the chat continues, as chats do, filling the silence with the next thing and the next thing and the next, because the alternative — sitting with the comparison, letting it settle — is too expensive.

Chidi Nwosu [2:29 PM]

Anyone know if Google is doing phone screens for L5/L6? My recruiter went quiet

Wale Bakare [2:31 PM]

Google recruiters are quiet because Google is doing another round next month. Source: my guy in Kirkland

Chidi Nwosu [2:32 PM]

■

Emeka Obi [2:33 PM]

The way this industry is going we'll all be farming by December

Wale Bakare [2:34 PM]

Farming is honest work o. My grandfather in Ekiti will show you the way

Emeka Obi [2:35 PM]

Your grandfather didn't have $8,000 rent in Cupertino

Someone posts a link to an article about tech companies rehiring the people they laid off six months later at lower salaries. Three angry-face emojis. Then a meme — a man in a suit shaking hands with the same man in a suit, captioned *Getting re-hired at your own company for 30% less*. The group laughs. The group always laughs. The laughter is the mortar between the bricks, the thing that holds the structure together when the individual pieces are too heavy to carry alone.

*

Dapo watched the group from a distance that was measured not in miles but in disclosure.

He was present. He responded to the job links with thumbs-up emojis. He answered a question from Chidi about data pipeline architecture — a technical query, safe, the kind of exchange that allowed him to be helpful without being visible. He posted a link to a job opening at a company in San Mateo that he had found on LinkedIn, a senior data engineering role whose requirements he matched precisely and whose application he had already submitted, though he did not mention this, because mentioning it would open a thread he could not control. Someone would ask how the application went. Someone would follow up. And then he would have to say something — *waiting to hear back* or *they passed* or *still in process* — and each update would be a small window into the progress of his search, a progress that, by the end of the first week, was already behind the curve he had projected.

He had applied to fourteen positions. Three had sent automated rejections within hours — the algorithmic no, instant, bloodless, a machine deciding his future in the time it took him to open the notification. Two had moved him to a phone screen. The rest were silence, the particular silence of a job application that has entered the system and is being processed by forces he cannot see or influence, the same silence he remembered from the H-1B years when his life existed in a filing cabinet in a government office and the only thing he could do was wait.

He did not share this with the group. He could not. The group was a performance space — he understood this with the clarity of a man who had been performing his entire adult life, who knew the difference between a room where you could be honest and a room where honesty was permitted only in the form of jokes, where *I'm struggling* had to be dressed in laughing emojis before it could be spoken. The group was necessary and the group was insufficient, and the distance between those two things was the space where Dapo lived.

Tola's update — *Stripe phone screen went well, moving to onsite next week* — arrived while Dapo was sitting in the public library in Fremont, at a desk near the back, his laptop open to a job board, the library's Wi-Fi connecting him to the world while the library's silence wrapped around him like a second office, the one Chinwe did not know about. She believed he was meeting a former colleague for coffee. He had told her this at breakfast, casually, with the offhand precision of a lie that has been designed to be uninteresting enough that it does not invite follow-up questions.

He read Tola's message. He read the responses — the congratulations, the teasing, the goat emoji from Emeka that meant *greatest of all time* and also meant *you are making the rest of us look slow*. He read Wale's advice about RSUs and Tola's reply — *I know my worth. They will pay me or I will walk* — and the seven-minute silence that followed, and he understood the silence the way he understood every silence in this group, because he was fluent in the language of what was not said.

He closed WhatsApp. He opened the job board. He applied to two more positions — a data engineering lead in Redwood

City, a staff role at a startup in Palo Alto whose job description used the word *disruptive* four times in three paragraphs. He customised each cover letter. He matched each keyword. He did the work with the same meticulous attention he had given to the junior engineer's migration script on Tuesday morning, the same care, the same generosity with his own effort, because this was the only strategy he knew: do the work. Do it well. Do it until the system recognises you.

The library was quiet around him. Two aisles away, a woman was reading to a child, the soft cadence of a picture book, and the sound reached him the way sounds reach you when you are underwater — muffled, distant, belonging to a world that is above you and still breathing.

His phone buzzed. A text from Chinwe: *How is the coffee? Say hi to Emeka for me.*

He typed: *Good. Will do. Home by 3.*

He pressed send. He put the phone face down on the library desk and turned back to the screen, where the cursor blinked in an empty search bar, patient, expectant, waiting for him to type the next query, the next application, the next version of himself that a company in a glass building might find worth hiring.

*

By Sunday evening, the group has become what every Nigerian WhatsApp group eventually becomes — a small country, complete with its own government, its own economy, its own unwritten constitution. The rules are understood, never stated: you share job leads without being asked. You congratulate without bitterness, or with bitterness so well disguised that it passes for humour. You do not post about your savings or your debts. You do not mention the calls from your mother asking why you sound different, why your voice has lost the particular brightness that a mother recognises the way a musician recognises pitch.

Segun has gone quiet. I notice because I notice absences — it is a habit I developed after Dapo, though I cannot say that yet, not in this telling, not at this point in the story where Dapo is still alive and present and sending two-emoji responses to threads he cannot bear to enter. But the habit is there, already forming, the way a crack forms in concrete before you can see it from the surface. Segun posted the tire-pressure joke on Thursday night. By Sunday he has not posted again. His last message — *The tires are very important Emeka* — sits in the chat like a door that was open and is now closed, and nobody has knocked.

I want to knock. I draft a DM three times. *Segun, you good?* Delete. *Bro, just checking in.* Delete. *Segun, I know the car thing wasn't really about the tires.* Delete. Each draft feels either too casual or too heavy, too much or not enough, and the calibration is exhausting — the work of being a man who wants to ask another man a real question without either of them having the language for what a real answer would sound like.

I don't send the message. I put the phone down and go to the kitchen, where Remi is making jollof rice for the week, the big pot, the one that serves as both cooking vessel and time capsule, and the smell of it — tomato and scotch bonnet and the particular sweetness of onions that have been cooked past gold into something darker and richer — fills the house the way certain sounds fill a room, completely, leaving no corner unoccupied.

She looks up when I come in. "You're quiet," she says.

"I'm thinking."

"About?"

"The guys in the group. Segun went quiet."

She stirs the pot. The wooden spoon moves in the slow circles that mean the rice is at the stage where attention matters. "Quiet how?"

"Just — stopped posting. He was active all week. Now nothing."

Remi nods. She does not offer advice or platitudes. She stirs. "You could call him," she says. Not *you should.* Not *why don't you.* Just *you could*, leaving the door open the way she leaves doors open now — without force, without pressure, just the acknowledgment that the door exists and my hand is near the handle.

"Maybe tomorrow," I say.

She lets it sit.

*

On Sunday night, Dapo composed a message to the group. He did not send it.

He was sitting in bed, the phone held close, Chinwe's breathing steady beside him. The cursor blinked in the text field. He had been staring at it for four minutes — counted, as always, the way he counted the time it took Chinwe to fall asleep, the way he counted the automated rejections, the way he counted the days since Tuesday as though the counting itself could impose order on what was falling apart.

The message he had composed was not long. It read: *Bros, real talk. How are you guys actually doing? Not the LinkedIn version. The real version.*

He read it back. The words sat on the screen like a key to a room he had never entered. He could see what would happen if he sent it — the pause, the shift in the group's register, the moment when the jokes stopped and the masks came down and thirty-seven men looked at the question and decided, each one separately, whether to answer it honestly or to respond with the performative laughter that had become the group's default currency.

Someone would answer honestly. He believed this. Segun, maybe. Jide. Possibly Wale, whose jokes were getting darker in a way that suggested the comedy was running out and the thing beneath it was beginning to show. Someone would say the thing that nobody had said yet — *I am afraid* or *I don't know how to tell my wife* or *I lie awake at night and my heart does things I cannot explain* — and the saying of it would change the room, the way Kolade's telling had changed his kitchen on Friday night, the way truth changes any space it enters, not by making it better but by making it real.

But he could not send it. Not because the words were wrong. Because sending them would mean he was one of the men who needed the answer. And Dapo Olusanya, who had crossed an ocean and survived Ohio and built a house and maintained a pipeline and provided for two families on two continents — Dapo Olusanya was not one of those men. Could not be. The architecture would not allow it. The instruction from the balcony would not allow it. The face in the mirror, checked each morning with the detached appraisal of a man inspecting equipment, would not allow it.

He deleted the message. Character by character, watching each word disappear from the screen the way channels had disappeared from Slack on Tuesday morning — quietly, without ceremony, as though they had never been there.

He typed instead: *Good night bros. We go dey alright.* ■■

He pressed send. He put the phone face down on his chest. He stared at the ceiling fan.

The group responded. Fist emojis. Fire emojis. *We move* from Chidi. *No shaking* from Wale. The affirmations arrived like small lights in a dark room, each one genuine, each one insufficient, the community doing what the community knew how to do — holding the shape, maintaining the structure, offering the words that kept the conversation in the register where everyone could breathe.

Dapo did not read the responses. His phone sat face down on his chest, rising and falling with his breathing, and the vibrations of each incoming message were small tremors he could feel but chose not to interpret, the way a man can feel the early signs of something wrong in his body and choose, with the full weight of his will, to call it nothing.

The house was quiet. The fan was still. The crack held.

*

I see Dapo's message on Monday morning, scrolling back through the night's chat while the coffee steeps.

Good night bros. We go dey alright.

Five words and a fist emoji. I read them twice. They sound like Dapo — steady, encouraging, the voice of a man who has processed the crisis and arrived at something solid enough to stand on. They sound like the Dapo I have known for eleven years, the man who makes the room calmer by being in it, whose competence is not a performance but a frequency, a station he has tuned to so long that it sounds like who he is.

But I am reading them on a Monday morning in a house where I told the truth on Friday, and the telling has changed my eyes. I see things now that I did not see before — the way Remi's hand on the legal pad made the problem real, the way naming the wound did not heal it but at least identified where to apply pressure. And reading Dapo's message through these new eyes, I notice something I would not have noticed a week ago.

He has not said how *he* is doing. Not once. Not in the group, not in the DMs, not in the message he sent me Thursday night — *Koly, you dey? Call me when you get chance. No rush* — that I answered with a phone call where we talked for twelve minutes about the job market and the severance timeline and Tola's preternatural speed, and at no point did either of us say the thing that the conversation was built to avoid.

I think about calling him. The thought has the specific weight of something I should do and probably will not do, at least not today, because today I am filing for unemployment and updating my résumé and meeting Marcus for coffee in San Jose, and the day has a shape that does not include the kind of conversation I would need to have with Dapo — the kind where I say *How are you really?* and mean it, and he says — what? What would Dapo say if the question were asked in a room with no audience, no group chat, no emojis to hide behind?

I don't know. I will think about this later, in the months that come, in the room where this story is no longer happening but being remembered, and the not-knowing will be the part I carry.

For now, I put the phone down. I rinse the mug. I open the laptop and begin.

The golden cage is open. The door has been there all along — a red door, a kitchen table, a hand left palm-up in the dark. Whether a man walks through it is not a question of courage. It is a question of what he has been taught a man is allowed to be.

Remi would say this is where it starts. The real part. The part that comes after the news and the silence and the jokes at 1 a.m. The part where you look at the life you built and ask: *What here is mine, and what is the shape someone else handed me, and can*

I tell the difference anymore?

Part One ends here. Not because the story is finished, but because the cage has been described and its dimensions measured, and the two men inside it are beginning — one of them aloud, one of them in silence — to feel its walls.

PART TWO

The Unravelling

Chapter Seven

The spreadsheet begins the way all my worst decisions begin — with the conviction that if I can just get the numbers right, the feeling will stop.

It is 1:53 a.m. on a Wednesday, two weeks after the Slack message, and I am at the kitchen table with the laptop open and the house dark around me and the only light is the screen and the small bulb above the stove that Remi leaves on because she believes a completely dark kitchen invites something she will not name. I have never asked what. The light stays on. It is not negotiable.

The chair I am sitting in is the same one I sat in on Friday when I told her. The same table where her legal pad still lives, pushed to the side, her numbers face-up, her pencil laid across the top like a blade at rest. She wrote the numbers as facts. I am writing mine as questions. That is the difference between us at 2 a.m. — Remi measures the wound and reaches for the bandage. I measure the wound and then measure it again, and again, as though precision is a form of anaesthesia.

Google Sheets is open. I have titled the file *Runway*, which is a word I learned from startup founders who used it to describe how many months of cash a company had before the money ran out and everyone went home. I used to find the term faintly absurd — the aviation metaphor, the implication that a business was a plane and you just needed enough concrete to get airborne. But at 1:53 a.m. in a kitchen in Fremont, looking at a grid I have been building for forty minutes with the focus of a man defusing something, the word feels less like metaphor and more like diagnosis. The runway is how long we have before this life stops being this life and becomes something I cannot yet bring myself to picture.

I start with what comes in. This is the easier column, because it is short.

Severance: $34,200. Twelve weeks at base, minus taxes, minus the deductions that continue even after the company has decided you are not a person it needs. The letter arrived on Thursday — cream-coloured stationery, because HR departments in Silicon Valley have apparently decided that the aesthetic of termination should match the aesthetic of a wedding invitation. Three disbursements, July through September. After September, it becomes a memory.

Remi's salary: $4,150 per month. She is a pharmacy technician at Walgreens. She has been a pharmacy technician for fourteen years — since before Yemi was born, since before this house, since before the word *senior* appeared in my title and the numbers on my pay stub made her salary look like a footnote. It was never a footnote. I know this now, at 1:53 a.m., the way you know things in the dark that you were too proud to know in the light. Her $4,150 is the only number in this column that does not have an expiration date.

Unemployment: approximately $2,100 per month, if the EDD processes my claim on schedule, which Emeka in the group says takes four to six weeks. I filed on Monday. The website looked like it was designed in 2003 by someone who believed the internet was a passing trend. The interface matched my mood — functional, graceless, offering no illusions about what it was for.

I type these into the income column and look at them. Severance plus Remi's salary plus unemployment. For the first three months: roughly $17,650. After the severance stops: $6,250.

I stare at the second number. $6,250. I let it sit on the screen the way Remi let the legal pad sit on the table — face-up, undeniable.

I move to the expense column.

*

The mortgage is $6,800.

I type it first because it is the number that does not negotiate. It does not care that I have been laid off. It does not restructure itself. It does not send a calendar invite with a euphemism and a virtual room link. The mortgage is $6,800 on the first of every month, and the first of every month arrives with the punctuality of a thing that has never once been told it could be late. We bought this house in 2021, when rates were low and my salary was high and the math worked the way math works when you are employed and the future is a line on a graph that only goes up. Remi wanted to put twenty percent down. I said fifteen was fine, that we should keep some liquidity, and the word *liquidity* came out of my mouth with the confidence of a man who read investment blogs and believed that the language of finance was a form of control.

$6,800. The cell holds it the way cells hold everything — neutrally, without opinion.

Below the mortgage, the rest of the life we built:

Property tax and insurance, escrowed: $1,640. The house costs $8,440 per month to exist inside, before anyone eats or drives or turns on a light.

Yemi's school: $4,200 per month. Academy of the Pacific. Where the brochure says *whole-child development* and the parking lot is a catalogue of vehicles that cost more than my father earned in a decade. Yemi is in tenth grade. He is good at mathematics in the effortless way that makes his teachers write notes about *exceptional aptitude*. He does not know what the school costs. He knows his friends' parents are engineers and doctors and partners at firms with their names on buildings in the Financial District. He does not know that the $4,200 is the price of his not-knowing — the cost of maintaining the fiction that his ground is concrete and not the thin crust of his father's salary.

Dara's school: $3,800 per month. Same school, lower grade, sibling discount. That word — *discount* — presented as generosity, received as arithmetic.

Two car payments: $1,140. My Accord and Remi's Civic. Both reliable. Both still carrying debt. These are not extravagant cars. They are the cars of people who understand that a vehicle is a tool, not a performance, and that the performance, if one is to be made, is made by the house, the school, the neighbourhood — the architecture of respectability a man constructs so that when people look at his life from outside, they see something that holds.

Health insurance: COBRA will cost $2,340 per month for a family of four. I am still on the company plan through end of July — a grace period that feels less like generosity and more like a countdown timer with a corporate logo on it.

Utilities: $380. Internet alone is $89, which I find darkly amusing — the infrastructure I need to search for jobs costs more than the water I drink or the gas that heats the food.

Groceries: $1,400. This is Remi's number, from her legal pad, and I do not adjust it, because Remi's relationship with the grocery budget is the relationship of a woman who can tell you the exact price of plantain at three different stores and has feelings about all of them.

Credit cards: $620 in minimum payments. One card carries the balance from Yemi's dental work in March — an impacted wisdom tooth, an oral surgeon who charged with the confidence of a man who knows parents do not comparison-shop while their child is in pain. The other carries the remnants of the trip to Lagos in December, the trip where I sat in my father's parlour and told him about the promotion and watched his face assemble pride the way a man assembles something he has been waiting his entire life to hold.

I did not tell him about the promotion because I was boasting. I told him because the telling was the return on his investment — the investment that began in Surulere, in a flat where the power went out and a man sat at the table with his hands flat on the surface and said *we will manage*. My promotion was his dividend. And now the salary is gone, and the dividend has stopped, and I am calculating how long the story he told himself about his son can survive the arithmetic.

Miscellaneous: $400. This covers what does not fit in columns — Dara's book fair, Yemi's boots for football, the birthday present for a classmate whose party cannot be missed without social consequence, the small toll of raising children in a community where participation is both optional and mandatory.

Remi's mother: $600. Every month. To Abeokuta. She has never asked my permission to send it. She has never presented it as a request. It is a fact of our marriage, as fixed as the mortgage — the understanding that the life we built here exists in conversation with the lives that made it possible, and that conversation has a cost.

I total the expense column. I total it again, because the first time made me close my eyes for three seconds and I need to confirm that the number is real and not a product of a 2 a.m. mind that has confused fear with arithmetic.

$24,960 per month.

I sit with this. I let it press against my chest the way a stethoscope presses — cold, deliberate, listening for something the body knows that the mouth has not said.

*

The savings account holds $52,000. I have checked it four times since Tuesday. Fifty-two thousand dollars. It sounds like a lot if you say it quickly, if you hear it in the voice of the boy in Surulere who watched his father count naira at the kitchen table. It sounds like enough. But enough depends on the rate of departure, and the rate of departure is $24,960 per month, and when I subtract what comes in during the severance period, the burn — the real burn, the gap between the life and the income — is $7,310 per month.

The savings cover seven months at that rate. Plus the three months of severance. So: roughly ten months if I have a job by the time the severance expires.

But the severance will expire. And after it does, the gap widens to $18,710 per month. At that rate, the savings last 2.8 months.

I create a second tab. I name it *Scenario B.* I copy the expenses. I begin to cut.

The gym membership: $89. Gone. The streaming services: I keep one, Yemi would notice, the others disappear. The miscellaneous: cut to $150. This means Dara's book fairs become something I feel in my chest. This means birthday presents come from Target, not the shop on Paseo Padre where the wrapping paper costs more than the gift inside it.

These cuts save $406 per month. The spreadsheet recalculates. The runway extends by six days. Six days. I have just taken birthday presents from my daughter and gained less than a week.

I stare at the screen. The cuts I have made are cosmetic. They are the financial equivalent of rearranging furniture on a boat that is taking on water. The numbers that matter — the numbers that would actually move the runway — are the ones I have been circling since I opened the laptop. The ones that sit in the grid like walls I have been walking toward since 1:53 a.m., hoping the smaller numbers would somehow rearrange themselves so I would not have to reach them.

The school. $8,000 per month. Combined. For two children to attend a place where they are known and challenged and held to a standard I chose for them because I believed — with the faith of a man who crossed an ocean and built a career and bought a house with a red door — that this was the irreducible thing. The foundation beneath the foundation.

I put them in this school. Not Remi — Remi was open to other options. She said so. *Kolade, there are good public schools in Fremont, Irvington is excellent.* I heard her and I understood her and I overruled her, not with argument but with the slow gravitational pull of a man who has already decided and is merely performing the deliberation. I chose the private school because I could afford it, and because affording it was proof — proof that the boy from Surulere had arrived somewhere his father could not have imagined, proof that my children would never sit in a classroom with forty students and one textbook between four, proof that the distance between where I began and where I landed was real and could be measured in the quality of their education.

The school was never just a school. It was the architecture of a story I told myself about who I had become. And now the architecture is too expensive for the life I am actually living, and the gap between the story and the spreadsheet is $8,000 a month, and the spreadsheet does not care about the story.

I type the numbers for Scenario B. Without the school: expenses drop to $16,960. During severance, the household nearly breaks even. After severance, the gap becomes $10,710 — still a cliff, but a cliff with a bottom I can see. The savings stretch. Four months comfortable, six if we cut everything, if I sell the Accord at a loss, if we pause the transfer to Abeokuta, which is a conversation that will cost more than any money it saves.

With the school: we have until October if I am careful. After that, the savings are gone and the severance is gone and what remains is Remi's salary and unemployment benefits that do not cover the mortgage alone, let alone the rest.

Four months. Maybe six.

I close my eyes. The spreadsheet glows behind my lids — green cells, white cells, the red cell I formatted for the deficit because even at 2 a.m., even in crisis, I cannot resist the instinct to make the data legible. To give the fear a grid reference, as though naming the coordinates is the same as solving it.

It is not. I know this. I know it the way I know the driveway is cracked and the light needs changing and the red door is six steps from the car. I know that the spreadsheet is not a plan. It is a mirror. It shows me the shape of the life I built and the shape of the life I can afford and the distance between them, and the distance is not a number. The distance is a question: *What are you willing to lose?*

*

At 2:31 a.m. I hear the floor creak above. A door. The bathroom light — I can see the glow beneath the kitchen door, the faint yellow that means someone is awake and the house is no longer mine. Footsteps, then quiet.

I minimise the spreadsheet. The reflex of a man who does not want to be seen counting. Who understands that sitting in a dark kitchen with a runway calculation is not the same as sitting in a dark kitchen with a plan. The spreadsheet is the room I enter before I am ready to enter the room where Remi waits with her legal pad and her pencil and her absolute intolerance for information that arrives late.

I think about the legal pad. The way she pulled it from the drawer on Friday without asking, without waiting, the way she began writing numbers she already knew because the architecture of this household was never a secret she needed me to reveal. I think about her hand, palm-up on the mattress. The grip when I took it. The contract it offered — not the old one, built on solo endurance, but the new one, still wet, still curing.

She will want to see this spreadsheet. She will sit across from me and study it the way she studies the legal pad — systematically, without flinching — and she will find something I missed. She always does. Not because I am careless but because she reads numbers the way she reads me: looking for the gap between what is presented and what is true.

I will show it to her. Tomorrow. In the morning. In the light, where the numbers will still be terrible but will at least be shared, held between two people instead of carried by one.

But right now, at 2:31 a.m., the spreadsheet is the private language of my fear. The numbers are how I hold the shape of the problem when the problem is too large for my hands. My father sat at the table with his palms flat on the surface. I sit at the table with my hands on a keyboard. The posture is different. The need is the same.

I think about Dapo. I think about Dapo most nights now, in the specific way you think about a friend who is going through the same thing and saying less about it. His message on Sunday — *We go dey alright* — sits in my memory the way his voice sits, steady, the voice of a man who has processed something and arrived at a conclusion. But I build spreadsheets for a living. I know what a clean output looks like when the inputs are hidden. *We go dey alright* is a summary row with no supporting data, a conclusion without a formula, and the absence of the formula is what keeps me awake.

He has a spreadsheet. He must. A man like Dapo — meticulous, systematic, the man who timed himself reaching for fabric bolts because his father taught him that order is survival — a man like that has done this calculation, in his own dark kitchen, at his own 2 a.m. And his numbers are the same shape as mine, adjusted for his mortgage and his school fees and his mother in Ibadan and the exchange rate that makes every naira a reminder that the distance he has travelled is measured in obligations.

I should call him. I should say: *Dapo, show me the real spreadsheet. Not the version for Chinwe. The cells.* But I have been saying *I should call him* for a week now, and the should is a word that is doing more work than it can carry, and at 2 a.m. the distance between *should* and *do* is a canyon I keep walking to the edge of and not crossing.

I add it to the list of things for tomorrow. Tomorrow, which is also doing more work than it can carry. Tomorrow, which is the word I use for every hard thing I am not yet brave enough to do today.

*

At 2:47 a.m. I close the laptop. The kitchen goes dark except for the stove light, Remi's small concession to whatever she believes a dark kitchen invites. My eyes adjust. The shapes of the room assemble — counter, sink, knife block, the legal pad, the chairs. The room looks the same. It will look the same in the morning when Remi comes down and the children come after her and they eat the breakfast she has made and they go to a school that costs $8,000 a month and they sit in classrooms where the textbooks arrive on time and the labs hum with machines that teach them futures, and they will not know that the future is a spreadsheet with a red cell that says the math does not work.

I stand. The chair scrapes the tile, too loud for this hour, and I freeze the way you freeze when you have made a sound in a sleeping house and are waiting to learn if the house heard. Silence. The house did not hear. The house is asleep, and the mortgage is $6,800, and the deficit after September is $18,710, and the runway is four months if we cut the school and six if we cut everything and the numbers will still be true at 7 a.m. when the light is different and Remi is at the stove and the morning is doing its best impression of a life that works.

I go upstairs. Past Yemi's door — the deep silence of a fifteen-year-old whose sleep is a fortress. Past Dara's door — quiet, but I know the book light is on, hidden beneath the covers, because my daughter reads the way I build spreadsheets: at night, in secret, as though the act of understanding something requires darkness and solitude and a light small enough that it belongs only to you.

I open the bedroom door. Remi is on her side, facing the window. The room smells like shea butter and the lavender she puts on her pillow because she read it helps with sleep, and I have never told her whether it works because what helps me sleep is not lavender but the sound of her breathing — the steady rhythm that has been the metronome of my nights for nineteen years.

I get into bed. I lie still. The spreadsheet is downstairs, closed, the screen dark, the numbers patient in their cells, waiting for morning when they will be opened and shared and argued with by two people instead of one.

I know now — from this distance, looking back — that the spreadsheet was both necessary and a kind of hiding. It was the last place I could be the man I was trained to be: the one who measures, who calculates, who sits alone with the problem. It was control dressed as planning dressed as competence. And it was also the first honest thing I did after the lie — the first time I looked at the shape of the crisis and refused to round the edges.

Four months. Maybe six. The mortgage does not move.

I close my eyes. Sleep comes slowly, the way it comes to a man who has spent two hours converting fear into arithmetic and is now, finally, too exhausted to keep counting. The numbers sit in the dark kitchen below — precise, implacable, true. Tomorrow Remi will open the laptop. She will look at the red cell. She will not flinch.

There is a gap between the spreadsheet and the life it describes. The spreadsheet knows the cost of the school and the mortgage and the groceries and the insurance. It does not know the cost of Yemi's face when he learns his world has changed. It does not know the weight of the conversation with my father that I have not yet had. It does not know what it means to carry a number like $6,800 in your body every night while your children sleep above you, dreaming of futures you are calculating how to afford.

The gap is where we live — in the space between what the numbers say and what the numbers mean. The spreadsheet can close. The gap stays open.

Tomorrow we will sit at the table. Together. And begin.

Chapter Eight

He went to the church on a Thursday, because Thursday was Pastor Femi Adesanya's open office hour, and because Thursday was the day Chinwe took the children to their aunt's in Hayward, and because a man who is hiding something learns very quickly which hours are his to use.

Grace Baptist Church sat on a quiet block of Tennyson Road in South Hayward, between a nail salon and a tax preparation office, in a converted storefront whose former life as a furniture showroom was still visible in the ceiling fixtures — long fluorescent tracks designed to illuminate sofas, now lighting rows of chairs. The sign outside was hand-painted, navy letters on white: GRACE BAPTIST CHURCH — *Where Every Soul Is Valued*. The paint on the V in *Valued* had chipped and been retouched in a slightly different shade, so it looked like the word was smiling in the middle.

Dapo had been attending Grace Baptist for seven years. Not every Sunday — Chinwe's work schedule and the children's activities made weekly attendance a negotiation — but often enough that Pastor Femi knew his name, knew his children's names, knew that Dapo preferred the seat three rows from the back on the left side because it was closest to the exit and farthest from the altar call, which was Dapo's way of being present without being available.

He arrived at 10:14 a.m. The church was empty except for Sister Bukola, who managed the office and regarded all visitors during non-service hours with the measured suspicion of a woman who had seen too many people come to the church needing something. She looked at Dapo, then at the clock, then back at Dapo.

"Pastor is inside."

"Thank you, ma."

"He has a meeting at eleven." This was either information or a boundary. With Sister Bukola, it was often both.

*

Pastor Femi's office was a small room behind the sanctuary, furnished with a metal desk, two chairs with fabric seats that had been reupholstered more than once, a bookshelf holding a mix of theology and Nigerian history, and a framed photograph of his ordination at Calvary Baptist in Ibadan, 1998. He was a compact man in his late fifties, bald by choice, with wire-rimmed glasses and the unhurried demeanour of someone who had learned that silence in a room was not a problem to be solved but a space to be inhabited. He was not the kind of pastor who filled every pause with scripture. He listened. He nodded. He waited. And when he spoke, he spoke with the careful economy of a man who believed that words, like money, were best spent deliberately.

He was not Pentecostal. This mattered. In the constellation of Nigerian churches scattered across the East Bay — from the Redeemed parishes in Oakland to the Winners' Chapel in Union City to the house churches that met in living rooms in Newark — Grace Baptist occupied a specific position: measured, liturgical, unhurried. There was no band. There was a choir. There were no prophecies. There were prayers. The sermons ran forty minutes, not ninety, and they were structured like arguments — premise, evidence, application — rather than performances. Dapo had chosen this church precisely because it was a place where a man could sit and think without being asked to raise his hand, fall to his knees, or declare his breakthrough.

"Dapo." Pastor Femi stood and extended his hand. The handshake was firm, brief, pastoral. "Sit down. How is Chinwe? The children?"

"They're well, sir. Everyone is well."

He sat. The chair creaked beneath him — a small sound that seemed louder than it should have in the quiet of the room. Through the wall, he could hear Sister Bukola's keyboard, the irregular percussion of a woman who typed with two fingers and absolute conviction.

"I wanted to talk to you," Dapo said. "About something that has happened."

Pastor Femi removed his glasses, cleaned them with the cloth he kept in his breast pocket, and replaced them. This was his way of creating space — a pause that said *I am preparing to listen.* "Go on."

*

He told him. Not the full architecture of it — not the half-truth he had given Chinwe, not the morning drives to the library, not the browser folder labelled *Research* — but the core fact, stripped of its scaffolding. He had been laid off. Six weeks ago. He had not yet found a new position. He was struggling.

The word came out before he could edit it. *Struggling.* He had not said it to anyone — not to Chinwe, not to the WhatsApp group, not to himself in the mirror at the library bathroom where he practised the expression that said *today was productive*. But here, in a room with a metal desk and a man who had known him for seven years, the word escaped the way air escapes a tyre — not with a bang but with a slow, steady hiss that, once started, could not be reversed.

Pastor Femi listened. He did not interrupt. He did not nod in the encouraging way that meant *keep going*. He simply sat with his hands folded on the desk, his glasses catching the light from the small window behind him, and waited for Dapo to reach the end of what he was willing to say.

When Dapo finished, the room was quiet. Sister Bukola's typing had stopped. The fluorescent light above the desk hummed — a thin, persistent sound, like a thought that would not leave.

"How are you sleeping?" Pastor Femi asked.

The question surprised him. He had expected scripture. He had expected *God is faithful.* He had expected the verse about casting burdens, which was the verse Nigerian pastors reached for the way doctors reached for paracetamol — the first prescription, the default.

"Not well," Dapo said. "Some nights. Not well."

Pastor Femi nodded. Then he leaned back in his chair and looked at the ceiling, the way he did when he was selecting from the catalogue of stories and lessons he had accumulated over thirty years of ministry. Dapo had seen this posture from the pew — the tilt, the pause, the moment before the pastor opened the text.

"Do you know the story of the disciples in the boat?" Pastor Femi said. "Mark chapter four."

Dapo knew it. Every child who had attended Sunday school in Lagos, in Ibadan, in Abeokuta, in any church in any city in the southwest, knew it. Jesus asleep in the stern. The storm. The frightened men. *Teacher, do you not care that we are perishing?*

"They were experienced fishermen," Pastor Femi said. "These were not men who were afraid of water. Peter, Andrew, James, John — they had spent their lives on the Sea of Galilee.

They understood weather. They understood waves. They knew what a boat could take and what it could not. So when the storm came and they were afraid — when they woke Jesus and said *don't you care?* — it was not because they had never seen a storm before. It was because this storm was different. This storm was beyond what their experience had prepared them for."

He paused. Removed his glasses again. Cleaned them. Replaced them.

"The fear they felt was not ignorance, Dapo. It was competence meeting its limit. They knew enough to know that their knowing was not enough. That is a particular kind of fear. It is the fear of the capable man who has reached the edge of his capability."

Dapo said nothing. His hands were in his lap, one thumb pressing against the other — a habit Chinwe had noticed years ago and interpreted, correctly, as the gesture of a man holding himself in place.

"And where was Jesus?" Pastor Femi continued. "He was in the same boat. Not on the shore. Not watching from a distance. He was in the same boat, in the same storm, on the same water. Asleep — yes. But present. The disciples' mistake was not that they were afraid. Their mistake was that they looked at the waves instead of looking at who was in the boat with them."

He leaned forward. His voice did not rise. It did not need to. Grace Baptist was not a church where volume did the work of conviction.

"Your bank balance is the wave, Dapo. It is real. I am not telling you it is not real. The bills are real. The applications that have not been answered are real. The weight of providing for your family — I know that weight. Every man in this church knows that weight. But the wave is not the whole picture. The wave is what you see when you are looking down. When you look up, you see that you are not alone in the boat."

*

Dapo wanted to believe this. He sat in the chair with the reupholstered fabric and the small creak and he wanted, with a force that surprised him, to feel what Pastor Femi was describing — the presence, the assurance, the calm at the centre of the storm. He had felt it before. Not often, but enough to remember what it was like: the Sunday mornings when the choir sang *Great Is Thy Faithfulness* and something in his chest opened, briefly, like a window, and he could feel the air of a different kind of knowing. A knowing that was not calculation. A knowing that was not spreadsheets or pipeline dashboards or the number of days since the last recruiter email. A knowing that rested.

But that was before. Before the half-truth at the dinner table. Before the library. Before the bathroom mirror where he practised the face. The window that used to open had been painted shut, one layer at a time, by the accumulated weight of what he could not say.

"Pastor," he said, "I hear you. I do. But the disciples — when Jesus calmed the storm, the storm actually stopped. The water went flat. The boat was safe. That is what the text says. The storm *stopped*."

"Yes."

"My storm has not stopped."

Pastor Femi was quiet for a moment. Not the strategic quiet of a man preparing his next point, but the genuine quiet of a man who had been met with something he could not dismiss.

"No," he said. "It has not."

"So what do I do while I am waiting for it to stop?"

"You keep your eyes on who is in the boat."

"And if I can't see Him?"

"Then you remember that He is sleeping. Not absent. Sleeping. There is a difference. A sleeping God is still a present God. The disciples forgot this. They looked at the water and forgot who was beside them."

Dapo nodded. It was the nod of a man receiving something he could carry for perhaps a day, perhaps two, before it would need to be renewed. A nod of temporary faith — borrowed, not owned.

Pastor Femi reached across the desk and placed his hand over Dapo's. The gesture was brief and firm — not the lingering hold of a Pentecostal altar call, not the emotional clasp of a man trying to transfer feeling through contact, but the short, deliberate grip of a Baptist pastor who believed that physical comfort, like everything else in his ministry, should be offered precisely and without excess.

"Come back next Thursday," he said. "We will talk again."

"Yes, sir."

"And Dapo." He held his gaze. "Tell Chinwe."

The words landed in the room like a stone in still water. Dapo felt the ripple move through him — through his chest, his stomach, the place where the second clock had started beating.

"She knows I was laid off. I told her."

"You told her something. I am asking you to tell her everything."

Dapo did not answer. He looked at the framed ordination photograph behind Pastor Femi's head — a younger man, the same glasses, the same careful expression, standing in front of a church in Ibadan with his Bible held in both hands like a man holding a door open.

"I will think about it," he said.

"Think quickly. The storm does not wait for you to decide whether to be honest about it."

*

He drove home on the 238, then the 880, the route that had become as familiar as breathing. The car smelled of the thermos Chinwe had given him — the one with his initials, DKO, etched into the steel — which he had filled that morning with coffee he did not drink because the coffee was not the point. The thermos was the point. The thermos was a prop, a detail in the performance of a man who was going to work.

The sermon — or not a sermon; a conversation, a counsel, whatever the word was for what had happened in that small office with the fluorescent hum and Sister Bukola's two-fingered typing — sat in his chest like something he had swallowed but not yet digested.

Keep your eyes on who is in the boat.

He understood the theology. He had understood it since he was a boy in Lagos, sitting in the front row at Calvary Baptist Yaba while his mother's voice rose above the choir with the conviction of a woman who believed that God's faithfulness was not a metaphor but a ledger, balanced and exact. He had grown up inside that faith the way he had grown up inside his father's shop — surrounded by its patterns, its logic, its careful arrangement of meaning.

But the theology did not know about the library. The theology did not know about the browser folder labelled *Research*, or the bathroom mirror, or the twenty-two minutes of highway between Dublin and the life he had constructed for Chinwe's benefit. The theology operated in a space where honesty was assumed — where the man in the boat was at least honest about the water rising around his ankles. Dapo was not honest. He was managing. He was performing. He was building a structure of half-truths so intricate that dismantling it now would require confessing not just the layoff but the weeks of deception that followed it, and that second confession — *I have been lying to you* — was heavier than the first.

Tell Chinwe, Pastor Femi had said. As if telling were a single act. As if telling did not mean unbuilding everything he had built since that Tuesday in June when the Slack message arrived and he placed his palms flat on the desk and the desk was the last solid thing.

He pulled into the driveway at 11:47 a.m. The house was empty. Chinwe and the children were still in Hayward. He sat in the car for a moment — not as long as Kolade had sat in his, not the forty minutes of a man paralysed by the distance between the driveway and the door, but long enough. Long enough to feel the engine tick as it cooled. Long enough to notice that the ceiling of the Camry had a small stain near the rear-view mirror that he had never seen before, or had seen and forgotten, which amounted to the same thing.

He went inside. He put the thermos on the counter. He opened the laptop and navigated to Indeed, then LinkedIn, then the folder called *Research*. He applied to three positions before lunch. Senior Data Engineer, each one. The titles were the same. The companies were different. The cover letters varied by approximately forty words.

At 1:15 p.m. he closed the laptop and sat in the quiet kitchen with the wooden cross on the wall above the doorframe — the one Chinwe's mother had sent from Ibadan when they bought the house, wrapped in newspaper and prayers — and he tried to see what Pastor Femi had told him to see. The presence in the boat.

The calm behind the waves.

What he saw instead was the bank balance. $14,200. Down from $22,000 when this started. The number falling at a rate he could calculate but could not stop, like the fuel gauge on a long drive where the exits are getting farther apart.

He closed his eyes.

Keep your eyes on who is in the boat.

But his eyes, when they opened, went to the number. They always went to the number. And the number — patient, indifferent, precise — looked back at him and did not blink.

Chapter Nine

The first interview arrives three weeks in, and I am ready for it the way a soldier is ready for a war he has studied but never fought — armed, trained, and completely unprepared for the part where someone shoots back.

It is a phone screen with a mid-stage fintech company in San Francisco. Series C. Four hundred employees. The recruiter's email arrived on a Tuesday morning and I read it standing in the kitchen while Remi made eggs and I felt something lift in my chest — not hope exactly, but the precursor to hope, the faint twitch of a muscle that has been held still for too long. The recruiter's name was Kaylee. She used exclamation marks the way some people use cologne — liberally, without apparent awareness of the effect.

Hi Kolade! Super excited to connect! Your background is exactly what we're looking for!

I replied within seven minutes, which is both too fast and too slow. Too fast because a man who replies in seven minutes is a man who has been refreshing his inbox. Too slow because I spent six of those minutes rewriting two sentences to remove the scent of desperation, which is a particular kind of editing — the kind where you are not improving the words but disguising the writer.

The phone screen lasted thirty-one minutes. The recruiter asked about my experience with distributed systems, my leadership philosophy, my reason for looking — the euphemism the industry uses for *what happened to you*, phrased as though leaving were a choice I had made rather than a decision made about me. I said *restructuring*. I said it with the practised cadence of a man who has rehearsed the word until it no longer stings, or stings in a place he has learned to not show.

She said she would pass me to the hiring manager. The hiring manager's calendar, she said, was *pretty packed* but she would *definitely circle back within the week.*

She did not circle back within the week. Or the week after. On day fourteen I sent a follow-up — polite, brief, one line below the previous thread. No response. On day twenty-one I sent another. Still nothing. The silence that follows a promising phone screen is a specific kind of silence. It is not the silence of *no*. It is the silence of *we have forgotten you exist*, which is worse, because *no* is an answer and silence is a void you can fill with anything — hope, humiliation, the desperate algebra of *maybe they're just busy*.

This was the first one. There would be eleven more.

*

LeetCode at midnight. I cannot describe this to someone who has not lived it, so let me try.

Imagine that you are a senior software engineer who has spent sixteen years building systems that serve millions of users. Imagine that you have led teams, designed architectures, mentored juniors, given conference talks, written documentation that people actually read. Imagine that you have done this work — real work, consequential work, the kind of work that required judgment and experience and the accumulated wisdom of a career — and that now, in order to prove you are qualified to do it again, you must solve puzzles.

Not design problems. Not system architecture questions. Puzzles. Algorithmic puzzles. *Given an array of integers, find two numbers that add up to a target. Implement a trie. Find the shortest path in a weighted graph.* The problems exist in a universe parallel to actual software engineering — a universe where the work is stripped of context, of teams, of users, of consequence, and reduced to pure abstraction, as though the essence of building software were not judgment but gymnastics.

I begin at ten each night, after the children are in bed and the house is quiet and Remi has settled into the breathing pattern that means she is asleep or close enough. The laptop is open on the kitchen table — the same table, the same spreadsheet, but now a different tab. The LeetCode tab. My profile shows fourteen problems solved, then thirty-two, then sixty-seven. The count climbs the way all counts climb when the count is the only thing moving.

Some nights the problems give easily. I see the pattern — the sliding window, the two-pointer, the memoization — and the solution arrives with the clean satisfaction of a lock turning. These are the good nights. These are the nights I go to bed at twelve thirty and sleep.

Other nights the problem stares at me and I stare back and the solution is somewhere in the space between what I know and what the problem is asking and I cannot bridge it, and the clock passes one, then two, and I am forty-four years old and I am sitting in a dark kitchen solving a problem about binary trees while my wife sleeps upstairs and my children dream of futures that depend on my ability to reverse a linked list in O(n) time, and the absurdity of this — the absolute, grinning absurdity of a man with sixteen years of experience proving himself via timed puzzle — is something I can only laugh at later. At 2 a.m. it is not funny. At 2 a.m. it is the price.

*

The interviews come in clusters. A phone screen on Monday, a technical on Wednesday, a system design on Friday. Then silence. Then another cluster. The rhythm is not a rhythm — it is the erratic pulse of a system built on no one's schedule, where each company operates as though it is the only company you are talking to and your time is a resource it has already purchased.

I will spare you the details of each one, because the details are the same and the sameness is part of the cruelty. The phone screens that lead nowhere. The take-home projects — eight hours of unpaid labour, submitted into a portal, acknowledged by an automated email, followed by silence. The live coding sessions where a twenty-six-year-old watches you share your screen and type while a timer counts down in the corner, and you can feel the evaluation happening in real time, the assessment not of your ability but of your performance under conditions designed to produce anxiety.

I pass some. I fail others. Each failure has a specific shape. The fintech — silence. A gaming company in Redwood City — four rounds, excellent feedback, *we've decided to go in a different direction*, which is the industry's way of saying *we chose someone else* without naming the someone or the else. A cloud infrastructure startup — I made it to the final round, presented my system design to four engineers and a VP, answered every question, walked out believing I had it. The rejection came by email at 6:47 a.m. on a Thursday, as though the algorithm that sends rejection emails had been programmed to arrive with the morning coffee, to merge seamlessly with the day's first dose of caffeine and disappointment.

Each rejection takes a piece. Not a large piece — not the kind that makes you fall. A small piece. The kind you do not notice missing until you try to stand and discover that the ground has shifted, that you are slightly less tall than you were a month ago, that the man who walked into this process with his shoulders back and his résumé open is not the man still in it.

*

I meet Uncle Ricky on a Thursday morning at the Fremont Athletic Club.

This is the gym I keep adding and deleting from the spreadsheet — the $89 membership that Remi says is not essential and I say is the only thing keeping me from becoming a person I do not want to be. We have agreed, in the silent way that married people agree on things they have argued about twice and will not argue about a third time, that the gym stays. It stays because Kolade at the gym is a better version of Kolade than the one who sits at the kitchen table at 2 a.m. with a spreadsheet, and Remi knows this, and I know she knows, and the $89 is the cost of that knowing.

He is on the stationary bike when I arrive at 7:15 — a tall man, mid-seventies, with the build of someone who has been moving his body with discipline for decades. He wears grey sweatpants, a faded SFPD t-shirt, and a pair of New Balance trainers that look like they have walked through several decades without complaint. He is reading the Wall Street Journal on an iPad propped against the handlebars, and he is pedalling at a speed that suggests the reading, not the exercise, is the primary activity.

I notice him because of the shirt. SFPD. San Francisco Police Department. The letters faded to a memory of themselves — the blue nearly grey, the seal cracked. It is a shirt that has been washed hundreds of times and kept for reasons that have nothing to do with fabric.

I take the bike next to him. We do not speak. This is the etiquette of the early-morning gym — a shared space of men who are here because the alternative is being somewhere else with their thoughts, and the bike or the weight or the treadmill is the machine they are using to process what cannot be processed sitting still.

On the third Thursday, he speaks.

"You're here every day now." Not a question. An observation. The voice is deep, unhurried, carrying the particular authority of a man who has spent a career being listened to.

"Trying to be."

"Mm." He pedals. The iPad screen changes. "Between jobs?"

The directness catches me. I glance at him. He is not looking at me — he is looking at the Journal — but the question is precise and unpadded and I understand immediately that this is a man who does not waste language.

"How did you know?"

"Brother, I've been at this gym fifteen years. I know what a man who just started coming every morning at seven looks like. He looks like you."

I laugh. The real one — the one from the belly that surprises the room. He smiles without turning his head.

"Richard Caldwell," he says. "Everybody calls me Uncle Ricky."

"Kolade Adeyemi."

"Ko-lah-deh." He says it correctly on the first try. "Nigerian."

"Yes, sir."

"Mm. My nephew married a Nigerian woman. Yoruba. From Ibadan. Beautiful wedding. *Owambe*, that's what they called it?" He pronounces it close enough. "Most fun I've had at a wedding since 1987."

*

Uncle Ricky does not tell me his story all at once. He gives it in pieces, over Thursdays, the way a man distributes weight across a structure — one beam at a time, never more than the frame can hold.

He graduated from the San Francisco Police Academy in 1982. Twenty-five years old, raised in Bayview-Hunters Point, one of seven children. His mother cleaned offices in the Financial District. His father drove a bus for Muni for thirty-one years. Uncle Ricky joined the SFPD because the city offered a pension, health insurance, and a path to a house that did not require becoming someone else.

He retired in 2006. Twenty-four years. Full pension. He was fifty. Not fifty-two — fifty, because the police retirement multiplier at twenty years was generous and at twenty-four years was better, and Uncle Ricky, who grew up watching his father calculate bus routes and overtime, understood compound decisions the way I understand compound interest.

But the part that matters — the part he tells me on the fifth Thursday, while I am still breathing hard from the treadmill and he is still pedalling at the same unhurried speed — is what he witnessed in between.

"Ninety-nine," he says. "Dot-com. You're too young for it, but you've heard the stories."

"I've heard the stories."

"The stories are wrong. The stories are about companies. About stock prices. About the kid who made a billion and the kid who lost a billion. That's the movie version. The real version is the guys I knew. Patrol officers, sergeants, guys on the force who quit in '97, '98, to go work for startups. Smart guys. Hard-working guys. Guys who looked at the money and said *I can't afford to not do this*."

He pauses. The iPad has gone to sleep. He does not wake it.

"You know where most of them are now?"

"Where?"

"Working. Still working. Seventy years old, seventy-two, seventy-five. Still working. No pension. No retirement. They cashed out their years for stock options that went to zero, and by the time they realised what they'd given up, the door was closed. You can't buy back time in a pension system. Once you leave, the clock stops."

He looks at me for the first time since we started talking. His eyes are clear and unhurried, the eyes of a man who has been looking at the same truth for twenty-five years and has never needed anyone to validate it.

"I'm not a rich man because I was smart, Kolade. I'm a rich man because I was steady. Pension, plus the rental properties I bought in the '90s when Bayview was still cheap, plus the index funds I put money into every month for thirty years. Nothing fancy. Nothing that makes a good story at a dinner party. But I'm seventy-three years old and I don't owe anybody anything, and every morning I come to this gym because I *want* to, not because I'm trying to outrun something."

I nod. I am thinking about the spreadsheet. I am thinking about the runway. I am thinking about the $89 gym membership and the twelve LeetCode problems I solved last night and the recruiter who said she would *definitely circle back.*

"The government hires engineers," he says. It is not a suggestion. It is a fact, offered the way facts are offered by men who have learned that advice works better when it arrives without instructions. "Federal, state, city. Good salary. Pension. Benefits your family can actually use. And nobody's going to make you reverse a linked list on a whiteboard to prove you can do work you've already been doing for fifteen years."

I open my mouth to say something — to explain that government work is not the same, that the prestige is different, that the trajectory is different, that a man who has spent sixteen years in the private sector does not simply *switch* — but Uncle Ricky has already turned back to the iPad, and the Wall Street Journal has woken up, and he is reading again with the patient focus of a man who has said what he came to say and is now finished saying it.

*

I do not think about Uncle Ricky's words that afternoon. I am too busy preparing for the next interview — a FAANG company, the big one, the one that would make everything else irrelevant. The recruiter has been responsive. The phone screen went well. The coding round is tomorrow and I have been solving medium-difficulty problems for six straight nights and my confidence is high and my preparation is thorough and I am a man who builds systems for a living and I will not be undone by a timed puzzle in a virtual room with a twenty-six-year-old watching me type.

But at 1 a.m., after the last practice problem, after the screen goes dark and the kitchen is quiet and the stove light glows with Remi's unnamed vigilance — at 1 a.m., Uncle Ricky's voice arrives in the room the way certain truths arrive, not when you are ready for them but when the rest of the noise has stopped.

Nobody's going to make you reverse a linked list to prove you can do work you've already been doing for fifteen years.

I close the laptop. I go upstairs. I do not think about it again until much later, when I am ready. When the FAANG interview has come and gone and the silence that follows it is the loudest silence of all, and Uncle Ricky's words are still in the room, patient and unhurried, waiting for me to catch up to what he already knows.

Chapter Ten

The pharmacist was a young woman with box braids and a nametag that read AMARA. She wrapped the cuff around his left arm with the efficient tenderness of someone who performed this action forty times a day and had learned to make it feel personal each time.

"Just relax your arm," she said. "Let it rest on the counter."

Dapo did as he was told. He had come to the Walgreens on Dublin Boulevard for ibuprofen — the headaches had been arriving every afternoon now, at roughly 3pm, with the punctuality of a recurring meeting his body had scheduled without his consent. The pharmacy was running a free blood pressure screening. A cardboard sign near the register said CHECK YOUR NUMBERS in red block letters above a cartoon heart wearing a stethoscope, and he had walked past it twice before something — not concern, not yet, but the faint hum of a system running a diagnostic it had not been asked to run — made him stop.

The cuff inflated. The pressure was firm, specific, the feeling of being held in a way that was clinical rather than comforting. Dapo watched the digital display. He was not anxious. He was a man in good health — he had always been a man in good health, had always passed the annual physical with the effortless scores of someone whose body was an ally rather than an adversary. The gym membership he had not used in seven weeks notwithstanding. The sleep that came in fragments notwithstanding. The headaches notwithstanding.

The cuff deflated. Amara looked at the screen. She looked at it for slightly longer than he expected.

"What was it?" he asked.

"One fifty-eight over ninety-seven."

The numbers meant nothing to him. He knew they should mean something — the way a man knows that a check engine light means something, even if he cannot name the component — but the specifics were not in his vocabulary. He had never needed them.

"Is that high?"

Amara's face did something careful. Not alarm — she was trained past alarm — but the calibrated adjustment of a person choosing how much truth to deliver at a pharmacy counter on a Wednesday afternoon.

"That's stage two hypertension," she said. "Normal is below one twenty over eighty. Your numbers are significantly elevated. Have you had your blood pressure checked recently?"

"Last year. At the physical. It was fine."

"Things can change." She said this gently, without accusation, the way one states a fact about weather. "I'd strongly recommend following up with your doctor. In the meantime — are you under any particular stress?"

The question hung in the air of the Walgreens pharmacy like a diagnosis in itself. *Are you under any particular stress.* He almost laughed. Not the laugh of humour but the laugh of a man who has been handed, by a twenty-something pharmacist in a fluorescent-lit drugstore, the most precisely inadequate question of his life.

"Some," he said. "Work has been busy."

She nodded. She did not press. She handed him a printout with his numbers and a list of recommended lifestyle modifications — reduce sodium, increase exercise, manage stress, limit alcohol — and told him again to see his doctor. The printout was warm from the printer. He folded it once, then again, and put it in his back pocket, where it would sit for the rest of the day, a small square of paper carrying information he was not yet ready to unfold.

*

He bought the blood pressure monitor at the CVS on Amador Valley Boulevard because he could not bring himself to buy it at the Walgreens where Amara had seen his numbers. The monitor was an Omron — white, digital, with a cuff that wrapped around the upper arm and a screen that displayed the reading in numbers large enough to be seen from across a room, which felt like a design choice made by someone who did not understand that the people who needed the numbers were the same people who might not want to see them.

$49.99. He paid cash because the transaction felt private — the kind of purchase that should not appear on a statement Chinwe might review, not because it was secret but because explaining it would require context he was not prepared to provide. *I went to the pharmacy. They checked my blood pressure. It was high. No, I don't know why. Well — actually, I do know why, and the reason is that I have been lying to you for eight weeks about the fact that I was laid off and I spend my days at the Fremont Public Library pretending to go to work and the stress of maintaining this architecture is expressing itself through my cardiovascular system, which is, I suppose, the body's way of telling the truth the mouth will not.*

He did not buy the monitor because of the number. He bought it because buying it was an action — a response, a step in a protocol — and Dapo was a man who responded to problems with protocols. Identify the issue. Gather data. Implement a solution. Monitor the output. This was how he had built data pipelines and it was how he would manage his blood pressure, and the fact that the blood pressure was a symptom of a problem the protocol could not reach was a complexity he filed under *later*.

He used the monitor that evening, in the bathroom, with the door closed. 154/94. He wrote it on the back of a receipt and put the receipt in his wallet.

He used it again the following morning, before the drive to the library. 149/91. Slightly lower. Progress, if progress was the word for a number that was still dangerously high but moving in a direction that allowed for optimism.

On the third day he did not use it. On the fourth day he put it in the drawer of the nightstand on his side of the bed — the bottom drawer, beneath the phone charger and the Bible he had been reading less since the conversation with Pastor Femi, not because the conversation had weakened his faith but because it had made faith feel like one more performance he did not have the energy to sustain.

The monitor sat in the drawer the way the printout sat in his back pocket — present, known, unexamined. The data existed. He had chosen not to look at it. In data engineering, this was called an unprocessed queue. In life, it was called something else. The word for it lived in the space between the drawer and the doctor's office he had not called, in the silence between the reading and the response, in the gap between the body's alarm and the mind's refusal to hear it.

*

Chinwe noticed in the way Chinwe noticed everything — not suddenly but accumulatively, the way a photographer notices a shift in light. Not by the thing itself but by the shadow it cast.

"You're not sleeping."

It was a Sunday morning. The children were at Sunday school — dropped off at Grace Baptist at 9:15 by Dapo, who sat in the parking lot for seven minutes after they went inside, not because he was praying but because the car was quiet and the quiet was a substance he had begun to need. Chinwe was at the kitchen table with her coffee, still in the grey dress she had changed into the night before, her hair wrapped, her face bare of the makeup she wore to work and church but not to the kitchen on Sunday mornings.

"I'm sleeping fine," he said.

"You're not. You were up at three again. I heard you in the kitchen."

He had been in the kitchen. He had been standing at the counter with a glass of water, looking at the wooden cross above the doorframe, trying to calculate something — not money, not this time, but the distance between who he was presenting to Chinwe and who he was becoming, a distance that was growing each day the way compound interest grows, invisibly at first, then with a speed that makes the original amount unrecognisable.

"I was thirsty."

"You were thirsty three nights this week."

He said nothing. Chinwe held her coffee with both hands — the gesture she made when she was choosing not to press, when the choice was deliberate, when the warmth of the cup was doing the work of the patience she was spending.

"Is everything okay at work?"

"Everything is fine. The project is in a busy phase."

The lie came so easily now that it frightened him. In the early days — June, July — the lies had required effort, the conscious assembly of sentences that could pass inspection. But now, nine weeks in, the lies arrived fully formed, pre-packaged, indistinguishable from the truth in the way that a well-made counterfeit is indistinguishable from currency. He did not decide to lie. The lie decided for him. It stepped into the space between the question and the honest answer and filled it so completely that the honest answer — *I am not sleeping because my body is telling me something I will not listen to and I am afraid and I do not know how to say that to you without dismantling everything I have built* — did not even have room to form.

"Okay," Chinwe said. She took a sip of coffee. She looked out the window at the backyard, where the fence Dapo had promised to stain in April was still bare, the wood greying in the Dublin sun.

"Will you call the doctor about the headaches?"

"I will."

"This week?"

"This week."

He would not call the doctor this week. He knew this even as the words left his mouth, the way he knew the ceiling fan had been broken since February and the fence needed staining and the monitor was in the drawer and the printout was in his wallet. He knew it the way a man knows the full inventory of the things he is not doing while he is not doing them — a running list, maintained with the same precision he once applied to data pipelines, each deferred action catalogued and time-stamped and filed under the expanding folder labelled *later*.

*

That night, in bed, Chinwe fell asleep first. She always fell asleep first now. In the early years of their marriage she had been the one who stayed up — reading, praying, making lists for the morning on the back of envelopes. But since Dublin, since the house and the commute and the two children whose needs arrived in overlapping shifts, her body had learned to take sleep the moment it was offered, the way a person in a drought drinks water without tasting it.

Dapo lay beside her and listened to her breathing. In. Out. The rhythm steady, untroubled, the breathing of a woman who believed the man next to her was employed, was healthy, was carrying nothing heavier than a busy project at work.

His left arm lay on the sheet. He could feel his pulse in the crook of his elbow — the faint, insistent knock of a heart working harder than it should. He counted the beats the way he had counted everything since June: job applications (forty-seven), days since the layoff (sixty-three), dollars remaining in the savings account ($11,400, down from $22,000), emails sent to recruiters who did not respond (nineteen). The pulse was another number in a life that had become nothing but numbers — numbers he tracked, numbers he hid, numbers that sat in drawers and wallets and the bottom lines of bank statements he opened alone, in the library bathroom, where the light was institutional and the mirror confirmed only that he was present.

His heart rate was elevated. He could feel it without the monitor, the way you can feel a machine running hot without reading the gauge. Something was wrong in a place the spreadsheets could not reach, in a system he could not debug, and the error logs were written in a language his body spoke and his mind refused to read.

He closed his eyes. Pastor Femi's words drifted through — *a sleeping God is still a present God* — and he tried to hold them, to let them be the anchor the pastor intended. But the words dissolved the way they always dissolved now, at night, in the dark, in the space between Chinwe's breathing and the pulse in his arm that would not slow.

In the drawer of the nightstand, beneath the charger and the Bible, the Omron monitor sat with its empty screen, waiting to tell him what he already knew.

Chapter Eleven

The invoice arrives on a Tuesday, because invoices do not know what day would be convenient. It appears in my email at 8:22 a.m. with the subject line FALL SEMESTER — TUITION STATEMENT and the quiet authority of a document that has never once been questioned.

Academy of the Pacific. Yemi Adeyemi — Grade 10. Amount due: $12,600. Payment due: September 1st.

Below it, a second email. Dara Adeyemi — Grade 6. Amount due: $11,400. Payment due: September 1st.

$24,000. Due in nineteen days.

I am standing in the kitchen. The coffee Remi made before she left for Walgreens is still warm. The house is empty — Yemi is at summer practice, football conditioning, the thing he does with his body while the rest of his life is decided by adults in kitchens — and Dara is at her friend Sophia's house, which is a ten-minute walk and a universe away, a house where the tuition invoice does not land like a grenade on a Tuesday morning in August.

I read the email twice. Not because I do not understand it the first time but because reading it twice is a way of converting shock into process, of giving my hands something to do while my chest recalibrates. $24,000. I have $9,200 in the savings account. The severance is finished. The unemployment deposits — $2,100 per month — arrive with the grudging regularity of a system designed to help you just slowly enough that you feel the wait in your body.

I sit down at the table. Remi's legal pad is in the drawer now — she moved it after the second spreadsheet session, not because the numbers were resolved but because leaving them face-up on the table had become a form of surveillance neither of us could sustain. The pad is in the drawer. The numbers are in the drawer. And now $24,000 is in my inbox and the drawer is getting full.

*

Remi comes home at 4:47 p.m. I know this because I have been watching the clock the way I have been watching all clocks since June — not to track time but to track the distance between now and the conversation I know is coming. She enters through the garage, the way she always enters, and I hear the sequence: door, keys on the hook, shoes off, the soft pad of socked feet on the tile. She appears in the kitchen doorway and sees me at the table and she knows. She always knows. The shape of me at this table at this hour carries information she has learned to read the way I read error logs — by pattern, by deviation, by the specific quality of stillness that means something has broken.

"What happened?"

"The school invoice came."

She sets her bag on the counter. She does not sit. This is Remi in assessment mode — vertical, alert, the stance of a woman who processes standing up because sitting down is a posture of acceptance and she has not yet decided what to accept.

"How much?"

"Twenty-four thousand. Both kids. Due September first."

She is quiet. Not the quiet of calculation — she already knows the numbers, has known them since my first spreadsheet, has carried them in her head alongside her own set of numbers that she maintains with the rigour of a woman who grew up watching her mother count change at the market in Lagos. This is the quiet of a decision arriving.

"Kolade."

"I know."

"We cannot pay it."

The sentence fills the kitchen. It fills it the way the fluorescent light fills it — completely, without warmth, leaving nothing in shadow. *We cannot pay it.* Five words. Each one a brick removed from the structure I built when I chose this school, this neighbourhood, this version of our life.

"We can pay part of it," I say. "If I defer the—"

"Defer what? There is nothing left to defer. The credit card is carrying the dental work and the Lagos trip. The savings is at nine thousand. Kolade, we are three months from—" She stops. Not because she has run out of words but because the next words are the ones we have been circling, the words that sit in the centre of every conversation we have had since June like a drain neither of us wants to step near.

"Three months from what?"

"You know what."

I do. Three months from not being able to pay the mortgage. Three months from the kind of conversation that involves the word *forbearance*, which I looked up at 2 a.m. one night and which means *we will let you not pay for a while, and in exchange, the debt will grow, and the growing will cost you more than the not-paying saved.* Forbearance. A word that sounds like forgiveness but works like a loan.

"I'll find something before then."

"You've been saying that for three months."

The words are not cruel. That is what makes them land. Remi does not do cruelty — she does precision, and precision, when it is aimed at a truth you have been avoiding, cuts cleaner than anger. She is not attacking me. She is reading the spreadsheet out loud, the one we both know, the one with the red cells and the runway that is getting shorter, and she is saying what the spreadsheet says because someone has to say it and I have not.

"The school has to go, Kolade."

"Not yet."

"When? When the savings hits zero? When we're choosing between the mortgage and Yemi's chemistry lab fee? When is the right time to stop pretending we can afford the life we built on a salary that doesn't exist anymore?"

I stand. Not to leave — I am not leaving, I will not leave this kitchen, I learned in June that leaving a kitchen does not solve what happens inside it — but because my body needs to be a different shape than the one it has been holding. I stand and I put my hands on the counter and I look at the backsplash Remi chose when we renovated — the pale blue tile she spent three weeks selecting, visiting showrooms on her days off, bringing home samples she held up to the light at different times of day because Remi believed that a kitchen should be beautiful in the morning and the evening and not just one.

"It's not about the money," I say, and even as the words leave me I can hear how they sound — how they sound to a woman who has been tracking every dollar for three months, who has adjusted the grocery budget twice, who cancelled the subscription to the meal kit service and the cleaning service and the after-school tutoring Dara didn't need but attended because her friends did.

"Then what is it about?"

"It's about—" I stop. The sentence has a shape but the shape is something I am not sure I can say in this kitchen at this hour to this woman who is looking at me with the expression that is not anger and not disappointment but the third thing, the thing that is worse, which is *I see exactly who you are right now and I am choosing to stay in this room anyway.*

"It's about what we promised them."

"We promised them a good education. We can give them that at Irvington."

"It's not the same."

"You're right. It's not the same. It's free."

The word *free* enters the room and rearranges it. Free. The public school in Fremont that ranks in the top three percent in the state. The school Remi suggested before I overruled her with the gravitational pull of a man who had already decided. Irvington. Where the textbooks arrive on time and the teachers are qualified and the only thing missing is the parking lot full of Teslas and the annual gala and the feeling — the specific, irreplaceable feeling — of walking your children through a door that your father could not have imagined and knowing that you earned the right to be there.

"It's not about free," I say. "It's about—"

"It's about your pride."

*

The silence after that sentence is the longest silence of our marriage.

I do not know how long it lasts. I know that the kitchen light hums — the fluorescent, the one I still have not replaced. I know that the coffee machine clicks off, the automatic timer, the small sound of an appliance completing its cycle and moving on. I know that Remi is standing four feet from me and the distance feels like geography, like the space between two countries that share a border but not a language.

"My pride," I say.

"Your pride. The school was never for them, Kolade. It was for you. It was proof. You said it yourself — in the car, when we were driving back from the open house. You said *my children will never sit in a classroom with forty students.* You said that. And I heard you and I loved you for it and I also knew, even then, that the person you were protecting was not Yemi or Dara. It was the boy in Surulere who sat in that classroom. It was him."

I want to argue. I want to say she is wrong, that the school was about opportunity, about access, about the compound returns of a world-class education that begins in kindergarten and carries through. I want to cite the college admission statistics and the AP offerings and the science lab that smells like ambition and new equipment. I want to argue because arguing is what I do when someone has located the exact centre of the wound and pressed.

But I cannot argue. Because she is right. And because my wife has the particular gift of being right in a way that does not allow you to pretend she isn't — not with deflection, not with data, not with the careful architecture of a counter-argument assembled at 2 a.m. when she is asleep and cannot rebut it.

"Okay," I say.

"Okay what?"

"Okay, it's about my pride. And my pride is too expensive. And we can't afford it."

She exhales. Not a sigh — something deeper, something that has been held for weeks, the exhalation of a woman who has been waiting for her husband to arrive at a conclusion she reached in July and has been standing beside patiently, not pushing, because she understood that a man who is losing something needs to believe he chose to let it go.

And then, from the hallway — from somewhere between the kitchen and the staircase, in the space that is neither room nor corridor but the no-man's-land of a house where sound travels through walls the builders said were insulated — a sound.

A door. Closing.

Not slamming. Closing. Quietly. The kind of quiet that is louder than any slam, because a slam is a child's anger and a quiet close is a child's understanding, and understanding, at fifteen, is a wound that does not show.

Yemi.

Remi and I look at each other. The look contains everything — the recognition, the failure, the shared knowledge that our son has heard something we believed was private, that the architecture of protection we built around his life has a crack in the hallway, and through that crack he has heard his parents discuss the cost of the life he thought was his.

"How long?" Remi says.

"I don't know."

"I'll go."

"No." I move toward the hallway. "I'll go."

She lets me. This is the gift Remi gives when she knows the repair is mine to make — she steps back, not out, creating the space for me to do what a father does when his child has overheard the machinery behind the scenery.

I stand at the bottom of the stairs. I can hear Yemi's music — the bass through the door, the muffled percussion of whatever he has put on to fill the room with sound that is not his parents' voices. He is fifteen. He understands more than we credit him for and less than he believes he does, and the gap between those two quantities is where the damage lives.

I climb the stairs. The third step creaks. The same step that Remi's feet found at 3 a.m. when she came down with orange juice and the word *okay*. The house keeps its own record of our movements — each creak a timestamp, each sound a footnote in the running transcript of a family learning how to hold together when the numbers say it should not.

I stop at his door. I raise my hand. I knock.

The music lowers. Not off. Lower. The volume of a boy who is willing to listen but wants you to know he was doing something else first.

"Yemi."

Silence. Then: "Yeah."

"Can I come in?"

A pause. The pause of a fifteen-year-old calculating how much he is willing to give. Then: "Yeah."

I open the door. He is at his desk. Headphones around his neck. The laptop is open to something — homework, a video, the digital camouflage of a boy who does not want to be caught feeling. His eyes are dry. His jaw is set in the way that Remi's jaw sets — the muscle along the hinge, tight, holding.

I sit on the edge of his bed. The bed is unmade, which Remi has stopped correcting because there are only so many battles a household can fight at once, and the state of a teenager's bedsheets has been triaged to the bottom.

"You heard us," I say.

He does not confirm or deny. He looks at the laptop screen. Then he looks at me. His eyes are mine — the shape, the colour, the specific way they hold a question without releasing it.

"Are we broke?"

The word is Yemi's. Fifteen years old, the vocabulary of a boy whose understanding of money is built from context clues and overheard fragments and the particular literacy of growing up in a house where the adults speak in code and the code has started to crack.

"No," I say. "We are not broke. We are in a difficult season. I lost my job, and I am looking for a new one, and while I look, we have to make some choices about what we spend."

"Like my school."

"Like your school."

He is quiet. I watch him process — the face moving through something I cannot name, something between the boy who was dropped off at Academy of the Pacific in kindergarten with a backpack that was too big for his body and the young man who is sitting in this room understanding, for the first time, that the world his parents built for him was built on a salary, and the salary is gone, and the world is negotiable.

"Is the school the choice?" he asks. "Or is the school already decided?"

I look at my son. He is asking me to be honest. He is asking the way children ask when they already know the answer and want only to see if their parent will respect them enough to say it.

"The school is decided," I say. "I'm sorry."

He nods. One nod. The nod of a boy who is learning, in this bedroom, on this August evening, that the adults who built his world are also the adults who can unbuild it, and that the unbuilding is not betrayal but arithmetic, and arithmetic does not care about backpacks or chemistry labs or the parking lot where his friends' parents drive Teslas.

"Irvington?" he says.

"Irvington."

Another nod. Then he puts his headphones on. Not to shut me out — to shut the rest of it out. To be, for a few minutes, in the only room where the music is his and the volume is his and the world is exactly the size of the sound he has chosen.

I sit on the bed for another minute. Then I stand. I close the door the way he closed his — quietly, with the care of a person who understands that the sound a door makes is a sentence, and some sentences are better whispered.

Downstairs, Remi is sitting at the table. The legal pad is out. The pencil is in her hand. She has already started writing — the new numbers, the numbers without the school, the numbers that will carry us further because they carry less.

I sit across from her. She does not look up. She does not need to. The room holds us the way it has held us through every hard thing — not gently, not warmly, but completely, with the indifferent loyalty of a space that does not leave when the people inside it are breaking.

"He's okay," I say.

"He will be," she says. Which is different, and she knows it, and I know she knows, and the difference is the space we will live in for a while — the space between *okay* and *will be*, where parents sit after the conversation they hoped would never come, waiting for the future tense to become the present.

Chapter Twelve

The routine had a precision that would have impressed his father.

7:02 — alarm. Not the alarm he set when he was employed, which was 6:15, but a later alarm, carefully calibrated to the minute Chinwe left for work. She departed at 6:50, every morning, with the punctuality of a woman who regarded lateness as a character flaw. Twelve minutes of buffer. Enough time to hear her car reverse out of the driveway, to listen for the garage door closing, to confirm that the house was his.

7:04 — shower. Brief, functional. The water temperature set to a degree that was warm enough to feel human and cool enough to feel awake. He did not linger. Lingering was for men with nowhere to be, and Dapo was a man with somewhere to be. The somewhere was not real, but the schedule was, and the schedule was the load-bearing wall of the structure he had built.

7:22 — dressed. Slacks, button-down, the kind of clothes a senior data engineer wore to an office that operated on a business-casual spectrum between *we have a dress code* and *we have a foosball table*. The clothes were the costume. He understood this. He understood that putting on the shirt and the slacks and the shoes — the brown oxfords Chinwe had given him for his fortieth birthday, the ones she chose because she said they were *the shoes of a serious man* — was a performance. But understanding it did not stop him from performing it, the way understanding that a drug is a drug does not stop a man who needs it.

7:31 — breakfast. Two slices of toast. The thermos — DKO etched in the steel, Chinwe's Christmas gift from 2022 — filled with coffee. He made the coffee in the kitchen, under the wooden cross, standing at the counter where eleven weeks ago he had told Chinwe a version of the truth and watched her receive it with the practical grace of a woman who believed the worst was a temporary condition.

The worst was not temporary. The worst was still arriving.

7:38 — the car. The Camry, backed out of the driveway at the same speed and angle he had used for three years. Amaryllis Court to Dublin Boulevard. Dublin Boulevard to 580 West. The commute that had once carried him to Santa Clara now carried him to the Fremont Main Library, which opened at nine and closed at six, and the gap between a tech campus and a public library was a distance the Camry crossed in thirty-seven minutes without knowing the difference.

*

The library had become a country.

He did not think of it this way — the metaphor was too literary for a man whose interior life was built on schemas and logic models — but the library had its own borders, its own customs, its own unspoken laws. He entered through the south entrance because the north entrance faced the parking lot of a Peet's Coffee where, once, he had seen a former colleague through the window and had turned so quickly he spilled his thermos and burned the inside of his wrist. The south entrance faced a courtyard with a small fountain that worked intermittently and a bench where an elderly Vietnamese man read the same newspaper every morning with the concentration of a person who regarded the news not as information but as routine.

His station was the long desk by the east-facing windows, third seat from the end. The seat had an outlet — a necessity. The chair had a cushion — a luxury he had not expected and was quietly grateful for. The light from the windows moved across the desk in a slow arc through the morning, warming his hands at 10:15, reaching the edge of his laptop by 11, and retreating by noon, as though the sun had its own schedule and was not available in the afternoon.

He knew the librarians. Not by name — learning their names would have made the arrangement too real, would have converted the library from a waypoint to a destination — but by rhythm. The morning librarian was a white woman in her fifties with reading glasses on a beaded chain who shelved returns with the gentle authority of a woman restoring order to a disordered world. The afternoon librarian was a younger man, Filipino, who wore earbuds and processed holds with the mechanical efficiency of someone whose real life was happening somewhere inside the music.

Neither asked what he was doing. This was the library's gift — the unspoken contract of a public space that did not require you to justify your presence. You could be there to read, to research, to sleep in a chair with a book on your lap as a cover story, to use the bathroom, to charge your phone, to sit in a room where other people existed without any of them needing anything from you. The library did not ask. The library held.

The work of pretending to have work had its own workflow.

9:05 — open the laptop. Navigate to Indeed. Refresh the saved searches. Note which postings had been updated, which had been removed, which had appeared overnight with the desperate optimism of a company that believed posting a job at 11 p.m. signalled urgency rather than disorder.

9:20 — LinkedIn. Check messages. Check the feed. Endure the feed. The feed was a particular kind of torture — a stream of former colleagues announcing new roles, sharing insights about *resilience* and *growth mindset* and *the power of pivoting*, each post accompanied by a photograph of the author smiling in a way that suggested the photograph had been taken after the announcement, not during the search. Nobody posted photographs of themselves at the library at 9:20 a.m. in business-casual clothes they no longer had a reason to wear.

9:45 — applications. He had a system. The system involved a spreadsheet — not Kolade's kind, not the runway calculation of a man measuring the distance to the edge, but a tracking spreadsheet, a pipeline dashboard for the pipeline that did not exist. Company name. Date applied. Role. Status. Contact. Follow-up date. The spreadsheet had fifty-eight rows by the ninth week. Fifty-eight applications. Eight phone screens. Three technical interviews. Zero offers.

The numbers were not the problem. The numbers were what they were — the output of a market that had absorbed 260,000 layoffs in eighteen months and was not absorbing them quickly. The problem was what the numbers did to the space between 9:45 and 12:30, the hours when the applications were sent and the inbox was refreshed and the time between sending and hearing was a texture Dapo had never known before — the texture of a man waiting to be chosen by people who did not know he was waiting, who processed his application through systems that reduced sixteen years of experience to keyword matches and ATS scores and the algorithmic indifference of a process that was not designed to see him.

*

At 12:30 he would close the laptop, walk to the bathroom, and wash his face.

The bathroom was institutional. Beige tile, fluorescent light, a mirror bolted to the wall above a sink that ran cold for the first three seconds and warm after. The mirror was small and positioned at a height that assumed all visitors were five foot nine, which Dapo was not — he was six one, and he had to angle his head slightly downward to meet his own eyes, a posture that felt, each time, like a small act of submission.

He practised the expression. Not consciously — not the way an actor practises, with awareness and adjustment — but in the reflexive way a man checks his appearance before entering a room where he will be evaluated. The expression said: *today was productive*. The expression said: *the pipeline is strong*. The expression said: *I am a man who is working, who has purpose, who is moving through the world in the direction of something rather than the absence of it*.

The expression was a lie. But it was a well-made lie — constructed from the same materials as the truth, assembled with the same care Dapo brought to everything he built, indistinguishable at the surface from the face of a man who was fine. The difference was underneath. The difference was the pulse he could feel in his temples now, not just in his elbow. The difference was the headache that arrived at 3 p.m. with the regularity of a recurring calendar invite. The difference was the drawer at home with the Omron monitor he had not touched in two weeks, its screen dark, its data uncollected, its silence a choice he was making every day he did not open it.

He dried his face with a paper towel. He looked at himself one more time. The man in the mirror was dressed for work. The man in the mirror had a thermos with his initials and a laptop bag and a spreadsheet with fifty-eight rows. The man in the mirror was a senior data engineer between opportunities, and the mirror — small, institutional, bolted to the wall — confirmed this without comment.

✳

The drive home was the performance within the performance.

Twenty-two minutes. 580 East. The route had become so automatic that his body drove it while his mind composed the evening — selecting details from the library day and reassembling them into a day at the office. A meeting that went long. A deployment that needed monitoring. A conversation with a colleague about the new data governance framework, a phrase so specifically boring that no spouse would ask follow-up questions.

He had learned that the most effective lies were the most mundane. Chinwe would not question a meeting that went long — she had sat through her own share of long meetings. She would not question a deployment — she understood, in the general way a non-technical spouse understands, that deployments were events that required attention. What she might question was novelty. What she might question was a story that deviated from the pattern of his ordinary days. So he kept the lies ordinary. He kept them within the bandwidth of the life she expected, and the bandwidth was wide enough to carry the deception without distortion.

At 5:14 he would pull into the driveway. Earlier than his old arrival time — he used to get home between 5:45 and 6:30, depending on the 680 — but close enough. Close enough because he had explained, during the first week of the deception, that the new project schedule allowed him to leave earlier, and Chinwe had said *good, you should be home more*, and the tenderness in her voice when she said it was the worst thing he had heard since the layoff, worse than the Slack message, worse than the calendar invite, because the Slack message was a company deciding he was disposable and Chinwe's tenderness was a wife believing he was truthful, and both were things he could not control, and only one of them was his fault.

*

On the eleventh Thursday — he counted the Thursdays now, the way prisoners count days, the way patients count treatments, marking time in the units of the thing that contains you — on the eleventh Thursday, a man sat down at his station.

Not at the desk. Not in his chair. The man sat two seats over, in the fourth seat from the end, with a laptop and a coffee cup and the particular stillness of someone who was not visiting the library but inhabiting it. He was Indian — south Indian, Dapo guessed, from the cadence of the phone call he took outside at 10:15, the Tamil or Telugu or Kannada that Dapo could not identify but could recognise as the sound of a man speaking to someone in a language that was not the one he used for work.

They did not speak. They did not need to. The recognition was immediate and silent, the way two soldiers recognise each other in civilian clothes — not by uniform but by bearing, by the specific posture of a man who is trained for something he is not currently doing. The man had a spreadsheet open. Dapo could see it from two seats away — the columns, the colour-coding, the rows that meant *applied*, *screening*, *rejected*, *no response*. The same spreadsheet. The same pipeline dashboard for the pipeline that did not exist.

They sat together for three hours without exchanging a word. At 12:30, when Dapo closed his laptop to go to the bathroom, the man glanced up. Their eyes met. The man gave a small nod — not greeting, not sympathy, but acknowledgment. The nod of a man who understood that the library held others like him, that the long desk by the east-facing windows was not a workspace but a ward, and that the patients in it were recovering from the same thing and did not need to name it.

Dapo nodded back. Then he went to the bathroom, washed his face, and practised the expression.

*

That evening, at the kitchen table, Chinwe asked: "How was work?"

"Fine," Dapo said. "Long meeting in the afternoon. The migration is behind schedule."

"Again?"

"Again."

Femi looked up from his homework. Thirteen years old, the age when a boy's attention to adult conversation is intermittent but targeted — he listens to nothing until he hears something, and then he hears everything.

"Baba, can we get the ceiling fan fixed this weekend?"

"I'll look at it."

"You said that in July."

"Femi." Chinwe's voice. The boundary. Femi returned to the homework.

Dapo ate. The egusi was good — Chinwe's egusi was always good, the spinach wilted to the exact degree, the stockfish shredded fine, the way his mother would not have done it but the way Chinwe did it, which had become, over thirteen years, the way it was done. He ate with the careful attention of a man who understood that this meal — this table, this woman, these children, this house with the broken fan and the unstained fence — was the thing the spreadsheet was trying to protect. That every row in the pipeline dashboard, every application submitted into the void, every morning at the library in clothes he no longer had reason to wear, was in service of this. This kitchen. This moment. The sound of Sade's spoon against the plate. The glow-in-the-dark stars he knew were waiting on her ceiling. The life he had built and was now borrowing time inside of, the way a man borrows against a house — spending the equity of a future he is no longer certain will arrive.

After dinner, he washed the dishes. Chinwe dried. They stood side by side at the sink, not speaking, performing the choreography of a marriage that had learned to share a small space without collision. His hands in the water. Her hands on the towel. The silence between them was warm and habitual and entirely false, because her silence was contentment and his silence was architecture, and the architecture was getting heavier every day he did not put it down.

He thought about Pastor Femi. *Tell Chinwe.* He thought about the man at the library with the same spreadsheet. He thought about the Omron in the drawer and the printout in his wallet and the number that was $8,700 now, down from $22,000, falling at a rate that would reach zero in six weeks if nothing changed.

He dried his hands. He kissed Chinwe on the temple — the gesture he made every evening, the small press of lips to skin that said *I am here, I am present, I am the man you married* — and the gesture, tonight, felt like the last honest thing his body could do. The mouth lied. The hands performed. But the lips on her temple, for one half-second, told the truth.

Then he went to the living room, sat in the chair by the window, and opened his phone to the job alerts. Forty-three days until the savings reached zero. The number sat in his chest the way the pulse sat in his elbow — constant, elevated, refusing to be ignored.

He did not open the Omron. He did not call the doctor. He did not tell Chinwe.

The architecture held. For now.

Chapter Thirteen

The message arrives at 11:42 a.m. on a Thursday. I am at the kitchen table — the table that has become my office, my confessional, my war room — with a LeetCode problem open in one tab and a rejection email open in another, and my phone lights up with the green pulse of WhatsApp, and I glance at it the way I glance at all notifications now, which is to say with the specific anxiety of a man who is waiting for something and has been waiting long enough that the waiting itself has become a condition.

Severance Package FC

Tola Balogun [11:42 AM]

Guys. I got it. ■

Three words and an emoji. I stare at them. I know what they mean before the next message confirms it, because in the grammar of this group, *I got it* has only one meaning, and the meaning is the thing we are all chasing and some of us are beginning to suspect we will not catch.

Tola Balogun [11:42 AM]

Senior SWE at Meta. Start date October 14th.

The group explodes. I watch the messages arrive in real time — the speed of thirty-seven phones buzzing across the Bay Area, thirty-seven men and women in kitchens and libraries and home offices reading the same two lines and producing, with the practiced reflex of a Nigerian community that celebrates loudly and quickly, the required response.

Emeka Obi [11:43 AM]

TOLAAAA ■■■

Wale Bakare [11:43 AM]

My person!! God is faithful!!

Chidi Nwosu [11:43 AM]

Bro congrats!! What level??

Tola Balogun [11:44 AM]

E6. Infrastructure team. Menlo Park.

Emeka Obi [11:44 AM]

E6 at META. Tola you don enter oh ■

Chidi Nwosu [11:44 AM]

The TC? Drop the numbers let's celebrate properly ■

Tola Balogun [11:45 AM]

■ let me start first before I start quoting numbers. But Alhamdulillah it's good. Very good.

Wale Bakare [11:45 AM]

We need to do dinner. All of us. Proper celebration

Segun Akindele [11:46 AM]

■ Congrats Tola!

Segun's single emoji. I notice it the way I noticed his silence in the early weeks — the economy of a man who is spending less and less language in this group, whose presence has been thinning the way a signal thins at the edge of its range. One emoji. One exclamation mark. The minimum viable contribution to a celebration he cannot afford to feel.

I type my message. I do not send it.

Congratulations Tola. Well deserved. You worked hard for this.

I look at the words. Fifteen words. Each one true. Tola did work hard — she applied three hours after the layoff email, she interviewed while the rest of us were still sitting in our driveways and building spreadsheets and pretending the shock would wear off before the money did. She is Remi's cousin, which means I have watched her navigate this from a proximity that is close enough to see but not close enough to share, and I know — I know in the way you know things about the people adjacent to your family — that Tola's speed was not callousness. It was clarity. She is thirty-one, single, renting a one-bedroom in Sunnyvale, no mortgage, no children, no school fees, no ceiling fan that has been broken since February. Her runway was her entire life, and she spent it moving.

I am not angry at Tola. I want to be clear about this, because the feeling in my chest as I stare at the unsent message is not anger. It is something more complicated — something that lives in the neighbourhood of anger but pays rent to a different landlord. It is the feeling of watching someone cross a finish line you are still running toward, and understanding that the distance between you is not talent or effort but circumstance, and circumstance is the thing you cannot LeetCode your way past at midnight.

Tola does not have a $6,800 mortgage. Tola does not have two children at a school she just pulled them from. Tola does not have a father in Surulere who framed the scholarship letter before reading it and whose pride is a debt that compounds silently. Tola has herself, and a one-bedroom, and the freedom to take a FAANG interview loop without calculating whether the childcare for the onsite rounds would consume the last of the savings.

I do not begrudge her. I celebrate her. These two things exist in the same chest, in the same breath, and the fact that they coexist without cancelling each other out is, I think, one of the more honest things about being human.

I press send.

The message appears in the thread. *Congratulations Tola. Well deserved. You worked hard for this.* Fifteen words. Two minutes from composition to delivery. Two minutes during which I sat with a feeling I am not proud of and chose, deliberately, to send the version of myself I want to be rather than the version I am at 11:44 a.m. on a Thursday in September with a rejection email still open in the next tab.

*

The group continues. The celebration is genuine — Nigerian WhatsApp groups do not perform joy; they generate it, produce it in surplus, distribute it with the generosity of a community that understands that one person's breakthrough is a data point for everyone's hope. If Tola can get Meta, then Meta is gettable. If E6 is possible, then the system is not broken, only slow. The celebration is fuel. It powers the next round of applications, the next phone screen, the next midnight session with a medium-difficulty problem and a cold cup of coffee.

But underneath the celebration — in the pauses between messages, in the members who react with a thumbs-up but do not type, in the ones who read and do not react at all — underneath it, there is a recalculation happening. Each person in the group is running the same internal query: *If Tola applied in June and received an offer in September, what does my timeline look like? If Tola, who is younger and more mobile and carries less, took three months, what does that mean for me, who is older and mortgaged and carrying the weight of a family on a salary that no longer exists?*

The math is different for each of us. The fear is the same.

Dapo Olusanya [12:03 PM]

Congratulations Tola. ■■ Very well done.

Twenty-one minutes. That is how long it took Dapo to respond. I notice the delay the way I notice everything about Dapo in this group now — the gaps, the brevity, the formality of *very well done*, which is the phrase of a man who is selecting his words from a shelf rather than pulling them from a pocket. Kolade-who-knows-Dapo reads this message differently from the group. The group sees a congratulation. I see a man who took twenty-one minutes to produce eleven words, and the space between those minutes and those words is the space where the real story lives.

I think about calling him. I think about it the way I have been thinking about it for weeks — the should that is doing more work than it can carry, the canyon between should and do. *Dapo, how are you really?* Four words. I have been unable to say them. Not because I do not care but because asking the question means being prepared for the answer, and the answer might be something I am not equipped to hold while holding my own.

Uncle Ricky's voice arrives, the way it does now, at the margins. *The government hires engineers.* The words have been sitting in my head since the gym, not growing but not leaving, patient the way Uncle Ricky is patient — the patience of a man who has watched enough people learn the hard way that he no longer needs to insist on the easy one.

Meta. E6. Menlo Park. Tola's trajectory, drawn on the same graph as mine. She took the private-sector path and it carried her. But there are other paths. Paths that Uncle Ricky traced for me on a stationary bike, between pages of the Wall Street Journal, with the unhurried certainty of a man who retired at fifty and has never owed anyone anything.

I close the WhatsApp thread. I open a new browser tab. I type, slowly, with the deliberate keystrokes of a man who is not yet ready to commit to what he is searching for but is no longer willing to not search: *usajobs.gov senior software engineer California*.

The results load. I scroll. I do not apply. Not today. The FAANG interview is still out there — the big one, the one I have been preparing for, the one that would make this search unnecessary. But the tab stays open. It sits beside the LeetCode tab and the rejection email and the spreadsheet, and together the four tabs are a portrait of a man standing at a crossroads he has not yet admitted he has reached.

*

That evening, Remi comes home and asks about my day and I tell her about Tola.

"Meta," she says. She is at the counter, chopping onions with the rhythmic efficiency of a woman who turns vegetables into decisions. "Good for her."

"Good for her," I repeat.

Remi looks at me. The knife pauses. "How do you feel about it?"

"Happy for her."

"And?"

"And nothing."

She resumes chopping. The onion yields to the blade with the clean submission of something that was always going to be divided. "Kolade. You are allowed to feel two things."

"I feel one thing."

"You feel one thing you are willing to say out loud. That is not the same as feeling one thing."

I stand in the kitchen of a house that costs $8,440 per month and I watch my wife cut an onion and I understand that she has, in twelve words, described the entire architecture of my interior life since June. *You feel one thing you are willing to say out loud.*

That is not the same as feeling one thing.

"I opened USAJobs today," I say. I did not plan to say this. The sentence exits my mouth the way the word *struggling* exited Dapo's in Pastor Femi's office — unbidden, escaping a containment that was never as strong as it appeared.

The knife stops.

"USAJobs," Remi says.

"Government positions. Engineering roles. Federal, state."

"I know what USAJobs is."

She puts the knife down. She turns to face me. Her expression is not what I expected — not surprise, not the gentle concern of a wife managing a husband's dignity. It is something else. Something that looks, from where I am standing, almost like relief.

"The man at your gym," she says. "The retired one."

"Uncle Ricky."

"He suggested this?"

"He mentioned it. Weeks ago."

She nods. It is the nod of a woman who has been holding a thought she did not want to introduce too early, who has been waiting — the way she waits for everything, with the strategic patience of a person who understands that timing is not when you know something but when the other person is ready to hear it.

"I think you should look," she says.

"It's less money."

"It's money that comes every month. That's not less. That's different."

She picks up the knife. The onion resumes its division. The conversation is over in the way Remi's conversations end — not with a conclusion but with a door left open, a space created for me to walk through when I am ready, which may be tonight or next week or after the FAANG interview that I am still carrying in my chest like a lottery ticket I have not yet scratched.

I go upstairs. Yemi's door is closed, the bass leaking through. He started at Irvington three weeks ago. He has not complained. Not once. The absence of complaint is its own language — the language of a fifteen-year-old who understood something in the hallway that evening and has chosen to carry it the way his father carries things: silently, structurally, with no expectation of thanks.

I sit on the bed. I open my phone. The USAJobs tab is still there. I look at it the way I looked at Tola's message — not with anger, not with hope, but with the specific feeling of a man who is beginning to understand that the finish line he has been running toward may not be the one he needs to cross.

The tab stays open.

Chapter Fourteen

The headaches had stopped arriving at three o'clock. They no longer needed an appointment. They lived in him now — a low, persistent pressure behind both eyes that began when he woke and did not leave when he slept, assuming he slept, which was an assumption that had stopped being reliable somewhere around the tenth week.

Dapo catalogued the symptoms the way he had once catalogued data anomalies — noting the time, the severity, the conditions. The headache: constant, bilateral, worse in the afternoon, worsened by screens. The fatigue: not the fatigue of exertion but the fatigue of carrying — the kind that sits in the marrow and does not lift with rest, because the thing causing it does not stop when the body stops moving. The chest tightness: new. A feeling like a hand resting on his sternum, not squeezing, not pressing, just present — the weight of something that had decided to make itself known.

And the stairs. The stairs in his own house had become a diagnostic.

Fourteen steps from the ground floor to the hallway where the bedrooms were. He had climbed them ten thousand times without thought — carrying Sade as a baby, carrying groceries, carrying laundry, carrying the ordinary cargo of a life built on two floors. But in the thirteenth week he noticed that by the seventh step his breathing changed. Not gasping — he was not gasping, he would have called someone if he were gasping — but quickening. A shift in rhythm. The lungs reaching for air that should have been there and finding it thinner than expected, as though the house had altered its atmosphere while he was not looking.

He stopped on the landing the first time it happened. Stood with his hand on the banister and waited. Fifteen seconds. Twenty. The breathing settled. He continued up the stairs and into the bedroom and sat on the edge of the bed and did not tell Chinwe, who was downstairs giving Sade a bath, because telling Chinwe would require context, and the context was a chain that began with the stairs and led backward through the chest tightness and the fatigue and the headaches and the blood pressure reading at Walgreens and the Omron in the drawer and the library and the half-truth at the dinner table and the Slack message in June, and the chain was too long to pick up at any single link without pulling the entire thing into the light.

So he said nothing. He sat on the bed. He listened to Sade laughing in the bath — the high, unguarded laughter of a ten-year-old who had not yet learned that the walls of a house could carry sounds they were not meant to hold — and he pressed his thumb against his opposite palm, the gesture Chinwe had identified years ago, the gesture of a man holding himself in place.

*

The Google search happened at 11:47 p.m. on a Wednesday.

Chinwe was asleep. Femi and Sade were asleep. The house was in its night configuration — the dishwasher running its cycle, the porch light on, the hum of the refrigerator providing the baseline over which every other sound was measured. Dapo was in the living room, in the chair by the window, with his phone angled away from the hallway in case anyone came down. The angle was habitual now. Everything was habitual now — the concealment, the management of sightlines, the architecture of a man who lived inside his own house like a guest managing his host's expectations.

He typed: *persistent headache fatigue chest pressure elevated blood pressure.*

The results loaded. He scrolled.

The first link was WebMD. The second was the Mayo Clinic. The third was a cardiac health foundation with a logo that included a heart and an EKG line, the universal symbol for *your body is trying to tell you something you are not listening to.* He opened the Mayo Clinic link because the Mayo Clinic had the aesthetic of institutional authority — clean, clinical, the font of a place that did not traffic in alarm but in information — and information, even frightening information, was preferable to the void he had been operating in.

Symptoms of hypertensive crisis may include severe headache, chest pain, shortness of breath, nausea, blurred vision...

He read the list. Each item was a checkbox, and beside each checkbox his body had, without his consent, placed a mark.

Uncontrolled hypertension significantly increases the risk of stroke, heart attack, heart failure, kidney disease...

The word *stroke* sat on the screen. Six letters. He had never thought about strokes — they were things that happened to old men, to grandfathers, to the uncle in Lagos his mother mentioned in phone calls with the particular tone reserved for catastrophes that happened at a safe distance. Strokes were not things that happened to forty-two-year-old data engineers who played football on Saturday mornings — before the layoff, before the mornings became library mornings — and who ate Chinwe's cooking and who walked through the world with the upright bearing of a man whose body had always been reliable.

Risk factors include: chronic stress, untreated hypertension, family history, male sex, African descent...

He read the last two risk factors and felt something shift in his chest — not the tightness, not the familiar hand on the sternum, but something colder. The recognition of a category. He was not reading about a condition. He was reading about himself. The page was describing him — not Dapo the individual, not Dapo the husband and father and engineer, but Dapo the demographic, the data point, the man whose race and sex and stress level placed him inside a statistical corridor that led, with the cold indifference of probability, toward outcomes he could not name in this living room at this hour.

He thought about his father. Emmanuel Olusanya, who had run the fabric shop on Bode Thomas Street with the precision of a man who believed that order was survival, who had never missed a day, who had eaten his wife's cooking and climbed the stairs to the flat and sat at the head of the table and said *eat, eat* while the portions on his own plate were smaller. Emmanuel, who had died at sixty-one of a heart attack that arrived on a Tuesday morning in the shop, between a bolt of aso-oke and the ledger book, while Dapo was three years into his first job in Ohio and did not get the call until evening because the time difference meant that his father was dead for six hours before his son's phone rang.

He had not thought about the connection. He had not allowed himself to think about it — the straight line between a man who carried everything silently in a shop in Lagos and a man who carried everything silently in a library in Fremont. The line was there. It had always been there. It ran through the genes and the culture and the lessons taught at kitchen tables by men who believed that the cost of providing was theirs alone to bear, and that bearing it was not a choice but an identity, and that the identity was non-negotiable even when it was killing them.

He closed the tab.

The screen returned to the home page — the apps, the wallpaper photograph of Sade and Femi at Half Moon Bay from last summer, the notification badge on the WhatsApp icon showing seven unread messages from the group he had not opened since Tola's announcement. The phone looked the way it always looked. The chair felt the way it always felt. The room held him the way it always held him — gently, in the dark, without questions.

He locked the phone. He set it face-down on the armrest. He sat for a long time in the silence of a house where everyone was sleeping and nothing was wrong except for the thing that was wrong with him, which he had just read about and confirmed and catalogued and closed, the way he closed every tab that contained information too heavy for the room it was in.

*

On Saturday morning Chinwe found the printout.

Not the one from Walgreens — that was still in his wallet, folded into a square the size of a postage stamp, compressed by weeks of being carried without being read. She found the second printout, the one the monitor produced each time it was used, the narrow strip of thermal paper that recorded the reading and the date and the time with the indifferent precision of a machine that did not know it was documenting a man's deterioration.

She found it in the laundry. In the pocket of the slacks he had worn to the library on Tuesday — the slacks he had forgotten to check before putting them in the hamper, because the architecture of deception had so many components that eventually one was bound to fail, and the one that failed was a two-inch strip of thermal paper with the numbers 161/99 printed in faded ink.

She brought it to him in the garage, where he was standing in front of the workbench pretending to organise the tools he had not used since May. She held the strip between her thumb and forefinger, the way a person holds evidence — not accusingly, but with the careful neutrality of someone who is allowing the evidence to speak before they do.

"What is this?"

He looked at the paper. He knew what it was. The numbers were facing him — 161/99, Tuesday, 10:14 AM — and the numbers were the truth the way numbers always were, precise, implacable, uninterested in the story he had constructed around them.

"It's a blood pressure reading."

"I can see that. Whose?"

"Mine."

"When?"

"Tuesday."

She was quiet. The garage was quiet. The neighbourhood was quiet — Saturday morning in Dublin, the lawns being watered by automatic timers, the distant sound of someone's leaf blower performing its weekly service.

"One sixty-one over ninety-nine," she said. "Dapo, that is—"

"I know."

"That is dangerous."

"I know. I'm going to call the doctor."

"When?"

"Monday."

"No. Today."

"Chinwe, the office isn't—"

"Then urgent care. Today. Now."

He looked at her. She was standing in the garage in the Saturday clothes she wore when the morning was hers — leggings, an oversized sweatshirt, her hair in the scarf she slept in. She was not angry. She was frightened, and she was showing it, which was something Chinwe did rarely and with the full commitment of a woman who believed that fear, when it was real, deserved to be expressed without apology.

"I'll go," he said. "I'll go today."

"I'll drive you."

"I can drive myself."

"I will drive you, Dapo."

He understood that this was not negotiable. He understood, too, that something had crossed — not the full truth, not the layoff or the library or the fifty-eight applications, but a bridge between what his body was doing and what Chinwe was allowed to know about it, and the bridge, once crossed, could not be uncrossed. She had the reading. She had the number. And the number — 161/99, printed on thermal paper in faded ink — was the first piece of the real story she had ever held in her hands.

She drove him to the urgent care on Tassajara Road. He sat in the passenger seat of the Accord and watched the Saturday morning pass the windows — the families at the farmers' market, the joggers on Iron Horse Trail, the ordinary beauty of a weekend in a town where people did not carry blood pressure readings in their slacks pockets because they were too afraid to show them to their wives.

At the urgent care, a nurse took his vitals. Blood pressure: 157/96. Pulse: 94. The doctor — a young man, Indian, with the brisk warmth of someone who had learned to deliver concern efficiently — looked at the numbers and asked the questions. Family history? Yes — father, heart attack, sixty-one. Current medications? None. Stress? Dapo opened his mouth to say *some, work has been busy* — the rehearsed line, the one he had given Amara at Walgreens, the one that passed for an answer in a world that did not want the real one — but Chinwe was sitting in the chair by the door, and her eyes were on him, and the lie that had served him in the drugstore could not serve him here. Not with the reading on the screen. Not with his wife in the room.

"Yes," he said. "A significant amount of stress."

The doctor prescribed lisinopril — 10mg, daily. He recommended a follow-up with a cardiologist. He said the words *lifestyle modifications* and *stress management* and *regular monitoring*, and each phrase landed on the floor of the exam room like a pamphlet — useful, well-intentioned, and entirely insufficient for a man whose stress was not a lifestyle issue but a structural collapse he had been managing with silence and thermal paper and a bathroom mirror at the Fremont Public Library.

They drove home. Chinwe did not ask about the stress. She did not connect the reading to anything beyond the reading — not yet, not today. She accepted the prescription and the follow-up appointment and the doctor's reassurance with the practical grace that Dapo both relied on and was terrified of, because the grace was built on a version of the truth that was missing its load-bearing wall, and the wall was the thing he could not give her without bringing everything down.

At home, she put the lisinopril on the kitchen counter, next to the salt grinder, where he would see it every morning. She did not say *take it*. The placement said it for her.

That night, in bed, she lay closer than usual. Not touching — Chinwe was not a woman who touched as a reflex — but close. Close enough that he could feel the warmth of her, the steady geography of her body beside his. She was awake. He knew she was awake the way he knew everything about the nighttime version of their marriage — by breathing, by stillness, by the particular quality of a silence that is shared rather than solitary.

"Dapo," she said.

"Yes."

"Is there anything else you need to tell me?"

The question was a door. Not a demand — a door. Open, unlit, leading to a room he could choose to enter or choose to walk past. She was giving him the choice. She was doing what Chinwe always did, which was to create the space and then wait for him to fill it, because she understood that a man who is pushed tells you what you want to hear, and a man who is invited tells you what is true.

He lay in the dark. The door was open. The room behind it contained everything — the layoff, the library, the fifty-eight applications, the savings at $8,700, the thermos with his initials that he carried every morning to a building that was not an office, the face he wore at the door, the half-truth that had become a whole lie. All of it was behind the door. All he had to do was walk through.

"No," he said. "Just the blood pressure. I'll take the medication. I'll be fine."

She was quiet for a long time. Then she placed her hand on his chest — over the sternum, over the place where the tightness lived. Her palm was warm. It pressed lightly, the way you press on something to see if it is solid.

"Okay," she said.

The door closed. Not slammed. Closed. Quietly.

He lay in the dark with his wife's hand on his chest and the lisinopril on the kitchen counter and the Omron in the drawer and the reading of 161/99 now somewhere in the laundry or the garbage or wherever Chinwe had put the thermal paper after she brought it to the garage, and the numbers were all known now — not all of them, not the ones that mattered most, but the numbers the body was producing, the vital signs, the data his cardiovascular system was generating with the urgency of an alarm that had been ringing for weeks in a room no one would enter.

He did not walk through the door. The door was there. Chinwe had opened it. He stood in the hallway of himself and chose not to enter.

This was the moment, looking back, when the architecture could have been dismantled and the man inside it could have stepped out into the air. This was the moment when *tell Chinwe* — Pastor Femi's instruction, the simplest sentence in the world, three syllables that weighed less than a strip of thermal paper — could have changed everything.

He chose the hallway. The architecture held. And the body, which had been speaking for weeks in a language of pressure and tightness and pulse rates that climbed in the dark, continued to speak. It would not stop speaking. It would speak louder, and louder, until the room it was speaking in was no longer large enough to contain what it had to say.

PART THREE

The Breaking Point

Chapter Fifteen

Six interviews. Three weeks. Two phone screens, a technical coding round, a system design round, a behavioural with the hiring manager, and a final presentation to a panel of four engineers and a VP whose name I had rehearsed until it sat in my mouth like a coin I could spend at the right moment.

I was ready. I want you to understand this. I was not hopeful in the vague, ungrounded way of a man who submits applications into a void and prays. I was ready in the specific, molecular way of a man who had spent three weeks preparing for something and had done it well. The system design was clean — a distributed event processing pipeline I had actually built at my last company, scaled for their use case, diagrammed with the precision I once brought to production architectures. The coding round I passed in twenty-three minutes with time to spare. The behavioural I answered with stories that were true and structured and landed in the room the way I intended them to. The VP asked about my approach to team leadership during crisis, and I told him about the time we migrated thirty million records over a holiday weekend and the junior engineer found the bug at 2 a.m. and I let him fix it because the fix was his to make, and the VP nodded in the way that means *I am filing this story in the column marked yes*.

I walked out of the final round on a Friday afternoon and I called Remi from the car — from the car, the place where every important call in this story happens, the confessional on wheels — and I said *I think I got it* and she said *don't celebrate yet* and I said *I know* and we both knew I was celebrating, quietly, in the way that people celebrate who have been hungry long enough that the sight of food makes them careful.

The recruiter said she would have feedback by Wednesday. She did not have feedback by Wednesday. On Thursday I sent a follow-up — one line, measured, professional, the email of a man who had learned to compress desperation into politeness. On Friday, nothing. On Monday, nothing. The silence was not the silence of forgetting — recruiters at this level do not forget candidates who have completed six rounds — it was the silence of a decision that had been made and had not yet been formatted into the language of *unfortunately*.

The email arrived on Tuesday at 6:47 a.m.

I know the time because 6:47 a.m. is the time I check my phone each morning before I get out of bed, in the thirty-second window between the alarm and the first movement, the window where I am still horizontal and the day has not yet begun and the inbox is the oracle I consult to learn whether today will be different from yesterday.

Dear Kolade, Thank you for taking the time to interview with us. After careful consideration, we've decided to move forward with another candidate whose experience more closely aligns with the current needs of the team. We were impressed by your technical depth and leadership qualities, and we encourage you to apply for future opportunities...

I stop reading at *future opportunities*. I have read this sentence before. I have read it eleven times, in eleven emails, from eleven companies that were impressed by my technical depth and encouraged by my leadership qualities and moved forward with someone else. The sentence is a template. It was not written for me. It was written for the category of person I have become — the rejected candidate, the almost, the man whose qualifications were sufficient and whose luck was not.

I put the phone face-down on the mattress. Remi is in the bathroom. I can hear the water running. The sound is ordinary and specific — Remi's morning routine, the sequence she has performed for nineteen years, the water and the toothbrush and the particular rhythm of a woman who begins each day by putting herself in order before she puts anything else.

I do not get out of bed.

*

I want to be careful about what I tell you next, because the telling is the part I have revised most often in my memory, the part I have smoothed and reshaped until the original texture is hard to recover.

Here is what happened: I lay in bed. Remi came out of the bathroom and saw me and asked if I was okay and I said I had a headache and she placed her hand on my forehead — the gesture of a woman who knows this is not a headache and is offering the cover story the dignity of a medical response — and she said *rest* and went downstairs and I heard her making breakfast and I heard Yemi's door open and I heard Dara's voice saying something about a permission slip and I lay in the bed and listened to my family perform the morning without me.

The ceiling was white. The ceiling is always white. But on this particular Tuesday in October the white was a specific shade — the shade of nothing, of zero, of a surface that reflects back exactly what you bring to it, and what I brought was the accumulated weight of four months of rejection and spreadsheets and midnight LeetCode and the specific, private shame of a man who was certain — *certain* — and was wrong.

Remi came back at eight fifteen. The house was quiet. The children had been delivered to school — Yemi to Irvington, where he had made two friends in three weeks and had not once asked about Academy of the Pacific, a generosity I did not deserve and could not repay. Remi sat on the edge of the bed. She did not say *what happened*. She had seen the phone face-down. She knew.

"Which one?"

"The big one."

She was quiet.

"Six rounds," I said. "Three weeks. I was—"

"I know."

She let the sentence live in the room. She did not fill it with *you'll find something else* or *their loss* or any of the phrases that well-meaning people offer to cushion a landing that has already happened. She let the silence hold the shape of the thing — the rejection, the certainty that preceded it, the gap between what I prepared for and what I received — and the silence was, in that moment, the most generous thing she could have given me.

"I opened USAJobs again last night," I said.

She said nothing. But her hand, which had been resting on the comforter, moved to my arm. Not gripping. Resting. The weight of a hand that is choosing to stay.

"There's a position. GS-14. Senior software engineer. Department of—it doesn't matter. Federal. Bay Area. The salary is—" I paused. The salary was $143,000. With locality pay, closer to $168,000. Less than half what I made before. Less than what Tola was making at Meta. Less than what the company that just rejected me would have paid. "The salary is enough."

"Enough for what?"

"Enough for the mortgage. The insurance. The schools — the public schools. Enough for us."

"And the pension?"

I looked at her. "You've been reading about it."

"I've been reading about it since you mentioned it. FERS. Federal Employees Retirement System. One percent of your salary per year of service, plus the Thrift Savings Plan with five percent matching. Kolade, do you know what five percent matching on a federal salary for twenty years looks like?"

I did not. I had been so focused on the salary — on the gap between $168,000 and the $380,000 I was making before, on the shrinkage, on the reduction — that I had not looked at the structure underneath. Remi had. Remi had been looking at it the way she looked at everything — from below, from the foundation up, measuring not the height of the building but the depth of what held it.

"It looks like retirement," she said. "It looks like never having to worry about a Slack message again."

Uncle Ricky's voice: *I'm seventy-three years old and I don't owe anybody anything.*

I lay in the bed with the ceiling above me and my wife's hand on my arm and the rejection email face-down on the mattress and the USAJobs tab open somewhere in my phone, and I felt something I had not felt since June. Not hope — hope was too bright, too clean, too much like the feeling I had walking out of the final round three weeks ago. Something quieter. Something closer to the ground. The feeling of a man who has been looking at the horizon and has decided, finally, to look at his feet, and discovered that the ground, while not spectacular, is solid.

"I'm going to apply," I said.

"Today."

"Today."

*

I got out of bed at nine fifteen. The house was empty and clean and filled with the evidence of Remi's morning — the wiped counter, the rinsed coffee pot, the lunch boxes she had packed and delivered while I lay upstairs calculating the distance between where I was and where I had planned to be.

I showered. I dressed. Not the interview clothes — not the blazer and the dress shirt and the shoes I had polished on Sunday in preparation for a week that would, I was certain, bring good news. I wore the jeans and the grey henley and the running shoes. The clothes of a man who is not performing anything for anyone.

I sat at the kitchen table. I opened the laptop. The USAJobs listing was still there — the tab I had opened the day of Tola's announcement and had not closed, the tab that had been sitting patiently beside the LeetCode tab and the rejection emails and the spreadsheet, waiting for me to arrive at it.

The application was different. No LeetCode. No whiteboard. No system design presented to a panel of engineers timing your pauses. The application was a form — a long, detailed, government form that asked for your experience in plain language and expected you to describe what you had done rather than prove you could do it again under artificial pressure. The form wanted your resume. The form wanted your references. The form did not want you to reverse a linked list.

I filled it out in forty-seven minutes. Sixteen years of experience, translated from the vocabulary of Silicon Valley into the vocabulary of the federal government. I did not embellish. I did not optimise for keywords. I wrote what I had done, plainly, the way Uncle Ricky spoke — without performance, without the need to impress, with the quiet confidence of a man who knows his work is real and does not require a timed demonstration to prove it.

I pressed submit.

The confirmation page said: *Your application has been received. You will be notified of your status within four to six weeks.*

Four to six weeks. In the private sector, this timeline would have been an insult. In the federal system, it was a promise. A promise that the process would be slow and thorough and indifferent to the urgency of a man's mortgage, and that the indifference was not cruelty but structure, and that the structure, once you were inside it, would hold.

I closed the laptop. I sat in the kitchen. The fluorescent light was on — the one Remi had asked me to replace, the one I had not replaced, the one that cast its flat white gaze across a room where every hard thing in this story had happened. I looked at the light and I thought: *I will replace it this weekend.*

Not because it mattered. Because it was something I could do. Because the distance between a man who replaces a light fixture and a man who lies in bed staring at a white ceiling is the distance I needed to cross today, and the light fixture was the bridge.

I went to the gym at eleven. Uncle Ricky was on the bike. The Wall Street Journal was on the iPad. He looked at me over the top of his reading glasses as I took the bike beside him.

"You look different," he said.

"I applied."

"Federal?"

"Federal."

He nodded. One nod. The nod of a man who has been waiting for this moment without rushing it, who planted a seed on a Thursday morning and watched it grow at the speed of a man's pride being slowly, painfully, replaced by his need.

"Good," he said. He turned back to the iPad. "How's the market doing?"

"I don't know."

"Me neither. That's why I read the Journal. So I can not know in detail."

I laughed. The big one. The one from the belly that surprises the room. Uncle Ricky smiled without looking up, and the smile was the smile of a man who has seen enough of the world to know that the distance between the worst day and the next one is sometimes no wider than a laugh you did not expect.

I pedalled. He read. The gym held us the way the kitchen held Remi and me — without judgment, without schedule, with the simple physics of a space that exists so that the people inside it can do the work of becoming whoever they are going to be next.

Chapter Sixteen

The morning began with the ceiling fan.

Not the broken one — the one in the master bathroom, which worked, which spun on its lowest setting with the faint wobble of a machine that had been functional for long enough to develop a personality. Dapo stood beneath it at 7:34 a.m. on a Sunday in October, tying his tie — the navy one with the small diagonal stripes, the tie he wore to Grace Baptist because it was sober and appropriate and did not call attention, and calling attention was the thing Dapo Olusanya had spent seventeen weeks learning not to do.

The mirror showed him what the mirror always showed: a man dressed for church. Clean-shaven. The white shirt pressed — Chinwe ironed on Saturday evenings, the iron's hiss a sound so woven into the rhythm of the house that its absence would have been louder than its presence. The suit was charcoal, not black, because Chinwe believed black suits were for funerals and interviews and that church required a colour that suggested devotion without severity.

He looked well. The mirror was not equipped to show what was underneath the looking-well — the 4 a.m. waking, the pulse he could feel in his jaw now, the headache that had become so constant it no longer registered as pain but as climate, the weather inside his skull that he had stopped trying to change. The lisinopril sat on the kitchen counter where Chinwe had placed it, and he took it most mornings, though not this morning, because this morning he had woken late and the sequence — alarm, shower, dress, medication, coffee — had been compressed, and the medication was the step that could be skipped without anyone noticing. He would take it after church. He would take it with lunch. The pill was small and white and patient, and it would wait.

He finished the tie. The knot was a half-Windsor — his father's knot, the one Emmanuel taught him in the flat on Bode Thomas, standing behind him at the mirror in the narrow bathroom, his large hands guiding the silk through the loop with the tenderness of a man teaching his son the grammar of manhood. *The knot must be symmetrical, Dapo. A crooked knot tells people you are not paying attention. And a man who is not paying attention is a man people do not trust.*

He was paying attention. He was paying attention to the knot and the mirror and the fan above him and the sound of Chinwe downstairs getting Sade into her dress and Femi into his shoes, and he was paying attention to the fact that his left hand, which was pulling the narrow end of the tie through the loop, was shaking.

Not trembling. Shaking. A fine, rapid vibration that ran from the wrist to the fingertips, as though the hand were receiving a signal the rest of the body had not yet decoded. He stopped. He held the hand in front of him and watched it the way a mechanic watches an engine — looking for the source, the origin, the component that had failed. The hand shook. He clenched it into a fist. Opened it. The shaking had stopped. Or paused. The distinction was not clear.

He returned to the tie. The knot was almost done. The narrow end was through. All that remained was the tightening — the small pull that brought the silk to the collar and completed the presentation.

Then the room moved.

*

Not the room — the room did not move. The room stayed where rooms stay. What moved was the space between Dapo and the room, the invisible architecture of balance and orientation that a body maintains without conscious effort, the gyroscope of the inner ear, the feedback loop between the eyes and the floor and the brain that says *you are standing, the ground is here, you are upright*. That loop stuttered. The signal dropped. And in the half-second between standing and not-standing, between vertical and whatever comes after vertical, Dapo understood that something was happening to him that he could not manage, could not defer, could not file under *later*.

His hand went to the counter. The marble was cold. His other hand went to the wall. Between the two surfaces he held himself in a geometry that was not standing and not falling but the space between, the liminal posture of a man whose body had decided to make itself heard.

The vertigo passed. Or receded — pulling back the way a wave pulls back, not gone but gathering. He stood. He breathed. The bathroom fan wobbled above him. The mirror showed a man in a charcoal suit with an unfinished tie and an expression that was no longer the expression he had practised.

He pulled the tie tight. He straightened the collar. He looked at himself and performed the assessment: upright, dressed, presentable. The assessment was a checklist, and the checklist was a protocol, and protocols were how Dapo Olusanya had survived every crisis from the scholarship exam in Lagos to the H-1B renewal in Ohio to the Slack message in June. You identified the status. You determined the next action. You executed.

Status: dizzy. Next action: drink water. Execute.

He turned toward the door.

The room moved again.

This time it did not stutter. It swung — a long, slow rotation, as though the bathroom were on a turntable and someone had given it a push. The mirror tilted. The counter tilted. The floor became a surface that was no longer trustworthy, and Dapo's hands — both hands, the shaking one and the steady one — reached for something and found nothing, because the space between the counter and the door was three feet of open air and open air does not hold a man who is falling.

He went down. Not slowly — not the cinematic descent of a man sinking gracefully. He went down the way bodies go down when the systems fail — suddenly, gracelessly, with the full weight of a six-foot-one man landing on bathroom tile without the intermediary of decision. His left knee hit first. Then his right hand. Then his shoulder, striking the base of the vanity with a sound that was neither loud nor soft but specific — the sound of bone meeting wood, of a body meeting a surface it was never supposed to meet at this speed.

He lay on the tile. The ceiling fan spun above him. The wobble was the same wobble it had always been — the same rotation, the same faint asymmetry — and the sameness of it was the thing that registered first, before the pain, before the fear, before anything else. The fan was the same. The fan did not know that the man beneath it was on the floor instead of standing in front of the mirror tying a half-Windsor with his father's hands. The fan just turned.

His chest. The hand that had been resting on his sternum for weeks — the imaginary hand, the weight, the pressure — was no longer imaginary. It was there. It pressed with a specificity that left no room for metaphor. This was not anxiety. This was not stress presenting as sensation. This was the body doing what the body had been threatening to do since the Walgreens reading, since the Omron in the drawer, since the Google search at 11:47

p.m. — the body delivering the message it had been composing in the language of blood pressure and pulse rate and the slow accumulation of cortisol in a system that had been running on emergency for seventeen weeks without a shutdown.

"Chinwe," he said.

His voice was quiet. Quieter than he intended. The word left his mouth and did not travel — it stayed in the bathroom, absorbed by the tile and the closed door and the fan that turned and turned.

"Chinwe."

Louder now. Loud enough, he hoped, to reach the hallway, to pass through the door, to find his wife wherever she was in the choreography of a Sunday morning with two children and a church service at nine.

He heard footsteps. Quick. Chinwe's footsteps had a specific rhythm — purposeful, direct, the walk of a woman who did not wander — and the rhythm accelerated in a way that meant she had heard something in his voice that the word alone did not contain.

The door opened.

*

Later — much later, in the telling and retelling that would follow — Chinwe would say that the first thing she saw was the tie. The navy tie with the diagonal stripes, half-tied, trailing from his collar across the tile like a signal flag, and that the tie was what told her the severity, because Dapo did not leave ties unfinished. Dapo did not leave anything unfinished. The incompleteness was the alarm.

"Dapo. Dapo, what happened?"

She was on the floor beside him. Her hands were on his face, then his chest, then his wrist — the rapid triage of a woman who did not have medical training but had the instinct, sharper than training, to locate the centre of the emergency.

"I fell. I got dizzy and I fell."

"Your chest?"

"Tight. Pressure."

"How long?"

"I don't know. A minute. Two."

She was already standing. The phone was in her hand — she kept it in the pocket of her dress on Sunday mornings because Chinwe kept her phone within reach the way other women kept their keys, as a tool for the unexpected, and the unexpected had arrived.

"I'm calling 911."

"Chinwe, it might just be—"

"I am calling 911, Dapo."

The sentence left no room. It was not a discussion. It was Chinwe at the limit of her patience with the graduated approach — the blood pressure check, the urgent care visit, the lisinopril, the follow-up he had not scheduled — and the limit had been reached not because she was angry but because her husband was on the bathroom floor with chest pressure and an unfinished tie and she was not willing to graduate any further.

She dialled. He heard her voice — clear, measured, providing the information the way she provided all information, with the precision of a woman who understood that emergencies rewarded accuracy: the address, the symptoms, his age, his history. *Forty-two years old. High blood pressure. Currently on lisinopril. Chest pressure. Dizziness. He's conscious. Yes, he's breathing.*

Femi appeared in the doorway. Thirteen years old, dressed for church, his shirt tucked in the way Chinwe insisted and Dapo reinforced. He looked at his father on the floor. His face did not do what an adult face would have done — the performative concern, the managed alarm. His face did what a thirteen-year-old's face does when the world rearranges without warning: it went still. Perfectly, completely still. The stillness of a boy who is recording everything and processing nothing, who will carry this image — father on tile, tie undone, mother on the phone — in a place he does not yet have the language to name.

"Femi, take Sade downstairs," Chinwe said. "Now."

He moved. He moved without question, with the obedience of a child who understood that the voice his mother was using was not the voice of a Sunday morning but the voice of a thing that required immediate, unquestioning action. He backed out of the doorway. Dapo heard his footsteps on the stairs, and then Sade's voice — *"Where's Baba?"* — and Femi's response, which Dapo could not hear, which lived in the space between the bathroom and the staircase, in the language siblings use when they are managing a situation they do not understand.

*

The paramedics arrived in nine minutes. Two men and a woman. They came through the front door that Chinwe had unlocked and entered the bathroom with the efficient choreography of people who did this every day — the questions, the blood pressure cuff, the pulse oximeter, the ECG leads placed on his chest with the adhesive pads that pulled at his skin when the charcoal suit jacket was opened.

Blood pressure: 182/108.

The number was said aloud by one of the paramedics — a man in his thirties with a shaved head and the calm voice of someone who had been trained to say frightening numbers in a non-frightening way. One eighty-two over one oh eight. The number hung in the bathroom. Chinwe, standing in the doorway because there was no room for her beside the gurney, heard it. Her hand went to the doorframe. She gripped it.

"We're going to transport you," the paramedic said. "UCSF or Stanford?"

"UCSF," Chinwe said. She said it before Dapo could answer, because Chinwe had already made this decision the way she made every decision — before it was asked, in the space between the question forming and the mouth opening, in the quiet, relentless engine of a woman who planned for contingencies that other people had not yet imagined.

They lifted him. The gurney was narrow and firm and rattled slightly on the tile. He was strapped — the chest strap, the leg straps, the small indignity of being held in place by a machine designed for bodies that could not hold themselves. The ceiling passed above him — the bathroom ceiling, then the hallway ceiling, then the front porch and the October sky, which was blue in the particular way that Bay Area skies are blue in autumn, clear and high and indifferent to the man being wheeled beneath it on a Sunday morning in a charcoal suit with a half-tied tie.

Sade was at the window. He saw her as the gurney passed the living room — her face in the glass, the glow-in-the-dark stars somewhere above her in the room he had put them in, the room where her private sky lived. She was not crying. She was watching. Watching with the quiet attention of a child who catalogued the world, who had inherited her father's way of entering a room as though she had already studied it from a distance. She watched him being taken from the house, and the watching was the thing that broke him — not the blood pressure, not the chest pressure, not the tile or the tie or the paramedics. The watching. The ėyes of his daughter in the window of the house he had built for her, seeing her father leave in a way he had never left before.

In the ambulance, the doors closed. The siren did not start — the paramedic explained that the siren was for critical situations and that Dapo was stable, which was a word that meant *you are not dying right now* and carried, in its careful specificity, the unspoken corollary of *but the margin is thinner than it should be.*

Chinwe was in the front seat. She had kissed Femi on the forehead and told him to call Auntie Ngozi and stay with Sade and not open the door for anyone and to pray, and the instruction to pray was the last thing she said before climbing in, and the way she said it — not as theology but as assignment, the same voice she used for homework and chores — told Dapo that his wife was operating in a mode he had never seen, the mode of a woman who was holding the entire structure by herself because the man who was supposed to be holding it with her was strapped to a gurney with ECG leads on his chest.

The ambulance moved. The neighbourhood passed the small square windows — the lawns, the automatic sprinklers, the Saturday cars still in driveways because it was Sunday and Dublin was the kind of place where people stayed home on Sunday mornings. Dapo lay on his back and watched the sky through the window above him and he thought about the library. He thought about the bathroom mirror. He thought about the spreadsheet with fifty-eight rows and zero offers. He thought about the half-truth at the dinner table and the whole lie it had become, and he understood — for the first time, lying on a gurney with the blood pressure cuff inflating on his arm and the paramedic writing numbers on a clipboard — he understood that the architecture he had built to protect his family was the architecture that was destroying him.

Tell Chinwe, Pastor Femi had said. *Tell Chinwe everything.*

The ambulance turned onto 580. The freeway that carried him to the library every morning now carried him to UCSF, and the difference was that this time he was not driving, and this time there was no expression to practise, no face to compose, no twenty-two minutes of rehearsal. He was a man on a gurney. He was, for the first time since June, unable to manage the narrative.

His eyes were open. The sky was blue. His chest was being monitored by a machine that beeped in a rhythm he could not control.

He was frightened. Not the fear of the disciples in the boat — not the fear of competent men meeting their limit. A simpler fear. The fear of a man who has been holding his breath for seventeen weeks and can feel, in the tightness and the pressure and the number 182 that was said aloud in his bathroom while his children were downstairs, that the breath is running out.

Chapter Seventeen

The call comes at 8:51 a.m. and I am at the kitchen table replacing the light fixture.

I want you to hold this detail, because it matters: the morning Dapo collapses on a bathroom floor in Dublin, I am standing on a chair in my kitchen in Fremont, unscrewing the fluorescent tube Remi has asked me three times to replace, holding the new fixture — a warm LED panel, thirty-two dollars at Home Depot, the specific shade of light Remi described as *the one that doesn't make everything look like evidence* — and my phone rings, and the phone is on the counter, and the screen says CHINWE OLUSANYA, and Chinwe Olusanya does not call me.

Chinwe calls Remi. That is the protocol. The women talk to the women. The men talk to the men. The streams occasionally cross — at parties, at church, at the children's events where the two families overlap — but the primary channel between our households runs through our wives, and the fact that Chinwe is calling me, on a Sunday morning, bypassing the protocol, is the first piece of information, and the first piece is enough.

I step down from the chair. I answer.

"Kolade." Her voice is controlled. Not calm — controlled. The distinction is everything. Calm is the absence of turbulence. Controlled is the presence of turbulence being managed by a woman who has decided the turbulence will not manage her. "Dapo collapsed this morning. We're at UCSF. He's stable. I need you to come."

"I'm coming."

"Emergency department. Parnassus."

"I'm coming."

She hangs up. Chinwe does not do conversational closings when the situation has rendered them irrelevant. She called. She delivered the information. She ended the call. The economy of it is frightening.

I am in the car in three minutes. The light fixture is on the chair. The old fluorescent tube is on the counter. Remi is not home — she took Dara to a friend's house at eight — and I text her as I reverse out of the driveway, one-handed, the text composed of fragments: *Dapo collapsed. Going to UCSF. Call Chinwe.* The text is not a sentence. It is a dispatch. It is the language of a man who is driving and afraid and cannot afford the luxury of grammar.

The 880 to the Dumbarton Bridge. The bridge to 101. 101 to 280. 280 to Parnassus. I know this route the way I know all Bay Area routes — by muscle memory, by the accumulation of a thousand drives across a geography that connects our lives with concrete and traffic and the specific quality of light on the water as I cross the bridge. The bay is silver this morning. Silver and flat and indifferent, and I drive across it at seventy-three miles per hour with my hands tight on the wheel and my chest doing something I cannot name.

The UCSF emergency department is a room designed to hold people in the space between one life and the next.

I know this is not what the architects intended. The architects intended a functional triage area with appropriate lighting and sufficient seating and the regulatory minimum of distance between the reception desk and the waiting chairs. But what the room is — what it becomes, when you are inside it, waiting for information about a person you love — is a holding pattern. A place where time does not pass but accumulates, layering on itself like sediment, each minute heavier than the last because each minute is a minute without news and a minute without news is a minute in which the mind produces its own.

I sit in a plastic chair. The chair is orange. The colour is presumably meant to be cheerful, or at least non-threatening, but in this context it reads as the colour of a thing that has been chosen by committee and approved by no one who has ever sat in it while waiting for someone to emerge from behind a set of double doors and tell them whether their friend's brain is intact.

The coffee. There is a machine in the corner — the kind that dispenses liquid that the machine calls coffee and that the recipient accepts as coffee because the act of holding a warm cup is the act of holding something, and holding something is better than holding nothing. I get a cup. I do not drink it. The cup sits in my hands, warming them, performing the only function a cup can perform when the person holding it is not thirsty but afraid.

Chinwe is inside. She went with Dapo when the ambulance arrived, and she has not come out, which means either the doctors are still working or the doctors have finished and the information they have requires the kind of delivery that happens in rooms with closed doors and tissue boxes and the particular tone of voice that medical professionals use when the news is the kind that changes the shape of a person's day, or week, or life.

I wait. The waiting room has seven other people in it. I do not see them. I see the double doors. I see the clock above the doors — analog, round, the second hand moving with the steady indifference of a mechanism that does not know what it is counting toward. I see the fluorescent lights — the same lights, always the same lights, the flat white gaze that follows me from kitchen to emergency room as though fluorescence is the official illumination of crisis.

*

Chinwe emerges at 10:47. One hour and fifty-six minutes after the call.

She looks the way she looked at the repast — or she will look the way she looks now at the repast; I am telling this out of order, because the order does not matter, what matters is the expression, which is the expression of a woman who is holding. Not together — Chinwe does not need to hold herself together, because Chinwe was never in danger of falling apart. She is holding something else. She is holding information, the way she held the thermal paper in the garage, with the careful neutrality of a person who is allowing the evidence to speak.

"He's stable," she says. "It was a TIA. A warning stroke. No permanent damage, they think, but they're keeping him overnight for monitoring."

I exhale. I did not know I was not breathing until the exhale informed me.

"Can I see him?"

"In a little while. They're finishing the imaging."

She sits beside me. The orange chair receives her the way it receives everyone — without comfort, without resistance. She sits the way Remi sits when a conversation is about to change direction — upright, hands in her lap, the posture of a woman who is preparing the room for what she is about to say.

"Kolade."

"Yes."

"How long has Dapo been unemployed?"

The question arrives and rearranges the room. I feel it in my chest — not the fear of the drive over, not the dread of the waiting room, but something sharper. The question is not a question. It is a door Chinwe is opening, the same way she opened a door for Dapo last week in the dark of their bedroom — *is there anything else you need to tell me?* — except this time she is opening it for me, and behind the door is not my secret but his.

"What did he tell you?" I say. Not answering. Stalling. The instinct of a man who does not want to be the one to dismantle another man's architecture.

"He told me he was laid off in June. That he's been interviewing. That the stress caused the blood pressure." She pauses. "He told me in the ambulance. On the gurney. With the ECG on his chest. That is when my husband chose to tell me the truth."

The way she says *chose* carries the weight of seventeen weeks.

"He also told me," she continues, and her voice is steady, so steady that the steadiness itself is the tell, the sign that beneath it something is moving at a speed that the voice is working hard to contain, "that he has not been going to work. That he has been going to the library. Every morning. In his clothes. With the thermos."

She looks at me. Her eyes are dry. This is not a woman who has been crying. This is a woman who is past crying, who has processed the tears and converted them into something harder, something that can be used.

"Did you know?"

I open my mouth. The truth and the lie are both there — side by side, the way they have been side by side for months in the WhatsApp group, in the phone calls I did not make, in the *should* that never became *do*. Did I know? I knew something. I knew the way you know that a sound in the engine means something without knowing what. I knew from the twenty-one-minute delay on his congratulations to Tola. I knew from the brevity of his messages. I knew from the way his voice sounded on the phone — the flatness, the careful management of tone that a man performs when the tone, left unmanaged, would tell you everything.

"I suspected," I say. "I didn't know for certain. But I suspected."

"You suspected your friend was in trouble and you did not ask."

This is not an accusation. Chinwe does not accuse. She states. She places the fact on the table between us the way she places everything — with precision, without cruelty, letting the fact do its own work. And the fact — *you suspected and you did not ask* — does its work. It enters my chest and sits beside the coffee I have not drunk and the fear I have not named and the guilt that has been building since the first time I thought *I should call Dapo* and did not.

"No," I say. "I did not ask."

She nods. One nod. Not forgiveness — acknowledgment. The acknowledgment of a woman who is collecting information from every source available and will sort it later, when the emergency has passed and the husband is home and the architecture has been fully dismantled and the rubble is on the floor and the work of understanding what was underneath can begin.

"He's been going to the library since July," she says. "Eleven weeks. Applying for jobs. Eating lunch alone. Coming home and telling me about meetings that did not happen."

I say nothing. There is nothing to say. The sentences she is speaking are not sentences that require a response. They are sentences that require a witness — someone to hear them, to hold them, to confirm by their presence that the thing being described is real and happened and was happening three miles from my house while I was building spreadsheets and solving LeetCode problems and replacing a light fixture.

"The savings are almost gone," she says. "Eight thousand dollars. We started with twenty-two."

"Chinwe—"

"I am not telling you this so you can help. I am telling you this because you are here and my husband is behind those doors and I need to say it to someone who will not tell me that God is testing us."

Pastor Femi. The sermon about the boat. The waves, the sleeping God, the instruction to keep looking up. I hear it in her voice — not the theology but the failure of the theology, the moment when the words that were supposed to hold a man in place became another thing he carried instead of the thing that carried him.

"I'm sorry," I say.

"Don't be sorry. Be here."

I am here. I am in an orange chair in a waiting room at UCSF with a cup of coffee I will not drink, and my friend is behind double doors with monitors on his chest, and his wife is beside me learning the shape of a lie she lived inside for seventeen weeks without knowing it, and I am here, which is the thing I should have been months ago when the phone was in my hand and the should was in my mouth and the canyon between them was narrow enough to cross if I had been braver.

I stay. Chinwe sits beside me. We do not talk for a long time. The clock moves. The fluorescent lights hold us in their flat, impartial gaze. The coffee cools. And somewhere behind the double doors, Dapo Olusanya is lying on a bed with electrodes on his temples and a truth in his chest that has finally, on a gurney, on a Sunday, in the language of an emergency he could no longer manage, come out.

*

I see him at 12:15. Chinwe takes me back. The room is small and curtained and lit with the same fluorescent light — the light that will not leave this story, the light that reports without flattering.

He is in a hospital gown. The charcoal suit is folded on a chair. The tie — the navy one with the diagonal stripes, the half-Windsor his father taught him — is on top of the suit, still half-tied, and the incompleteness of it is the thing I see first, because Dapo does not leave things incomplete.

He looks at me. His eyes are the same — dark, intelligent, carrying the quiet that I have always read as composure and now understand as containment. But something is different. Something behind the eyes has shifted, the way a building shifts after a tremor — still standing, still functional, but the alignment has changed, and the change is permanent.

"Koly," he says. The childhood nickname. The name only Dapo and my mother use. He has not called me Koly since the phone call in the first week, the one where we both said *we go dey alright* and neither of us meant it.

"How are you feeling?"

"Like a man who fell on his bathroom floor and was brought here by strangers." A pause. "I am tired, Kolade."

The word *tired* does not mean what it usually means. It does not mean he needs sleep. It means he needs to stop. To stop performing, stop managing, stop building the architecture of a life that requires his body to carry what his mouth will not say.

He is tired the way a machine is tired when it has been running past its maintenance schedule and the warnings have been ignored and the system, finally, has produced an error that cannot be closed.

"I know," I say.

"She knows everything now. The library. The applications. The money."

"I know. She told me."

He closes his eyes. When he opens them, they are wet. Not crying — Dapo does not cry the way I cry, with the full-body surrender of a man who has given up control. Dapo's tears arrive the way everything about Dapo arrives — managed, contained, permitted to exist only at the edges. Two tears. One from each eye. Symmetrical, like his father's knot.

"I should have told her," he says.

"Yes."

"In June. At the table. When she made the egusi."

"Yes."

"She would have carried it with me."

"She would have."

He looks at the ceiling. The hospital ceiling, white, featureless, not unlike the ceiling of the library bathroom where he practised the face, not unlike the ceiling of his bedroom where he lay awake counting the numbers. Ceilings, I think. The surfaces we stare at when we cannot look at each other. The blank spaces above our lives where we project the things we are too afraid to say aloud.

"I thought I was protecting her," he says. "I thought the silence was a kindness."

I reach across and take his hand. The gesture is not something I do — I am not a man who holds other men's hands, not in this culture, not in the vocabulary of Nigerian masculinity that Dapo and I were both raised in. But I take his hand because the moment requires something the vocabulary does not have, and the hand is what I can offer, and the offer is enough.

We sit. The monitors beep. The curtain moves in the air conditioning. Outside the window, the city of San Francisco goes about its Sunday, and in a small room on the fourth floor, two men from Surulere and Yaba hold hands and say nothing, because the nothing they are saying contains everything — the sorry and the fear and the should-have and the will-now — and the silence, for once, is not the problem. The silence, for once, is the bridge.

Chapter Eighteen

Kolade left at two o'clock. He held Dapo's hand a moment longer than either of them had language for, and then he stood, and Dapo watched his friend walk through the curtain and out of the room, and the curtain swung and settled, and the room was quiet again — the beeping of the monitor, the hum of the IV pump, the distant sound of the hospital's Sunday afternoon: footsteps, a phone ringing, the hydraulic sigh of an elevator arriving on the wrong floor.

Chinwe came back at two fifteen. She had been in the hallway. He knew this because he could hear her shoes — the low heels she wore to church, the ones that made a particular sound on hospital linoleum, measured and deliberate, the walk of a woman who was choosing when to re-enter a room rather than being pulled into it.

She sat in the chair beside the bed. The chair was blue vinyl, the kind that could be wiped clean, which was a design consideration Dapo found both practical and devastating — the chair anticipated spillage, anticipated mess, anticipated the bodily cost of what happened in this room. The chair was ready. He was not.

She did not speak first. This was Chinwe's way — not silence as punishment, not silence as withdrawal, but silence as invitation. The door she had opened last week in their bedroom (*is there anything else you need to tell me?*) was open again, and this time it was not a question. It was a room she was already standing inside, waiting for him to enter.

"Chinwe."

"I'm here."

"I need to tell you everything."

"Yes," she said. "You do."

*

He began with the morning. Not this morning — the other morning. The Tuesday in June. The Slack message. The calendar invite. The eleven-minute meeting in a virtual room with a woman from HR whose face he had never seen and a manager whose face he had seen every day for three years and who looked, during the meeting, like a man reading lines from a script he had not written and did not agree with but would deliver because the delivery was his job and his job was the only one in the room that was safe.

He told her about the drive home. The 680. The missed exit. The rehearsal — the drafts, the corporate language, the passive voice doing its work. He told her about the driveway, the Camry, the twelve minutes between arrival and the door.

He told her about the half-truth. *Between opportunities.* The phrase he had selected with the care of a man choosing which wire to cut, hoping the structure would hold.

Chinwe listened. She did not interrupt. Her hands were in her lap — folded, the right thumb pressing against the left palm, a gesture he had not seen her make before and which he understood, in the grammar of their marriage, as the gesture of a woman holding herself in a new way, a way she had not needed until today.

He told her about the library.

This was the part he had rehearsed least — not on the 580, not in the bathroom mirror, not in any of the spaces where he had practised the face and the lines and the careful management of what was known and what was hidden. The library had no rehearsal because the library was the thing itself, the architecture's foundation, the structure on which every other deception was built. To tell Chinwe about the library was to tell her that every morning since July — every kiss at the door, every *how was your day*, every *the migration is behind schedule* — had been a performance. That the man she slept beside and ate with and held in the dark was not the man she thought he was, or rather was the man she thought he was in every way except the one that mattered, which was that he was employed, and he was not.

"I drove to the Fremont Main Library every morning," he said. "I parked in the south lot. I sat at a desk by the east windows. I applied for jobs."

The monitor beeped. The IV dripped. The room held its breath.

"I ate lunch alone. Usually at the Subway on Mowry. Sometimes I brought a sandwich from home — from the groceries you bought, with the money that was running out."

Chinwe's thumb pressed harder against her palm. He could see the whitening of the skin around the knuckle.

"I came home at five fifteen. I told you about meetings. Deployments. A colleague named Raj who does not exist." He paused. "Raj does not exist, Chinwe. I invented him because I needed someone to mention in passing, someone whose name would make the day sound real."

She exhaled. Not a sigh — an exhalation, the release of air that had been held too long, the sound a body makes when it is recalibrating. The exhalation was followed by silence, and the silence was followed by more silence, and the silence filled the room the way the fluorescent light filled it — completely, without warmth, leaving nothing hidden.

"How much is left?" she said.

"In the savings?"

"Yes."

"Eight thousand seven hundred."

"We started with twenty-two."

"Yes."

She nodded. The nod was not the nod of acceptance. It was the nod of a woman assembling a structure — not the structure of deception that Dapo had built, but the structure of understanding that she was building on top of its ruins. She was counting. He could see her counting. Not on a legal pad, not on a spreadsheet, but internally, the way women count who have been managing households since before the men in those households learned what things cost.

"The thermos," she said.

"What?"

"The thermos I gave you. With your initials. You took it every morning."

"Yes."

"You filled it with coffee. In our kitchen. Under the cross."

"Yes."

"And you carried it to the library."

"Yes."

She looked at him. The look was the most honest thing he had ever received — more honest than the blood pressure reading, more honest than the ECG, more honest than the doctor's measured words about TIA and risk factors and lifestyle modifications. The look said: *I gave you a thermos because I loved you, and you used it as a prop in a performance you were staging to keep me from knowing you were drowning, and the fact that you did this with something I gave you out of love is the part that I will carry longest.*

She did not say this. She did not need to. Seventeen years of marriage had given them a language that operated beneath language, a subtext of gestures and glances and the particular quality of silence that contained more information than words could hold.

"Why?" she said.

The question was simple. Three letters. The smallest question in the English language and the only one that mattered. Not *what happened* — she knew what happened. Not *how long* — she knew how long. Not *how much is left* — she knew how much was left. *Why.* Why the silence. Why the library. Why the thermos carried like a talisman to a building where no one was expecting him. Why the face practised in a mirror. Why the lie, when the truth would have cost nothing except the one thing Dapo could not afford to spend: the admission that he was not what he had promised to be.

"I thought I was protecting you," he said.

"From what?"

"From — me. From the version of me that lost his job and didn't get another one and couldn't provide for his family and sat in a library applying for things nobody wanted him for." His voice broke. Not dramatically — the break was small, a fracture in a single syllable, the word *nobody* catching on something in his throat that was not phlegm but the accumulated weight of seventeen weeks of unsaid things. "I didn't want you to see that man."

"That man is my husband."

The sentence landed in the hospital room with the weight of every sentence Chinwe had ever spoken — direct, unpadded, arriving at the centre of the thing without detour. *That man is my husband.* Five words that dismantled seventeen weeks of architecture in the time it took to say them. Five words that said:

the man you were hiding from me is the man I married, and the hiding was not protection — the hiding was the injury.

"I know," he said.

"No. You don't know. Because if you knew — if you understood that I married Dapo, not Dapo's salary, not Dapo's title, not the version of Dapo that goes to an office and comes home and tells me about Raj — if you understood that, you would have come home in June and sat at the table and said *Chinwe, I lost my job, and I am afraid*, and I would have said *okay*, and we would have built a spreadsheet together, the way Kolade and Remi built theirs, and your blood pressure would be one twenty over eighty and you would not be in this bed."

The tears came. Not two, symmetrical, managed. The tears came the way they come when a man stops managing — the full, graceless release of a body that has been holding and holding and has finally been given, by the woman sitting in the blue vinyl chair, permission to stop.

He cried. He cried in a hospital gown with the ECG leads on his chest and the IV in his arm and the monitor beeping the rhythm of a heart that was still, despite everything, beating. He cried the way his father never cried — openly, audibly, with the sound that men from Lagos are taught to make only in private, if at all, and only before God, if anyone.

Chinwe did not move to hold him. Not immediately. She sat in the chair and she watched him cry and she let the crying be what it was — not a performance, not a negotiation, not the managed display of a man who is showing emotion to achieve an outcome. She let it be grief. The grief of a man who had lost his job and his health and seventeen weeks of his marriage to a lie he told to protect a woman who did not need protecting.

Then she moved. She stood from the chair. She sat on the edge of the hospital bed, which was narrow and not designed for two people, and she put her hand on the back of his neck — the place where the tension lived, the knot of muscle and tendon that had been tightening since June — and she held it. Not softly. Firmly. The grip of a woman who was holding a man in place, who was saying with her hand what she had said with her words: *you are here, I see you, the man you were hiding is the man I want, and the hiding is over.*

"We are going to figure this out," she said. "Together. The way we should have been figuring it out since June."

He nodded. The nod was wet, ungraceful, the nod of a man who was crying on a hospital bed on a Sunday afternoon while his wife held the back of his neck and the monitor beeped and the IV dripped and the city outside the window went about its business of being a city.

"The children," he said.

"The children are with Ngozi. They're fine."

"Femi saw."

"Femi saw. And Femi will be okay. Because we will tell him the truth, the way we should have told everyone the truth, and the truth is heavy but it is lighter than what you have been carrying."

She held him for a long time. The room was small. The curtain moved in the air conditioning. The fluorescent light held them in its flat, impartial gaze — the same light, always the same light, but for the first time since June it was illuminating something it had not seen before in the spaces where Dapo lived: honesty.

*

He slept. Chinwe did not.

She sat in the blue vinyl chair with her phone in her lap and her shoes still on — the church shoes, the heels she had not changed out of because changing shoes would have required leaving this room and she was not leaving this room — and she watched him sleep. The sleep was different from the sleep she had watched at home, in their bed, in the dark of the Dublin bedroom where the ceiling fan was broken and the glow-in-the-dark stars glowed above Sade's bed one room over. That sleep had been a man's performance of rest — the closed eyes, the measured breathing, the body lying still while the mind, she now understood, was running calculations it could not share.

This sleep was something else. This was the sleep of a man who had been emptied — who had taken the thing he was carrying and set it down, not neatly, not in an organised pile, but in a heap on the floor of a hospital room, and the setting-down had left him too exhausted to do anything but close his eyes and let the machines monitor what his body was doing while his mind, finally, did nothing.

She looked at her phone. She opened the banking app. She looked at the number: $8,700. She looked at it the way she looked at everything — directly, without flinch, with the intelligence of a woman who had been raised by a mother in Ibadan who could tell you the price of yam in three markets and the exchange rate from memory and who had once told her, on the porch of the family house, *Chinwe, money is not the problem. Not knowing is the problem. Know the number and you can fight. Don't know the number and the number fights you.*

She knew the number now. $8,700. She knew the mortgage, which she had never seen — Dapo managed the finances, had always managed them, and she had let him because trust is a kind of delegation and she trusted him the way she trusted the ground. She would learn the mortgage. She would learn the insurance, the utilities, the car payments, the remaining balance on the credit cards. She would learn every number Dapo had been carrying alone, and she would carry them with him, because that is what the word *together* means when a woman says it in a hospital room to a man who has just finished crying — it means *give me the weight.*

She opened her contacts. She scrolled to her supervisor at the dental office. She typed a message: *I need to increase my hours. Can we discuss this week?*

She sent it. Then she opened the calculator app. She began to count.

The hospital hummed around her. The machines beeped. Her husband slept. And Chinwe Olusanya — proud, capable, the woman whose grief would become the book's moral centre in the chapters to come, though neither of them knew it yet — Chinwe began to build the spreadsheet that Dapo never built, from the vinyl chair beside his bed, with her church shoes on and her phone in her hands, in the flat white light that reports without flattering, that holds without judging, that illuminates whatever is placed beneath it and calls it, simply, what it is.

Chapter Nineteen

The email arrives on a Wednesday at 2:14 p.m. — a time of day I have learned to distrust, because the good news and the bad news both arrive in the early afternoon, and the difference between them is not visible in the subject line.

The subject line reads: TENTATIVE JOB OFFER — GS-14 Senior Software Engineer.

I am at the kitchen table. The light fixture — the new one, the warm LED, the one Remi said doesn't make everything look like evidence — is on, and the kitchen looks different under it. Softer. More like a room where a family lives and less like a room where a man sits alone with spreadsheets and self-pity. I replaced the fixture the day I applied. Remi did not comment on the timing. Remi does not comment on the things she has already understood.

I open the email. I read it slowly, because reading it slowly is a way of not reacting, and not reacting is a way of protecting myself from the hope that has burned me eleven times in four months.

Dear Mr. Adeyemi, We are pleased to extend a tentative offer of employment for the position of Senior Software Engineer (GS-14, Step 5) with the United States Digital Service, based in San Francisco, CA...

The salary is listed. $143,736 base, plus locality adjustment bringing it to $168,979. Below the salary, the benefits: FEHB health insurance, FERS pension (1% per year of service, 1.1% after twenty years), Thrift Savings Plan with 5% agency match, thirteen days of annual leave accruing to twenty-six after fifteen years, thirteen days of sick leave per year, ten federal holidays.

I read the benefits list twice. Not because I don't understand it — I understand it the way I understand any system, by its components and their relationships — but because the list describes something I have never been offered. Not stock options that vest over four years and evaporate when a Slack message arrives. Not unlimited PTO that is unlimited in theory and monitored in practice. Not the equity refresh that is contingent on performance ratings administered by managers who are themselves contingent on the company's quarterly numbers. The list describes stability. The list describes a floor.

The salary is $168,979. My last salary was $347,000 in total compensation — base, bonus, RSUs. The gap between the two numbers is $178,021. The gap is a house. The gap is two private school tuitions. The gap is the distance between the man I was building and the man this offer is asking me to be.

I close the laptop. I do not reply.

*

The not-replying lasts three days.

On Thursday I go to the gym. Uncle Ricky is on the bike. The Journal is on the iPad. I take the bike beside him and I pedal and I say nothing, because I am not ready to say the thing and Uncle Ricky is a man who can sit in silence with a friend and not convert the silence into a conversation.

On Friday I look at the email again. I read the salary. I read the benefits. I read the words *United States Digital Service* and I think about what it means — what it actually means, beyond the salary and the pension and the TSP match — to build software for the government. To build systems that process veterans' claims, or manage immigration cases, or deliver healthcare data.

To build things that are used by people who did not choose to use them, who are not customers but citizens, who are not users but human beings interacting with the machinery of a country that promised them something and is trying, imperfectly and slowly, to deliver it.

I close the laptop again. The gap is still $178,021.

On Saturday morning I tell Remi.

"I got the offer."

She is at the counter. She is chopping something — she is always chopping something, the kitchen is her workshop the way the laptop is mine, and the rhythm of the knife is the rhythm of a woman who thinks with her hands. The chopping stops.

"Federal?"

"USDS. GS-14."

"The salary?"

"One sixty-nine. With locality."

She does not react. Not because she is not processing — Remi processes the way a computer processes, quickly and completely, with the output arriving fully formed — but because she is waiting for the rest. She knows there is a rest. She knows me.

"I'm thinking about not taking it."

The knife goes down. Not dramatically — Remi does not do dramatic — but with the specific finality of a utensil being placed on a surface by a woman who has decided that the conversation requires her full attention and the knife cannot have any of it.

"Tell me why."

"It's half what I was making."

"It's more than what you're making now."

The sentence is a scalpel. Clean, precise, no wasted tissue. *It's more than what you're making now.* Which is zero. Which is unemployment insurance and diminishing savings and a spreadsheet with a red cell that I no longer open because the red has become the default colour of the life we are living.

"It's not just the money," I say. "It's the—"

"The prestige."

I stop. She has named it before I could package it in a more acceptable word — *trajectory*, *career alignment*, *long-term positioning*. She has reached past the vocabulary I was assembling and pulled out the word I was trying to hide inside it. Prestige. The thing that cannot be deposited or withdrawn or calculated on a spreadsheet but that sits at the centre of every decision I have made since the scholarship letter arrived in Surulere and my father framed it before he read it.

"I was going to say trajectory."

"You were going to say trajectory because trajectory sounds like strategy and prestige sounds like vanity, and you are a man who would rather be strategic than vain, even when they are the same thing."

I stand in the kitchen under the new light fixture and I look at my wife and I understand that she has been waiting for this moment — not the offer, but the hesitation. She has been waiting for me to arrive at the crossroads Uncle Ricky described, the place where the path that looks like success and the path that looks like enough diverge, and she has been waiting to see which way I lean.

"Kolade," she says. "Sit down."

I sit. She sits across from me. The table is clean — no legal pad, no spreadsheet, no evidence of crisis. Just two people and the warm light and the morning.

"I need to tell you something about who you have become," she says. "And you are not going to enjoy hearing it."

"Okay."

"You have spent four months trying to get back to a place that no longer exists. The company is gone. The salary is gone. The title is gone. The RSUs — gone. And every night you sit at this table trying to find a door back into that building, and every morning you wake up and the building is still gone, and you are still here, and *here* is not a failure. *Here* is a kitchen with a new light fixture and two children who are adjusting and a wife who has been standing beside you for four months waiting for you to see what I see."

"What do you see?"

"I see a man who is more than the number on a pay stub. I see a man who replaced a light fixture and drove to a hospital and held his friend's hand. I see a man who sat with his son in a bedroom and told the truth when the truth was the hardest thing in the room. That man — *that* man — is not a man who needs a three-hundred-thousand-dollar salary to prove he exists. That man exists already. He has been existing this whole time. He just couldn't see it because the spreadsheet was in the way."

I am quiet. The quiet is not the quiet of disagreement. It is the quiet of a man hearing something he knows is true and needing a moment to let the knowing settle into the places where the other story — the story of prestige, of trajectory, of the boy from Surulere who would not stop climbing — has been living.

"Uncle Ricky told me something," I say. "He said he's rich because he was steady. Not because he was smart. Steady."

"Uncle Ricky is a wise man."

"He retired at fifty."

"And what has he been doing since?"

"Living. Coming to the gym. Reading the Journal. Not owing anyone anything."

Remi reaches across the table. She takes my hand. The gesture is simple and complete, the same gesture she made on the night I told her about the layoff, the same gesture that says *I am here and the hand is a contract and the contract says we do this together.*

"Take the job, Kolade."

"It's government."

"It's a pension. It's health insurance that doesn't disappear when someone sends a Slack message. It's a salary that arrives on the first and the fifteenth, and on the first and the fifteenth you can pay the mortgage, and on the day after you pay the mortgage you can sleep. When was the last time you slept?"

I do not answer. She knows the answer. The answer is June.

"Take the job. Build something that matters. Come home at five. Watch Yemi play football on Saturday. Replace another light fixture. Be the man you already are instead of the man you think you're supposed to be."

*

I accept the offer at 10:47 a.m. on a Sunday morning, sitting in the kitchen, under the light Remi chose, with a cup of coffee that I actually drink — the first cup I have finished in months, because finishing a cup of coffee requires the specific luxury of not being in a hurry, and for the first time since June I am not in a hurry, I am not running, I am a man sitting in his kitchen accepting a job that pays less than the one he lost and knowing, with a clarity that feels like the first clean breath after a long illness, that less is not the same as not enough.

The acceptance form is a PDF. The government communicates in PDFs the way tech companies communicate in Slack — relentlessly, unapologetically, with the absolute conviction that the format is appropriate for every occasion. I fill in the fields. I sign with the Adobe signature I created four months ago for the severance agreement, the same digital signature repurposed for a different kind of contract — not the ending of one thing but the beginning of another.

I press submit.

The confirmation page loads. It is plain. It is functional. It does not congratulate me with exclamation marks or tell me it is *super excited to welcome me to the team.* It says: *Your acceptance has been received. Your start date is November 18th. You will receive onboarding instructions by email within ten business days.*

I close the laptop. I sit in the kitchen. The house is quiet. Remi is at the store. Yemi is at a friend's house. Dara is in her room with the book light that we all know about and nobody mentions. I am alone, and the aloneness is not the 2 a.m. aloneness of spreadsheets and runways. It is the Sunday morning aloneness of a man who has done a thing and is sitting with the having-done-it, letting it settle.

I think about calling Dapo. He is home from the hospital — discharged Monday, on medication, Chinwe managing the recovery with the systematic thoroughness of a woman who has just learned the full dimensions of what she is managing and has responded, as Chinwe responds to everything, by building a plan. I think about calling him and saying *I got the job, the government job, the one that pays half and lasts forever*, and I think about how he would hear it — from the couch where Chinwe has installed him, with the lisinopril on the counter and the cardiologist appointment on the calendar and the truth finally out, all of it, the library and the spreadsheet and the face in the mirror.

I will call him. Not today. Today is for sitting. Today is for the coffee and the light and the quiet house and the knowledge that on November 18th I will walk into a building — not a glass campus with a cafeteria that serves açaí bowls and a gym nobody uses because everybody is too busy performing productivity to actually move their bodies — but a building. An office. A place where the work is steady and the salary is steady and the leaving is at five o'clock, and at five o'clock I will drive home on the 880 and the drive will not be a confessional or a rehearsal or a space of suspension. The drive will be a drive. And I will arrive in the driveway and I will not sit in the car.

I will go inside.

PART FOUR

What Remains

Chapter Twenty

I call him on a Tuesday evening, from the car, because the car is where every important conversation in this story happens and I have stopped pretending otherwise.

I am parked in the driveway. Not sitting in it the way I sat in it in June — not the forty-minute paralysis of a man who cannot cross the threshold. I am parked because I came home from the gym and Uncle Ricky said something that made me laugh, and the laughter reminded me of Dapo, and the reminder became a phone call before I could talk myself out of it. The engine is off. The October light is doing the thing it does in Fremont — golden, personal, the light that knows your name.

The phone rings three times.

"Koly."

His voice. I have not heard it in two weeks — since the hospital, since the hand-holding, since the curtain and the gown and the half-tied tie. The voice on the phone is different from the voice in the hospital bed. It is lighter. Not light — not the voice of a man who has recovered — but lighter. The difference between a man carrying a suitcase and a man who has set the suitcase down and is standing beside it, catching his breath.

"How are you?"

"I am sitting on my couch," he says, "and Chinwe has placed a pillow behind my back that I did not ask for, and my blood pressure medication is on the table next to a glass of water she has refilled three times because she is monitoring my hydration, and my daughter has drawn a card that says GET WELL BABA with a picture of a heart that has legs, and I am, Kolade, the most managed man in Dublin, California."

I laugh. The real one. The belly one. And on the other end of the phone, I hear something I have not heard since before June — Dapo laughing. Not the careful laugh of the WhatsApp group, not the two-emoji response, not the measured chuckle of a man performing levity. The real thing. Rusty, unfamiliar, slightly surprised at itself, the laugh of a man who has forgotten the sound of his own amusement and is hearing it for the first time in months.

"A heart with legs," I say.

"The legs are wearing trainers. She was very specific about the trainers."

"Sade is a detail person."

"Sade is her mother's daughter."

We are quiet for a moment. The quiet is not the old quiet — the quiet of the WhatsApp group, the quiet of *we go dey alright*, the quiet that was doing more work than it could carry. This quiet is thinner. Transparent. The quiet of two men who are on the other side of something and know it.

"I got a job," I say.

"Where?"

"USDS. Federal. Senior software engineer. GS-14."

The pause that follows is not the twenty-one-minute pause of the WhatsApp group. It is two seconds. Maybe three. The length of a man processing good news that is genuinely good and does not require him to perform anything — not congratulations, not envy, not the complicated calculus of watching a friend succeed while you are still falling.

"Government," he says.

"Government."

"Pension?"

"Pension. TSP. Five percent match. The whole thing."

"Kolade." He says my name the way he said *Koly* — with the weight of shared history, the specific gravity of a friendship that spans a geography from Lagos to the Bay Area. "That is — that is exactly right."

"It's half the salary."

"It's the whole salary. The other one was half a salary and half a lottery ticket. This one is the whole thing."

I sit in the car and I hold the phone and I feel something crack open — not the dramatic cracking of a wall coming down, but the quieter cracking of a seed, the kind that happens in the dark, in the dirt, when a thing that has been closed decides it is time to open.

"How's the blood pressure?" I ask.

"One thirty-two over eighty-four this morning. Chinwe checks it. She has a spreadsheet."

"Of course she does."

"It has columns, Kolade. It has colour-coding. She has turned my cardiovascular system into a data dashboard."

"You married the right woman."

"I married the right woman and lied to her for seventeen weeks and she is still here, and the fact that she is still here is the thing I will spend the rest of my life trying to earn."

The sentence arrives without performance. He says it the way he says everything now — plainly, without the architecture, without the half-truth and the rehearsed cadence and the corporate euphemism. The hospital stripped the architecture. Chinwe dismantled what was left. And what remains is a man who speaks in sentences that are shorter and truer and carry less weight because they are not carrying anything they weren't designed to hold.

*

Dapo held the phone with his left hand. His right hand was on the arm of the couch — Chinwe's couch, the grey sectional she chose when they moved to Dublin because it was large enough for a family of four to sit together and firm enough that nobody fell asleep during movies, though Femi always fell asleep during movies.

The living room was warm. The October light came through the west-facing windows and landed on the coffee table where Chinwe had arranged his medications — the lisinopril, the aspirin the cardiologist had added, the multivitamin she had added herself because Chinwe's approach to recovery was medical plus maternal, the overlap between the two indistinguishable to a woman who had been raised by a mother who believed that health was not a condition but a practice.

Sade's card was propped against the lamp. The heart with legs. The trainers drawn in blue marker, each lace individually rendered, the attention of a child who understood that the details were where the love was.

"Tell me about the job," he said.

Kolade talked. Dapo listened. The talking was different from the WhatsApp group — it was not bravado, not performance, not the careful management of tone that characterised every message in Severance Package FC. It was one man telling another man about a thing that had happened, plainly, the way men talk when the pretending has stopped and what remains is the conversation they should have been having all along.

Kolade described the application. The PDF. The lack of LeetCode. The confirmation page that did not use exclamation marks. Dapo laughed at the exclamation marks — Kaylee and her punctuation, the recruiter from the first phone screen, the one who was super excited and then disappeared.

"She ghosted you," Dapo said.

"She ghosted me."

"After saying she would definitely circle back."

"Definitely. With emphasis."

They laughed. The laughter moved through the phone like weather — clearing something, making room for what came after. What came after was quieter.

"I went back to the library," Dapo said.

Kolade was silent.

"Not to — I went back to return a book. Chinwe's book. She had a hold on a novel and I offered to pick it up because Chinwe will not let me drive yet, so she drove me, and I went inside and I walked past the desk — my desk, third seat from the end, by the east windows — and someone was sitting there. A woman. A laptop. A thermos. She was doing what I was doing. I could see it from across the room."

"How?"

"The posture. The way she was looking at the screen. The way her hand moved between the trackpad and the phone, refreshing, checking, waiting. You can see it, Kolade. When you've done it, you can see it in other people."

He paused. Chinwe was in the kitchen. He could hear her — the sound of the pot, the rhythm of her cooking, which had changed since the hospital. She cooked more now. Not because she hadn't cooked before but because the cooking had become something else — an act of management, of nutrition as architecture, of building a body back from the inside with egusi and greens and the broiled fish the cardiologist recommended and which Chinwe prepared with the same devotion she brought to everything, the full, concentrated attention of a woman who had decided that this man would not collapse again.

"I wanted to sit down next to her," Dapo said. "I wanted to say — I don't know. Something. That it ends. That the library is

not where you stay."

"Did you?"

"No. I picked up the book and I left. Chinwe was in the car."

"Maybe next time."

"Maybe next time."

✳

The call lasted fifty-three minutes. I know this because the phone logged it, and I looked at the log afterward, and fifty-three minutes is the longest phone call I have had with anyone since the one I made to my father in July to tell him about the layoff, which lasted forty-one minutes and ended with my father saying *we will manage* and me, for the first time in my life, believing him.

We talked about the children. Yemi at Irvington — the two friends, the football team, the math teacher who told Remi at the parent conference that Yemi's ability was *unusual* and that the word *unusual* in a public school math teacher's vocabulary was the same as the word *exceptional* in a private school's, just without the brochure. Femi and his questions — thirteen, the age where a boy's brain becomes a courtroom and every adult statement is cross-examined. Sade and the glow-in-the-dark stars. Dara and the book light.

We talked about the group. Emeka had landed at a startup in Oakland. Chidi was interviewing at Salesforce. Segun had gone quiet — really quiet, the kind of quiet that Dapo now recognised from the inside, and I said *I'll call him* and Dapo said *yes, call him* and this time the *call him* was not a should but a will, because we had both learned what happens when *should* stays in the mouth too long.

We talked about Uncle Ricky. Dapo wanted to meet him. I said I would arrange it — the gym, a Thursday morning, the bikes side by side, the Journal on the iPad. Dapo said *a man who retired at fifty from SFPD and reads the Wall Street Journal on a stationary bike is the most interesting person in this entire story* and I said *don't tell Remi* and he laughed and I laughed and the laughter was the thing, the actual thing, the sound of two men who had been silent for months discovering that their voices still worked.

At the end, there was a pause. Not the pause of men searching for words but the pause of men who have said enough and are resting in the having-said-it.

"Koly."

"Yes."

"Thank you for coming to the hospital."

"I should have come sooner."

"You came."

"I should have called in July."

"You're calling now."

The generosity of it — the absolute, unearned generosity of a man on a couch with a pillow he didn't ask for and a blood pressure dashboard and a heart drawn by his daughter forgiving me for the months I did not call — the generosity of it broke something and repaired something in the same motion, the way a bone resets, with pain and relief arriving in the same breath.

"I start November eighteenth," I said.

"The government."

"The government."

"Pension, TSP, five percent match."

"You sound like Remi."

"Remi is correct about everything. This has been established."

"Goodnight, Dapo."

"Goodnight, Koly. And Kolade—"

"Yes."

"Call Segun."

"I'll call him tomorrow."

"Good."

He hung up. I sat in the car. The driveway was dark now — the October light had gone, replaced by the streetlamp and the porch light and the glow from the kitchen window where Remi was moving, a silhouette, the shape of a woman in a house that was still standing.

I went inside.

Chapter Twenty-One

He woke before the alarm. Before the house. Before the light.

This was not unusual — Dapo had been waking before dawn for months, pulled from sleep by the pulse in his chest or the calculations in his head or the particular gravity of a body that had forgotten how to rest. But this morning was different. This morning he woke and the first thing he felt was not the tightness. Not the weight. Not the hand on the sternum that had been living there since September.

The first thing he felt was quiet.

He lay in bed for a moment. Chinwe was beside him, on her side, facing the window where the first grey suggestion of morning was beginning to separate the curtain from the dark. Her breathing was deep and steady — the breathing of a woman who was sleeping because she had earned the sleep, who had spent three weeks rebuilding the structure of their life from the hospital forward with the systematic thoroughness of a woman who had been given the full picture and had responded not with collapse but with architecture.

Chinwe's architecture was different from his. His had been designed to conceal. Hers was designed to hold. She had spreadsheets now — real ones, not pipeline dashboards for a pipeline that didn't exist, but the working documents of a household that had been repriced and reorganised and placed on a foundation that could carry the weight because the weight was shared. She had increased her hours at the dental office. She had called the mortgage company and negotiated a three-month forbearance — the word Kolade had looked up at 2 a.m. and feared, which Chinwe had looked up at 2 p.m. and used, because

Chinwe understood that financial instruments were tools, not judgments, and the tool was there to be used.

She had done this while he sat on the couch. While the lisinopril brought the numbers down and the aspirin thinned the blood and his body, slowly, began to speak in a tone that was no longer alarm. She had done this while he watched, and the watching — the specific, helpless watching of a man whose wife was doing the work he had tried to do alone and failing — was both the hardest and the most necessary thing the hospital had given him.

He got out of bed. Quietly. Not the quiet of concealment — he was done with that kind of quiet, or trying to be done with it, the way a man who has quit smoking is done with it: deliberately, with effort, with the awareness that the old habit is still in the house and may at any moment offer itself. This was the quiet of a man who wanted to let his wife sleep because she had been sleeping less, and less well, and the dark circles under her eyes were the ledger of what she was carrying, and the least he could give her this morning was another hour.

*

The kitchen was dark. He turned on the stove light — Remi's small precaution against unnamed things, he thought, and smiled, because Kolade had told him about the stove light on the phone and it had become, in the shared language of their friendship, a shorthand for the superstitions of wives who love you in ways they will not explain.

He made tea. Not coffee — the cardiologist had suggested reducing caffeine, and Chinwe had converted the suggestion into policy, replacing the coffee maker's position on the counter with an electric kettle and a tin of loose-leaf green tea that tasted like grass and virtue. He missed the coffee. He missed the thermos — the thermos was in a drawer now, not the nightstand drawer with the Omron but the kitchen drawer with the mismatched Tupperware lids and the spare batteries, the drawer of things that had a former purpose and were waiting to be assigned a new one.

He sat at the table. The wooden cross was above the doorframe, where it had always been, where Chinwe's mother had placed it when they bought the house. He looked at it. He had been looking at it differently since the hospital — not with the devotion of the boy who sat in Calvary Baptist Yaba, and not with the hollow performance of the man who sat in Grace Baptist Hayward while the lie expanded, but with something in between. Something cautious. A faith that was being rebuilt from the foundation, the way Chinwe was rebuilding the finances — not by pretending the collapse had not happened but by starting from the rubble and placing each stone with the care of a person who understood that the first structure had failed because it was built on the wrong thing.

Pastor Femi had visited on Saturday. He sat in the living room and he did not give a sermon. He sat with Dapo and Chinwe and he listened, and the listening was the best thing he had done — better than the boat, better than Mark chapter four, better than the sleeping God. The listening said: *I am here, and what happened to you is real, and I do not have a verse for it.* The absence of a verse was, paradoxically, the most pastoral thing he had ever offered.

He had also given Dapo a name. A counsellor. A Nigerian man — Yoruba, a psychologist in Oakland, whose office was on Broadway near the lake and who, Pastor Femi said, understood the specific weight that men like Dapo carried, because he had carried it himself, and had been trained to help others set it down.

Dapo had called on Monday. The appointment was next week. The appointment was the first thing he had ever done for himself that was not also a performance for someone else, and the doing of it — the dialling, the receptionist, the *yes, I'd like to schedule an initial consultation* — had felt like the lightest thing he had done in months.

*

The light came.

It came the way Bay Area light comes in October — gradually, then suddenly, the grey giving way to amber, the amber to gold, the gold to the specific, luminous clarity that made the hills across the valley look like they had been painted that morning by someone who understood that beauty did not require explanation. The light entered through the kitchen window and moved across the table and touched his hands, which were wrapped around the tea, and the warmth of the tea and the warmth of the light met at his fingers, and he sat in it.

He thought about the things he needed to do.

The cardiologist, Tuesday. The blood draw, Wednesday. The counsellor, Thursday. The follow-up with the primary care doctor, the one he had promised Chinwe he would see and had not seen, who was now scheduled for Friday because Chinwe had called and made the appointment herself while Dapo was in the shower, and had told him about it afterward with the matter-of-fact tone of a woman who was no longer leaving medical compliance to a man who had put a blood pressure monitor in a drawer.

He thought about work. Not the library — the library was over, the library was the country he had lived in and left, the country that existed for men who could not say what was happening to them and needed a desk and a window and the fiction of purpose. He thought about actual work. Chinwe had found a listing — a data engineer position at a healthcare company in Emeryville, smaller than what he'd had, a title that was lateral rather than a step up, a salary that was less, but a salary. A real one. She had bookmarked it on her phone and shown it to him on the couch and said *when you're ready*, and the *when you're ready* was the phrase that distinguished this from every other job conversation of the past five months, because *when you're ready* gave the timeline to him rather than to the savings account.

He was not ready. Not today. But soon. He could feel the soon the way he could feel the light — approaching, arriving, not yet here but no longer theoretical. Something was returning. Not the old Dapo — not the man who placed his palms flat on a desk and carried everything in silence and practised an expression in a bathroom mirror. That man was gone. What was returning was something smaller and truer. A man who could sit at a kitchen table with tea and watch the light come up and not need the watching to be a performance for anyone.

He thought about Kolade. The phone call, the laughter, the fifty-three minutes. The government job that started in two weeks. The pension. The TSP. Uncle Ricky and the stationary bike and the Wall Street Journal. He thought about how Kolade had held his hand in the hospital — the gesture that had no place in their vocabulary and had created a place by the doing of it. He would see Kolade soon. They would sit somewhere — the gym, a restaurant, the driveway — and they would talk the way they were learning to talk, which was plainly, without the architecture, without the half-truths and the managed silences and the cultural scaffolding that said men carry and do not speak about the carrying.

He thought about his father. Emmanuel, who carried. Emmanuel, who died in the shop with a bolt of aso-oke within arm's reach and the ledger book open to a page of numbers he was checking when his heart decided it was finished. Emmanuel, who was sixty-one. Dapo was forty-two. The difference was nineteen years, and the nineteen years were not guaranteed — the cardiologist had said this without saying it, in the way cardiologists speak, which is in probabilities and risk factors and the language of *if you make the changes, the outlook is good*, where *good* means *better than it was* and *if* is the word doing all the work.

He would make the changes. He was making them. The tea instead of coffee. The walks Chinwe insisted on — thirty minutes after dinner, the two of them and Sade, who chattered about school and the dog she wanted and the constellations she was learning, the real ones this time, not the glow-in-the-dark ones on her ceiling. Femi came sometimes. He walked beside his father without talking, which was its own kind of conversation — the conversation of a thirteen-year-old who had seen his father on a bathroom floor and was learning, in the particular language of adolescence, to be near him without requiring the nearness to be explained.

*

The tea was finished. The light was fully in the kitchen now — the room golden, warm, the wooden cross above the doorframe catching the morning in a way that made it glow. The house was beginning to wake. He could hear the sounds: a door, water in the pipes, Sade's alarm — the novelty ringtone she had chosen and

Chinwe had allowed because the battle over ringtones was a battle Chinwe had strategically lost in exchange for a won battle over screen time.

He stood. He rinsed the cup. He placed it in the rack — upside down, the way Chinwe did it, the way her mother taught her, the gesture so small and so borrowed that it felt like a kind of prayer.

He looked out the window. The hills were gold. The sky was the particular blue that Bay Area mornings produce in October when the fog has burned off early and the air is clean and the world, for a few hours, looks like it was made that morning.

He felt good. Not healed — he understood the difference now, the way he understood the difference between calm and controlled, between fine and fine. Not healed. But better. The blood pressure was down. The tightness had eased. The pulse no longer kept him awake, or kept him awake less often, the medication and the walks and the counsellor appointment and the truth — the truth most of all, the truth that had cost him everything and given him back the one thing the lie could not: the ability to stand in his own kitchen and not pretend.

He heard Chinwe on the stairs. Her footsteps — purposeful, direct, the walk of a woman who did not wander. She would come into the kitchen and she would see him standing in the light and she would say something ordinary — *good morning, did you take the pill, Sade needs her permission slip signed* — and the ordinary would be the most extraordinary thing, because the ordinary was the sound of a life that was real, that was not performed, that belonged to both of them.

He waited for her. The light held him. The cross glowed.

He was thinking about going back to work. He was thinking about the Emeryville company and the listing Chinwe had bookmarked and the word *ready*, which was getting closer, which was almost here. He was thinking about the phone call with Kolade, the laughter, the heart with legs, the trainers drawn in blue marker. He was thinking that the morning was beautiful and the tea was good and the house was waking and he was inside it, not in a library, not in a car rehearsing lies, not in a bathroom practising an expression, but here, in his kitchen, in the light, waiting for his wife.

He was not afraid.

For the first time since June, Dapo Olusanya was not afraid.

Chapter Twenty-Two

Chinwe calls at 6:12 a.m.

I am awake. I have been awake since five, lying in bed, listening to Remi breathe, thinking about nothing in particular and everything in general — the start date in nine days, the badge I will wear, the building I will enter, the smaller desk, the different life. The thinking is quiet. It is the thinking of a man who is, for the first time in months, looking forward, and the forward has a shape he can almost see.

The phone lights up. CHINWE OLUSANYA. And I know.

I do not know what I know. I do not have the information. But the body knows before the mind assembles the data — the body reads the screen and the hour and the name and produces a knowledge that arrives before language, that sits in the chest like a stone dropped into still water, the ripple moving outward before the stone has reached the bottom.

Chinwe does not call me. Chinwe calls Remi.

I answer.

"Kolade." Her voice. I have heard this voice three times in my life on a phone — once to tell me Dapo was in the hospital, once to tell me he was being discharged, and now. The voice is not controlled. The voice has passed the place where control is possible. The voice is the sound of a woman standing in a house where something has happened that is too large for the house to hold.

"Chinwe."

"He's gone."

Two words. The smallest sentence. The sentence that contains everything and communicates nothing, because *gone* is a word that the English language uses for departure and for death and for the thing that happens when you leave a room and also for the thing that happens when you leave the world, and the ambiguity of it is, in this moment, an act of violence against a woman who deserves a language that is more precise about the worst thing it can describe.

"He's gone, Kolade. This morning. Before I — before the ambulance. He was in the kitchen. The tea. He was making tea."

I sit up. Remi stirs. She opens her eyes and sees my face and the phone and she sits up too, and her hand goes to my back, and the hand is warm, and the warmth is the only thing in the room that is not the sentence Chinwe has just said.

"What happened?"

"Stroke. Massive — the doctor said massive. And cardiac arrest. He was — by the time I came downstairs he was on the floor. The kitchen floor. Kolade, I called 911 and they came and they tried and he was already—"

She stops. The stop is not a pause. It is the place where the sentence cannot go further because the further is a word she has not yet learned to say. The word is *dead*. She has not said it. She has said *gone* and *already* and the space between them is the word she is circling the way you circle a hole in the ground — close enough to see the depth, too close to the edge to look directly in.

"I'm coming," I say.

"The children are at Ngozi's. She came. I called her first and then I called you and I don't — Kolade, I don't know what to—"

"I'm coming. Right now. I'm coming."

I hang up. I do not remember hanging up. I remember the phone being in my hand and then not being in my hand and Remi's face, which has understood everything from the half of the conversation she heard, which is the half that contains all of it

— the name, the hour, the *I'm coming* repeated three times because the repetition is the only thing my mouth can produce when the rest of me has stopped.

"Dapo," Remi says. Not a question.

"Yes."

She does not ask how. She does not ask when. She puts her arms around me — in the bed, in the grey light of the bedroom, with the alarm that has not yet gone off and the day that has not yet begun — and she holds me, and I let her, and the letting is the hardest part, because a man who has spent his life holding does not easily become a man who is held.

*

I drive to Dublin. The 880. The same freeway, always the same freeway. The freeway that carried me home from the layoff and carried me to the hospital and carried me to the gym where Uncle Ricky read the Journal and now carries me to a house on Amaryllis Court where a man I have known since we were boys in Lagos is lying on a kitchen floor beside a cup of tea and is not going to stand up.

I do not remember the drive. I remember leaving the driveway and I remember arriving at Amaryllis Court, and the space between is a blur of concrete and light, the Bay Area morning doing what it always does — arriving, golden, indifferent — and the indifference of the light is the thing that will stay with me longest, because the world does not pause. The world does not dim. The world continues to produce its morning with the same luminous, unbroken beauty it produced yesterday when Dapo was alive and planning to go back to work and sitting in his kitchen feeling, for the first time since June, not afraid.

Chinwe is at the door. She has not changed. She is wearing what she slept in — the grey dress, the head wrap, the Saturday-and-Sunday clothes that are also, now, the clothes she was wearing when her husband died. She will remember these clothes. She will remember the dress and the wrap and the way the morning light hit the porch and the specific temperature of the air at 6:45 a.m. on a Wednesday in October. The memory will be precise and permanent, because trauma records in high resolution — every detail preserved, every sense sharpened, the mind's way of documenting a moment it will spend years trying to understand.

I hold her. She is shorter than me — she reaches my shoulder, the way Remi reaches my chest — and she presses into me with a force that is not grief but the precursor to grief, the physical state of a body that has not yet learned what it is carrying because the weight has not settled. The weight is still falling. It will be falling for months.

"Where is he?" I ask.

"They took him. The paramedics. They — he's at the hospital. They had to take him."

"Okay."

"I went downstairs and he was on the floor. By the table. The chair was pushed back. The tea was on the counter. He had made tea, Kolade. He was making tea."

She says this — *he was making tea* — as though the tea is the detail that refuses to compute, the data point that the system cannot process because the system was designed for a world in which a man who makes tea in his kitchen on a Wednesday morning is a man who drinks the tea and puts the cup in the rack and goes about his day. The tea is the ordinary. The tea is the thing that was supposed to happen. The tea is the life that was interrupted by the thing the body had been saying for months —

in blood pressure readings and pulse rates and the tightness on the sternum and the Google search at 11:47 p.m. — the thing the body said louder and louder until, on a Wednesday morning, in a kitchen in Dublin with the light coming through the window and the wooden cross above the doorframe, the body said it for the last time.

*

I stay. I stay all day. Remi comes at eight with food she has assembled in twenty minutes — jollof, fried plantain, the dishes that Nigerian women produce in crisis the way other cultures produce flowers, because food is the language of community and community is what you call when the individual has been overwhelmed. Ngozi is there. Two women from the church are there. Sister Bukola arrives at nine with a tray of chin chin and the expression of a woman who has typed two-fingered through thirty years of church life and has learned that grief requires not words but presence.

The house fills. It fills the way Nigerian houses fill — with food and bodies and the sound of women organising a thing that cannot be organised, because the organisation is the coping and the coping is the food and the food keeps arriving because to stop cooking would be to stop moving and to stop moving would be to feel the full weight of what has happened, and nobody in this house is ready for that weight yet.

I sit in the living room. The couch where Dapo sat two weeks ago, the phone against his ear, laughing. The pillow Chinwe placed behind his back. Sade's card is still propped against the lamp — the heart with legs, the trainers in blue marker. The card does not know. The card remains cheerful in the specific, terrible way that objects remain what they were before the world changed around them.

I think about the phone call. Fifty-three minutes. The laughter. The way he said *government* as though the word had a flavour he was tasting. The way he said *call Segun* — the instruction, the will instead of the should. I think about the last thing he said to me: *good*. One word. A closing. The period at the end of the last sentence he would ever say to me, though neither of us knew it, though neither of us could have known it, because the phone calls that end your friendship with a living man and begin your friendship with a memory do not announce themselves.

I did not call Segun. I was going to call Segun tomorrow. Tomorrow was the plan. Tomorrow is always the plan for the hard things, the things that require a courage we do not yet have but believe we will have after one more night of sleep, one more morning of coffee, one more day of the ordinary. I did not call Segun. And now I am sitting on Dapo's couch in a house that smells of jollof and loss, and the not-calling is another stone in the river of things I did not do in time.

I will call Segun today. Not tomorrow. Today. Because Dapo asked me to, and Dapo is gone, and the things a dead man asks you to do are not requests. They are obligations. They are the weight he is handing you on his way out, and the weight is light because the ask is small, and the ask is small because the man who made it understood, at the end, that the small things — the phone call, the tea, the cup placed upside down in the rack — are the only things that matter.

*

At four o'clock the house begins to thin. The women leave in pairs, carrying empty dishes, promising to return tomorrow. Ngozi takes Femi and Sade to her house for the night. Femi goes without argument. His face is the face from the bathroom doorway — still, recording, processing nothing. Sade holds Chinwe's hand at the door and does not let go until Chinwe kneels and presses her forehead to Sade's forehead and says something I cannot hear, something in the private language of a mother and a daughter that requires no witnesses.

Remi stays. She is in the kitchen, cleaning. Not because the kitchen is dirty — the church women have already cleaned it — but because Remi cleans the way she does everything in crisis: as a way of creating order in a space where order has been destroyed. She wipes the counter where the tea sat. She puts away the dishes that have accumulated. She does not look at the floor.

The floor where he fell. The kitchen floor, tile, the same tile as the bathroom where he collapsed three weeks ago. Two floors. Two falls. The first one a warning. The second one the thing the warning was warning about.

Chinwe sits in the chair by the window. The chair where Dapo sat in the evenings, the chair where he opened his phone to the job alerts, the chair where he counted the forty-three days until the savings reached zero. She sits in his chair and she looks at the backyard — the fence that needs staining, the fence he promised in April, the fence that will not be stained by his hands.

"He was happy this morning," she says. To no one. To the room. To whatever is left of the morning that held him. "He made tea. He was looking at the light. I could hear him from upstairs. The kettle. The cup. He was humming."

She pauses.

"He hasn't hummed in months."

I do not speak. There is nothing to say. The humming is the detail that will undo me — not now, not in this room, but later, in the car, on the 880, in the specific quality of silence that fills a vehicle carrying a man away from the house where his friend died happy on a Wednesday morning in October, humming in a kitchen where the light was gold and the tea was green and the wooden cross above the doorframe caught the morning in a way that made it glow.

Chapter Twenty-Three

The room asks me to speak.

Not formally — there is no microphone, no podium, no printed programme with my name in italics. But the room asks in the way Nigerian rooms ask: through the shifting of chairs, the lowering of plates, the specific quality of attention that gathers in a space when the people inside it have decided that someone needs to say the thing they have all been thinking and have not yet found the words for.

It is Wale who says it. Wale, who has known us since the early days — since the apartment in Fremont, since the company shuttle, since the WhatsApp group was just *Naija Tech Bros* and the only crisis it managed was who forgot to RSVP for Emeka's birthday. Wale puts his hand on my shoulder and says, "Kolade, say something. For Dapo."

I do not want to. I want to stand at the window with my warm ginger beer and watch the room the way I have been watching it — cataloguing, counting, measuring the distance between the performance of grief and the thing itself. I want to stay in the posture of the observer because the observer does not have to feel what the speaker does, and what the speaker will have to feel, if he opens his mouth in this room, is everything.

But Chinwe is looking at me. From the kitchen doorway, where she has been standing with Adaeze, one hand on the counter, the other holding nothing — the hand that should be holding Dapo's and is holding air. She is looking at me with the expression I saw in the hospital, the expression of a woman who is past crying and has converted the tears into something harder. She nods. One nod. Permission.

I set down the ginger beer. I step into the centre of the room. Forty-five people. I counted when I arrived, because counting is what I do when I am afraid, and I am afraid now — afraid of the silence, afraid of the words, afraid of the truth I promised to tell on the night Chinwe called and the morning I drove across the Dumbarton Bridge and the afternoon I held his hand in a hospital room and every day since, the truth that has been building in me chapter by chapter, waiting for the room that needed to hear it.

This is the room. These are the people. And the truth is not a eulogy. It is an accounting.

*

"I am not going to tell you that Dapo is in a better place," I say. "Pastor Femi has said that, and he said it well, and I do not doubt him. But I am not a pastor. I am an engineer. And what I have to say is not about where Dapo is now. It is about where Dapo was."

The room is quiet. The specific quiet of a Nigerian gathering that has been offered something other than the expected, something that does not fit the script of funeral oratory, and is deciding whether to receive it.

"Dapo was in a library. Every morning. For eleven weeks. In his work clothes. With a thermos his wife gave him for Christmas. Applying for jobs on a laptop at a desk by the east-facing windows, third seat from the end."

I hear a sound from the room — not a gasp, because Nigerians do not gasp at gatherings, but a shift, a collective inhale held at the top, the sound of people recalibrating what they thought they knew.

"He did not tell Chinwe. He did not tell me. He did not tell any of you. He dressed every morning and drove to the library and came home and described a day at work that did not happen, because the alternative — saying *I was laid off and I am afraid* — was a sentence he did not have permission to speak."

I look at the room. I look at the men. The men who are standing along the walls and by the sliding door and in the hallway, holding plates they are not eating from, wearing the suits they wear to church and to funerals and to the gatherings where the community performs its solidity. I look at them and I see Dapo. I see Dapo in every one of them — in the posture, in the contained expression, in the architecture of a masculinity that was built in Lagos and Ibadan and Abeokuta and shipped across the ocean and reassembled in Fremont and Dublin and Hayward without ever being inspected for the thing that was wrong with it, which is that it does not have a room for the sentence *I am struggling*.

"We built something," I say. "All of us. We came to this country and we built something. We got the degrees. We got the visas. We survived the H-1B lottery and the green card wait and the years of being the only person in the room who looked like us. We got the jobs. We got the houses. We got the schools for our children and the cars for our driveways and the salaries that let us send money home and call our parents on Sunday and say *everything is fine*."

I pause. The room is holding me the way rooms hold you when you are saying something they recognise but have not yet said aloud.

"And then a company sent a Slack message. And everything we built was contingent on a Slack message. The house, the school, the car, the insurance, the visa — all of it, contingent. We were not owners. We were tenants. We were tenants in a system that let us believe we owned something, and the rent was our labour and our silence and our willingness to perform our success without ever discussing its cost, and when the system decided it no longer needed us, it took everything back and sent a calendar invite to tell us."

Emeka shifts against the wall. Chidi looks at the floor. Wale's hand, which was on my shoulder, has dropped to his side. The room is not comfortable. The room is not supposed to be comfortable. Comfort is what we have been offering each other since June — *we go dey alright*, *God is faithful*, *the market will recover* — and comfort is what killed Dapo, because comfort told him the silence was sustainable and the performance was necessary and the lie was a kindness and the body could carry what the mouth would not say.

"I am not blaming the company," I say. "The company did what companies do. I am not blaming the economy. The economy does what economies do. I am talking about us. I am talking about this room. I am talking about the men standing along these walls who would rather die than say the words *I need help*."

The sentence lands. I watch it land. I watch it land on the men who were laid off and did not tell their wives for weeks. On the men who are still employed and afraid they will not be next month. On the men whose blood pressure they do not check and whose doctors they do not call and whose silence they have been told, since boyhood, is the shape a man is supposed to make when the load is too heavy.

"Dapo's blood pressure was one eighty-two over one oh eight the morning he collapsed. One eighty-two. The doctor at UCSF said his heart had been under severe stress for months. *Months*. While he drove to the library. While he sat at the desk. While he came home and said the migration was behind schedule. His body was screaming and he could not hear it because the silence he was inside was louder."

Chinwe has moved to the armchair. Dapo's chair. She sits in it with her hands on the armrests and her face compressed and her eyes on me, and I am speaking to the room but I am speaking for her, because Chinwe cannot say this — not today, not in this room, not with the grief still falling — and someone must.

"What the industry took from Dapo, it will never give back. Not the salary. Not the title. Not the years he spent building systems that processed millions of records while his own system — his heart, his blood, his brain — went unmonitored and unmentioned. The industry took his labour and his expertise and his time, and when it was finished with him, it sent an email."

I stop. I look at the photograph on the bookshelf. Dapo and me, 2019. The Heineken. The grin. My hand on his shoulder. Two men who thought the hardest part was behind them.

"But the industry did not kill Dapo. We did. This room. This culture. The culture that says a man provides and does not discuss the cost of providing. The culture that gives a man a thermos and a tie and a half-Windsor knot and says *carry it, carry it, carry it* and never once says *put it down*. The culture that sent Dapo to a pastor when he needed a therapist, and gave him a verse about a boat when he needed someone to say *brother, I see you drowning*."

I look at Pastor Femi. He is standing by the wall, his Bible under his arm, and his face is not defensive. His face is the face of a man hearing something he has suspected and is now being told, and the hearing is painful not because it is unfair but because it is true. He nods. A small nod. The nod of a man who will take this into his office behind the sanctuary and sit with it for a long time.

"I should have called him," I say. "I knew something was wrong. I felt it in the WhatsApp messages, in the delays, in the brevity. I should have picked up the phone and said *Dapo, how are you really?* Four words. I did not say them. And I will carry that for the rest of my life."

The room. The room with its jollof and its folding table and its forty-five people and its photograph on the bookshelf and the glow-in-the-dark stars on the ceiling upstairs where Sade's private sky waits for a father who will not come home. The room holds me the way rooms hold you when you have said the true thing and the true thing has changed the air and there is no version of the next sentence that makes it better.

"Dapo was forty-two years old. He was a senior data engineer. He was a father. He was a husband. He was my friend. And he died because he could not say five words: *I need help. I am afraid.*"

I stop. The sentence is the sentence. There is nothing after it that improves it.

"So I am saying them now. For him. To all of you. *Wetin we no go talk fit kill us.* What we will not speak can kill us. It killed Dapo. And it will kill the next man in this room who decides that silence is strength, unless we — all of us, the men and the women and the pastors and the friends — unless we build a room where the sentence *I am struggling* is not a failure. Where a man can put the thermos down. Where the half-Windsor can come undone."

I look at Chinwe. She is in the chair. Her hands are on the armrests. Her eyes are wet now — for the first time today, the first time I have seen — and the wetness is not collapse. It is the moisture on a surface that has been dry too long, the first sign that the grief beneath the compression is beginning, slowly, to move.

"That is what I wanted to say. For Dapo. For all of us."

I step back. The room holds for a moment — the long, full silence of a community that has heard something it needed to hear and is not yet sure what to do with it. Then Wale says *amen.* And Emeka says *amen.* And the room says *amen* — not the reflexive *amen* of a sermon's end, but the *amen* of recognition, the *amen* that means *yes, this is true, and we have been afraid to say it, and now someone has*.

The folding table holds the food. The photograph holds the grin. The chair holds Chinwe. And the room, for the first time, holds the truth.

Chapter Twenty-Four

Six months later, I leave work at 4:58 p.m.

I want you to hold this detail the way I hold it — not as an event but as a revolution. 4:58. Two minutes early. Because the meeting ended and the code was committed and the review was submitted and there was nothing left to do that could not be done tomorrow, and tomorrow the building would still be here, and the desk would still be here, and the work would still be here, because government work has the specific quality of permanence that private-sector work pretends to have and does not.

The desk is smaller than my old desk. The monitor is a single screen, not the dual curved setup I had in Santa Clara. The chair does not have adjustable lumbar support — it has a cushion Remi bought from Target that I placed on the seat during my first week and that has become, over six months, as much a part of the furniture as the desk itself. The office is a floor of cubicles in a federal building on 7th Street in San Francisco, and the aesthetic is institutional in a way that does not apologise for itself — grey carpet, fluorescent lights that are the same fluorescent lights from every room in this story, drop ceilings, a break room with a coffee maker that produces coffee of a quality I have learned to not only accept but appreciate, because the coffee, like the job, is not trying to impress me. It is trying to sustain me. And sustaining, I have learned, is enough.

My title is Senior Software Engineer. GS-14, Step 5. I build systems that process data for the Department of Veterans Affairs — specifically, the claims processing pipeline that determines how quickly a veteran who has served this country receives the benefits this country promised them. The work is not glamorous.

It does not produce a product that is reviewed on TechCrunch. It does not have a logo I can show at parties. But the code I write today will be running in five years, and in ten, and the people it serves are not users — they are veterans, and the difference between a user and a veteran is that a user can switch to a competitor and a veteran cannot switch to a different country.

I badge out. The badge is federal — blue border, my photo, the seal. It does not open with a tap on a phone. It requires a physical swipe, which feels, each time, like a small act of intention. I am entering. I am leaving. The building knows.

I take BART to Fremont. The commute is fifty-three minutes — longer than the drive, but the fifty-three minutes are mine. I read on the train. Not LeetCode. Books. I am reading a novel Dara recommended — she is twelve now, and her taste in books has surpassed mine, which I pretend to resent and secretly admire. The book is about a woman in Lagos who opens a bookshop. It is funny and sad and precisely observed, and I read it on BART surrounded by people who are also reading or sleeping or staring at their phones, and the shared anonymity of public transit is a comfort I did not expect — the comfort of being one person among many, moving through a system, not special, not performing, just going home.

The house is the same house. $6,800 per month. We are current on the mortgage — we have been current since January, when the government salary and Remi's hours and the careful architecture of the new spreadsheet (Remi's spreadsheet, the one with the columns she maintains with the devotional precision of a woman who has decided that financial clarity is a form of love)

— when the numbers aligned and the red cell turned amber and the amber, eventually, grudgingly, turned green.

The light fixture is warm. The kitchen does not look like evidence.

Remi is at the counter. She is chopping — always chopping, the rhythm of the knife the metronome of this household, the sound that means I am home and the world is functioning. She looks up. She does not ask how my day was. She can see how my day was. It was fine. Fine in the way that fine means when fine is the actual truth and not a performance — unremarkable, productive, adequate. I built a feature. I reviewed a pull request. I attended a meeting where people discussed timelines without urgency, because the timelines were generous and the funding was stable and nobody was going to send a Slack message that unmade the work.

"Yemi called," she says. "He made the varsity team."

"Football?"

"Wrestling."

"Since when does Yemi wrestle?"

"Since Irvington has a wrestling team and Academy of the Pacific did not, and your son has decided that being thrown on a mat by someone his own size is preferable to running back and forth on a field."

I laugh. Yemi at Irvington. Yemi who transferred without complaint and made two friends in three weeks and now wrestles. The boy who heard his parents through the hallway wall and closed his door quietly and put his headphones on and carried the knowing the way his father carries things — silently, structurally — except that Yemi is learning, at sixteen, to carry differently. He told Remi last month that he wants to talk to someone. A counsellor. Not because something is wrong but because, he said, *I want to learn how to not be like—* and he stopped, and Remi waited, and he did not finish the sentence, but the unfinished sentence was clear enough. *I want to learn how to not be like the men I come from.*

We are finding him a counsellor. Not Pastor Femi's kind. The kind Uncle Ricky's nephew recommended — a therapist in Fremont who works with teenagers and who, the nephew said, understands what it means to be a young Black man in a house where the ground shifted and nobody explained why.

Dara is in her room. The book light is on. We still know. We still don't mention it. Some things are better left in the agreement of silence — the good kind, the kind that is not concealment but respect, the privacy of a twelve-year-old girl who reads in the dark because the dark is where the best reading happens.

✳

On Saturday morning I drive to the cemetery.

Holy Sepulchre, in Hayward. The plots are arranged on a hillside that faces west, toward the bay, and on clear days you can see the water from the road, silver and flat, the same bay I crossed on the Dumbarton Bridge the morning Chinwe called. Dapo's plot is in the newer section — row 7, marker 14. The headstone is dark granite, polished, with his name and dates and the words Chinwe chose: *Beloved husband. Devoted father. Omo Olusanya.*

I bring flowers. I do not know what kind — Remi selects them, at the Safeway on Mission, and hands them to me in the car, and I carry them the way I carry all the things Remi gives me, which is with the trust that she has thought about the choice more than I would have and has arrived at the right one. They are yellow. I know that. Yellow flowers on dark granite, and the contrast is the kind of thing Dapo would have noticed and said nothing about, because Dapo noticed everything and narrated only what served the moment.

I sit on the grass beside the marker. The grass is green — January in the Bay Area, the rains have come, and the hills that were brown in October are the green of a postcard, impossibly vivid, the kind of green that makes you understand why people live here despite the cost, despite the fires, despite the Slack messages and the COBRA premiums and the $6,800 mortgages. The green is free. The green does not have a payment schedule.

"I replaced the light," I say.

This is how I begin. Each time. The light fixture. The small thing that I did on the day I applied for the job that changed the trajectory, the thing that connects the man I was — lying in bed, staring at a white ceiling, defeated — to the man I am — sitting on grass, holding yellow flowers, talking to a headstone. The light is the bridge. The light is how I got from there to here.

"Yemi wrestles now. I know. I didn't see that coming either. Remi says he's good. She goes to the matches. She says the other mothers are terrified and she is taking notes. I believe both of these things."

The wind moves the flowers. The bay is visible from here — a line of silver between the hills and the sky. The same bay. The same water. The same geography that holds all of us — the living and the dead, the employed and the laid off, the men who spoke and the men who did not.

"Chinwe is okay. She's more than okay — she is Chinwe. She has enrolled in a medical coding programme. She says the dental office was fine but fine is not a career plan, which sounds exactly like something Chinwe would say. Femi is in eighth grade. Sade still has the stars on her ceiling. I asked Chinwe if she wanted to take them down and Chinwe said *those stars are staying until Sade decides they go*, and that was the end of that conversation."

I sit with him. Not talking. Just sitting. The way we sat in the hospital room — two men from Surulere and Yaba, holding the silence between them, letting the silence be the bridge.

"I think about you every day. Not in the heavy way — not the way I thought about you in the first weeks, when the thinking was a weight I could not put down. I think about you the way you think about the weather. You're there. In the morning, when I make coffee — you're there. On the 880 — you're there. In the gym, when Uncle Ricky says something that only you would fully appreciate — you're there. You are the context I carry. The man who showed me what silence costs, and what honesty is worth, and that the distance between the two is narrower than any of us believed."

The cemetery is quiet. Not the quiet of absence but the quiet of accumulation — the gathered stillness of a place where many people have been loved and laid down and remembered by the people who drive here on Saturday mornings with flowers they did not choose and words they have been composing all week.

"I am okay," I say. "Not healed. Okay. The difference is — I know the difference now. Healed is a word for people who believe the wound closes. Okay is a word for people who have learned to walk with it open."

I stand. I place the flowers against the headstone — yellow on dark granite, the colour of October light in Fremont, the colour of the morning that came through Dapo's kitchen window on the last day, the colour of a world that does not stop being beautiful just because someone you love is no longer in it.

I walk back to the car. The Accord. The same car, the same driveway, the same drive. I start the engine. I sit for a moment — not forty minutes, not the paralysis of June, just a moment. A breath. The car smells like Remi's air freshener, the small tree she hung from the mirror that I said was foolish and she kept anyway. Three years. The same smell. The same life, rebuilt on a different foundation — smaller, steadier, the kind of structure Uncle Ricky would approve of. Not a mansion. A house. Built to hold, not to impress.

I drive home. The 880 carries me the way it always carries me — forward, without asking where I have been or what I am leaving behind. The freeway does not know the difference between a man going to work and a man coming from a grave. It just moves you. That is all it has ever done.

I pull into the driveway. The porch light is on. The kitchen window glows with the warm LED that Remi chose, the light that does not make things look like evidence.

I do not sit in the car.

I go inside.

Epilogue

Dapo.

I am writing this from the kitchen. The light is warm — I replaced the fixture, the one Remi asked about three times, the one I finally changed on the morning I decided to stop pretending that the small things don't matter. They do. You knew that. You knew it from your father's shop on Bode Thomas, where the bolts of fabric were arranged by colour and weight and occasion, and the arrangement was not decoration but survival. You knew that the small things are the architecture. You knew it, and you still put the blood pressure monitor in the drawer.

I am writing this because there are things I did not say at the repast. Not because I forgot them. Because a room full of people requires a certain kind of truth — the public kind, the kind that can be spoken standing up, the kind that generates amens. But there is another kind. The kind that can only be said sitting down, in a quiet kitchen, late at night, to a man who is not here to hear it.

So.

I am sorry I did not call. I know I said this at the hospital, and I know you forgave me, and I know the forgiveness was real because you are — you were — a man who forgave the way you did everything: completely, without performance, as though generosity were a reflex rather than a decision. But I need to say it again. Not for your sake. For mine. Because the sorry is not a debt I am paying. It is a weight I am learning to carry without letting it change the shape of my walk.

I should have called in July. I should have called when the WhatsApp messages got shorter. I should have called when Tola announced the Meta offer and your congratulations arrived twenty-one minutes late and I counted the minutes and did nothing with the count. I was afraid. Not of what you would tell me — I was afraid of what your telling would require of me, which was to hold something I was not sure I had room for while I was holding my own. That is not an excuse. It is the truth, and the truth is the only thing I can give you now that you can use.

You would laugh at the job. I know you would. Government. A federal building with fluorescent lights and a coffee maker that produces something the machine calls coffee and that I have learned to drink without grimacing. You would say something like *Koly, you are building software for bureaucrats* and I would say *I am building software for veterans* and you would say *same thing* and then you would ask about the pension and I would tell you and your eyes would do the thing they did when you were calculating something — that slight narrowing, the focus, the brain behind the eyes running the numbers faster than the mouth could report them — and you would say *that is smart* and you would mean it.

Uncle Ricky asks about you. He did not know you, but he knows about you, because I told him, and because Uncle Ricky is a man who understands that the people we carry are part of the weight he sees when he looks at us on the stationary bike at 7:15 on a Thursday morning. He said something last week that I have been holding. He said: *The ones who don't make it — they're not the weak ones. They're the ones the system used up fastest.* He said it while pedalling, without looking up from the Journal, and the sentence landed in the gym the way your sentences used to land — quietly, precisely, in the exact place it needed to be.

Chinwe is extraordinary. But you know that. You married her. You married the woman who found a blood pressure reading in your slacks pocket and drove you to urgent care in her church shoes and sat in a vinyl chair and built a spreadsheet while you slept. She is doing the medical coding programme. She says the work is boring in a way that is satisfying, which I think means the work has structure and the structure holds, and after seventeen weeks of a structure that was a lie, a boring structure that holds is exactly what she needs. Femi is growing. He is taller than Chinwe now, which she mentions with a tone that is fifty percent pride and fifty percent alarm. Sade's stars are still on the ceiling. They will be there until she decides they go. Nobody else gets a vote.

Remi sends her love. She does not use those words — Remi's love arrives in other forms: a pot of egusi dropped at Chinwe's door on a Tuesday, a text message that says *the children can come Saturday*, the quiet, steady machinery of one woman holding another woman's world while her own keeps turning. They talk on the phone most evenings. I do not ask what they discuss. I know it is everything, and I know it is theirs, and I know that the conversation between two women who have both lived through the thing our culture does to the men they love is a conversation I am not meant to overhear and would not understand if I did.

Yemi wrestles. I need you to know this because it is the funniest thing that has happened since you left, and you would appreciate it, and I need someone to appreciate it with me who knew him when he was a boy at Academy of the Pacific with a backpack too big for his body. He is sixteen and he wrestles and he is good at it, and when I asked him why he chose wrestling instead of football he said *because in wrestling, you can only blame yourself*, and the sentence was so perfectly Yemi — so precise, so unbothered, so exactly the kind of thing a boy says when he has decided who he is going to be without consulting anyone — that I sat in the car afterward and laughed until I cried, and the crying was not grief. It was something else. The something else that comes when you are holding loss and joy in the same chest and neither one will leave.

I think about what you said on the phone. The last call. Fifty-three minutes. You said the heart with legs. You said *call Segun*. You said *good* — one word, the period at the end of the last sentence — and I did not know it was the last sentence, and you did not know, and the not-knowing is the mercy and the cruelty of how we lose people, which is always in the middle of something, never at the end, because there is no end, there is only the place where the conversation stops and the silence begins.

I called Segun. That day. The day you left. I called him and he answered and his voice was the voice of a man at the edge and I said the four words — *how are you really?* — and he was quiet for a long time and then he told me, and I listened, and the listening was the thing I should have done for you and did not, and I will not make that mistake again. Not because I am a better man. Because you made me one, by dying, which is not how it should work but is how it worked, and I owe you the honesty of saying that.

I miss you. Not in the large way — not the way the movies show it, with the rain and the staring and the slow-motion montage of better days. I miss you in the small way. The way you said *Koly*. The way you tilted your head when you were cataloguing a room. The way you held a Heineken — by the label, always by the label, as though the bottle needed to know you were paying attention to its details. I miss the things about you that no one else will ever know to miss, because the things that make a person irreplaceable are never the things in the obituary. They are the angle of the head. The grip on the bottle. The laugh that arrived late because you were checking it for accuracy before you let it out.

You were not a cautionary tale. I need to say this because the speech at the repast — the speech I gave, the one about the industry and the silence and the thermos — that speech made you sound like a lesson, and you were not a lesson. You were a man. A man who loved his wife and dressed his children and drove the 580 and timed himself reaching for fabric bolts because his father taught him that order was survival. You were a man who built data pipelines and fried plantain diagonally the way your mother did and prayed at Grace Baptist and carried a thermos with your initials because the woman you loved gave it to you and you wanted something of hers with you every day. You were not a warning. You were Dapo. And the world that used you up and sent you a calendar invite does not deserve the full measure of who you were.

But I will give it to them anyway. Because the story is yours, and the telling is mine, and the least I owe you — the very least — is to make sure that when people hear what happened, they hear not the silence that killed you but the life that preceded it, the full, complicated, beautiful life of a man who came from Bode Thomas Street to Dublin, California, and built something with his hands and his mind and his heart, and whose heart, in the end, was the thing that broke, because it had been carrying too much for too long without anyone asking if it needed help.

I am okay. You asked me once — in the hospital, in the gown, with the ECG on your chest — you looked at me and said *Koly, are you okay?* And I said yes. And I meant it. And I mean it now. Not healed. Okay. Okay the way the house is okay after the earthquake — standing, functional, the cracks visible if you know where to look, but standing. The foundation held. The light is warm. The coffee is good. And every Saturday morning I drive to Hayward with yellow flowers and I sit on the grass and I talk to you about wrestling and spreadsheets and the small things that are the architecture.

The small things are the architecture. You taught me that.

Goodnight, brother. Rest.

O daaro ore mi, sun re o.

www.ingramcontent.com/pod-product-compliance
Lightning Source LLC
LaVergne TN
LVHW090558110826
845146LV00001B/182

* 9 7 9 8 9 0 4 1 7 4 5 4 5 *